G000067937

9500000136605

The Lost Girl from Far Away

The Lost Girl
from
Far Away

Elizabeth Gill

QUERCUS

First published in Great Britain in 2024 by

QUERCUS

Quercus Editions Ltd
Carmelite House
50 Victoria Embankment
London EC4Y 0DZ

An Hachette UK company

A CIP catalogue record for this book is available
from the British Library

HB ISBN 978 1 52942 109 5
EBOOK ISBN 978 1 52942 111 8

10 9 8 7 6 5 4 3 2 1

Typeset by CC Book Production
Printed and bound in Great Britain by Clays Ltd, Elcograf S.p.A.

Papers used by Quercus are from well-managed forests and other responsible sources.

This story is for the people of Tenerife, who live and work here and provide such great times and memories for those of us who visit their wonderful island.

I hope that the little girl in my book, Isabella, will one day be able to get back to Los Abrigos, the Red Mountain, and her beautiful home in the sunshine.

One

The Durham Felltops, Northern England

Isabella de Leon wanted to go home. She longed for a place that was as different from the fells of north-west Durham as it could possibly be. Her home was a land of almost constant sunshine, of friends and fish and fruit, a place where she had been a happy small child with family all around her: the tiny village of Los Abrigos on the southern coast of Tenerife in the Canary Islands off the coast of West Africa, where the winds blew in from the Sahara and the sun sank slowly in a fiery ball. The Red Mountain, an ancient volcano on the southern edge of the island, stood just beyond the village and could be seen from her home. She had thought when she was very small that the mountain had the power to grant her wishes. It was said that when Magellan sailed there in 1519 on his voyage around the world, he had called it the most beautiful place on earth. She had thought that she would live there all her life with her mother and father and her brother, Nico.

Her first memory was of being outside on Christmas Eve, when all the families had a big meal and before it, as her mother toiled in the kitchen, her father had taken her outside to see the sunset. The sun set in winter at about six in the evening and, just before it vanished, it sparkled gold in the sky and then disappeared beyond the mountain. Then, he had said to her, 'But wait, my most precious girl, because the best will come soon.'

She grew impatient, small as she was, but he lifted her into his arms and held her safely against him. Then, after she thought that night would darken quickly, there was a pause, which lasted for a long time to a tiny girl but was probably only a few minutes, and suddenly amidst the darkness there was light, pink and blue, very pale and two stars, one low and one high. Her father pointed them out to her and he said, 'Do not forget my little one, that you come from the most beautiful place on earth. Be proud.'

He had been right. It was as perfect a home as anybody had ever seen. The men in the village fished, the women kept house and looked after the gardens and orchards and animals, and the children ran freely, except on Sunday mornings, when they made their way to the little church where they had been baptized and since then had attended every Sunday along with all their families.

She would never forget the day that her life changed forever, when a wind bearing red sand had come across the Atlantic Ocean and brought with it a storm. To begin with, all it did was enshrine the village in fog. Her uncle and two cousins had already gone out in the boat that morning. The fog gave way to the biggest storm in the island's history and the three men were lost.

After that all her father wanted to do was leave. Her mother also, but they had different goals in mind and argued more than usual. That was bad enough, all the shouting and her mother throwing what was left of the pots she had not thrown at her husband the last time they had an argument, but in the end her father had decided to take her mother to her family home, leave her there and go on to Canada, the place he had always dreamed of.

Her mother's home was here in Weardale. Isabella's parents had met when her father had been a sailor in his young days and her mother had been a maid in a big house in Newcastle upon Tyne. His ship had come in and his heart had gone out, that was how he remembered it, but there was nothing left of the romance.

Her mother had wanted to go home when her father talked of leaving Los Abrigos and she had cried. Isabella found it hard to imagine anybody wanting to return to this bleak, freezing and desolate place in the middle of nowhere.

They had made their way overland to here after a long sea journey and the weather had got worse and worse.

Everything was cold and wet and there was fog too and her father had lost the way as he tried to find her mother's home and family.

Her mother was angry by then and tired, for she was about to have another child and badly needed to lie down. They had ended up in this huge old house, which stood alone at the head of a deserted village.

They were grateful enough to have reached shelter and had huddled here inside the walls, hoping that the rain would stop and the wind would not cut you in half as you tried to go forward.

Come morning, the storm had passed and her father did his best to make up the fire. It was not usually his job and in the end Isabella pushed him away and gently took over the building of the fire. At least it was something to do and warmth was the first thing they needed.

Isabella could not meet his eyes because he kept going to the window and she knew he was going to say that he would not stay for much longer, it was time to move on.

She was hoping that the fog would never lift so he couldn't leave but it was going, leaving a cold, wet land behind it. Canada beckoned, that was what he told them. Every day he talked of it as paradise. He kept his mind on his goal and would not give up the idea. Isabella knew that her mother had hoped they all would stay here but she had learned better.

Her mother, after many previous births, was about to

go into labour once again. She had lost more children than Isabella could remember but had never seemed any worse for it. At the moment, she was sitting up on the old sofa not far from the fire, taking from the small blaze the little warmth that it gave to her hands as she declared, as she had done so many times before, that she would go no further, not one more step. Isabella knew that her father no longer cared. He had taken her home, he had fulfilled his promise and now he longed to be gone.

Isabella began to look forward to him leaving. Her parents had been fighting her whole life. Sometimes she wondered why on earth they had got married. The trouble was that they were too much alike. The fighting was an integral part of their lives, and perhaps it provided some kind of excitement which the fishing village and their lives there had lacked.

The fighting had meant that Isabella and Nico were very quiet. There was no room for their voices in their parents' house. Now had come the moment she had initially feared, the anger wanted to explode from her but it would do no good. If he must go, why delay it? She couldn't stand much more.

'I've done what I said I would do,' her father said, his voice level. 'I've brought you home. The place you were born and brought up is but a few miles away and you can go nowhere until that child is born. Then you'll be able to walk the short distance. Your family will be bound to take you in.'

Her mother said nothing. Isabella concentrated on keeping the fire alive. Her father gave her all the money that he said he could spare and all the food he had, which did not amount to much, and then he urged Nico out of the door. Nico hesitated and Isabella began to understand why nobody was looking at anybody else. They could not. Nico stood there, glanced at her and then he followed his father. Such had always been the plan but now that it was happening, Isabella could not believe that her father and brother would go. She waited for Nico to change his mind and come back but nothing happened.

'But, Papa, what will they do?' Thirteen-year-old Nicolas de Leon turned to his father, at a loss.

Sebastian dismissed his wife and daughter with a nod. 'Will you come with me, Nicolas? There will be so many opportunities.'

Nico glanced at his sister and mother before he left the house. His father was right, his mother would give birth shortly and after that she would be well. She always was.

'I have been a good husband to her, you know it, but I could never belong in such a place and neither, I think, could you.'

'But Isabella—'

'She is like her mother. She will find a home here. She even looks like her mother, has the same ideas and needs.'

Nico knew that Isabella was a disappointment to his father. She was, for a start, fair-haired and green-eyed, whereas he looked like his father, dark and Spanish, though he was not. Spaniards came from so many places with so many different cultures and all of them proud, but he would not contradict his father. Isabella belied her name in that sense to his father and yet there were a good many people on their home island of Tenerife who were blond and blue or green eyed. Invaders had come from many different countries over the years and had fathered children there, so that it was very much a mix.

His father was proud that Nico looked like he did, and his father and his father before him.

Their mother, who came from this strange place, had never learned to speak Spanish well and she had never taken up Spanish customs or ideas. She could not, or would not, adjust to the village which was their home. She had always longed to be here. Now she was beginning to realize her dream and at huge cost to his father, he knew.

His father longed for a whole new life and he had done his best by his wife Marianna, or Marian as she was known in England.

'She'll be able to travel in a few days. The village below

7

can be no more than half an hour's walk from here. They will help her since she is one of them.'

His father had a very persuasive tongue and was looking hard and longingly at him. Nico knew that his father loved him very much and that in comparison he loved Isabella very little. It was sad but what could he do?

'Come with me, my son, and we will have an adventure. We have done our duty.'

It was bitterly cold but since Isabella had sharp ears, he had taken his son outside to talk to him like this. It was high time they were gone.

'Let me say goodbye,' Nico ventured.

He kept in mind that his father had wanted to go to Canada as directly as he could. This must have been the biggest diversion that anybody had ever taken and for the sake of someone else. Instead of going straight across the Atlantic, they had come to England, and it had taken such a long time that Nico's mind clouded whenever he thought of the journey.

They had set off in the autumn, his father hoping to get his family to where they wanted to go before the bad weather arrived. It had also cost his father a lot of money to bring them here and now he had to set off again in winter, which was the worst time of the year to be on a ship. Nico was not looking forward to that and yet he too longed for something new and not a single part of him thought this place had anything to offer him.

He went back inside. The huge house was freezing. The fire had gone out again. The wood was damp, Isabella had said. No one had apparently lived there for some time and although the house still had fuel in an outbuilding, the coal had been outside and was wet. The rooms were filled with furniture, as though people had had to leave quickly or could not take anything with them. Also, there were pots and pans and various kitchen items which he did not recognize. He had never felt less at home and he knew that his father felt the same.

It was true also that the nearest town was but a short walk down the hill, as his father said. No doubt they'd welcome his mother and sister. Why wouldn't they?

His mother was lying on a big sofa. His sister was trying to relight the fire. She was eleven and knew a great deal about lighting fires, for she did it every day at home and helped her mother in the kitchen with cooking, washing and cleaning.

In some ways he wished they had remained in the village where his father's family had lived for many generations. Would he ever see it again?

Isabella did not turn from what she was doing. She only acknowledged him with a quiet, 'So, you're going then.'

'I cannot let him go by himself. You'll be able to walk to the village and probably find Mama's family there. It will be a homecoming.'

'Goodbye then.'

'Goodbye.'

Nico was relieved that his sister made so little fuss. She didn't move and so he went outside and closed the door behind him. Then he felt better. A new life beckoned. Perhaps the biggest chapter of his existence was about to begin.

Two

After they had eaten once again, Isabella and her mother had nothing left but some bread and cheese, some coffee in a small pack, which smelled good. She had discovered the well outside at the back of the house and a kettle in the cupboards, but the fire was not making enough heat for coffee. When the day cleared and the wind died down, she would make her way to the village. Maybe there would be a shop open and she could get help for her mother, though to be fair, her mother had birthed all her children by herself and had seemed to suffer nothing from it, whether they lived or died. Her mother was tough, she would survive.

It would soon be Christmas. Isabella thought back to the Christmases they had had before, all such joyous times with carol services and midnight mass in the little church just up the street from their house. She missed the children she went to school with and being able to run in and out of the houses around her.

Isabella eventually managed to get the kettle to boil and felt almost triumphant when she was able to hand her mother coffee from one of several pots she had discovered. It gave out warmth and a sweet smell and she was pleased with herself. Her father had brought in fuel, so they would manage, she thought. This all made her feel much better, as though she was coping. What they had they would manage on until the child was born and then they could make their way down to the village and things would be easier.

Her mother was restless at first but as the time went by, she began to groan and moan and it became clear to Isabella that the child was not being born as the others had been, for it was taking a long time. It got worse until her mother was screaming in pain and writhing on the bed. Isabella could not do anything to help.

It was dark outside by then and snow had begun to fall. She went out but the snow came above the top of her shoes and there was no light anywhere. Her father had told her the village was just a short distance away but, as she ventured down from the house, she could see nothing through the blizzard.

She knew that she had to get help. What was this place they were in which was so far from the road?

They had kept walking up on the tops, as far as she could tell or remember now. Her memory was confused by what had happened and the realization that she and her mother were alone here, and she forced herself to think. Isabella tried to give her mother a second cup of weak coffee, but she would take nothing and the pain got worse.

In the end, the following day, as soon as it was light, Isabella left the house and struggled through the snow towards the little town.

The snow was thick and falling fast and sideways. After a while she could not tell whether she was going up or down and all she longed for was to get back to the house where her mother was in such a bad way.

She walked on and on until she couldn't walk any further. She kept falling over and getting colder and colder and it began to dawn on her that if she couldn't get up, she would die, so she kept on getting up until she couldn't do it anymore and then it didn't matter.

When she awoke, she was very cold but the sky was clear now and she could see everything around her. She got to her feet and there in front of her she saw the house she had left to try and find help. Was this as far as she had got? Had she wandered around in circles?

She went back into the house. The moon shone in through the open roof and she could see where her mother lay and that she was not moving any longer. She could not be dead. Isabella hadn't seen anybody dead before but her mother still didn't move and she didn't respond when Isabella said her name, at firstly softly and then louder.

Suddenly she was afraid and wondered how far her

father and Nico had got. Surely they would come back, surely she was not to be left here so alone?

She lay down beside her mother and waited. And grew colder. She made herself believe that it was just a dream, that she would wake up in the morning and they would be back in the sunshine and the warmth of Los Abrigos, with the Atlantic washing the shore just below the house, blue-green in the sunshine, and all would be well again.

Three

Sarah Charles had lived in Wolsingham for five years after Connie and the rest of the Butler family had left the Hilda House up on the tops. Sarah liked living in Wolsingham with Miss Hutton. The old lady treated her like a grandchild, making lovely frocks for her, feeding her well, and they worked together in the shop, which had been Miss Hutton's livelihood for as long as anybody could remember.

That December morning when Sarah got up first, as she always did, and made up the fire and put the kettle on to boil for tea, she took a cup to the old lady, only to find that Miss Hutton was no more. She was stiff and cold. Sarah was so shocked and horrified that she could not believe it.

She had no idea what age Miss Hutton was, but she had been very old, to the point where her cheeks sagged and she had to use reading glasses to sew, even in the mornings, and she had become bent and shaky. But Sarah had kept telling herself that Miss Hutton would never die because Sarah could not afford to lose the only person she loved.

Now it had happened. She tried thinking of her many friends in the village but Miss Hutton had been family to her. She didn't know what to do so she sat on the bed for a while, hoping that she would wake up and the old lady would still be alive, but nothing happened. So she took the cup and saucer downstairs and then banked down the fire, put on her boots and made her way through the fast-melting snow and across the street to the doctor's surgery.

She was too early.

'We're not open yet,' Jimmy said. He ran the pharmacy.

Sarah didn't like Jimmy. Nobody liked Jimmy. He was rude and brushed everybody off, but he had been there for a long time and presumably was good at his job or the doctor would have got rid of him.

'Miss Hutton died,' was all Sarah could manage to say.

Jimmy looked at her as though nobody had ever died before and then he left her standing in the hall, went into the gloom at the back of the house and disappeared.

Moments later he came back with Alexander Blair, who was the local doctor. He'd taken over from Dr Neville and for years folk had complained about him because he was nothing like the other man. He came from Edinburgh originally and his clipped tones told of his background.

He had been the doctor further up the dale for some years but had moved here after Dr Neville left. People said it was to make a new start because his wife and youngest child had died and his older children lived in Satley with his wife's parents.

He did not suffer fools gladly, that was the conclusion of the village when he had been there for a year. By the second year he was accepted and after that, nobody would have got in his way for they were grateful for his skill and understanding.

Also, when you really did have a problem, he could be cool but kind, and Sarah didn't think a doctor could give you more than that.

'Now, Sarah,' he said and he came to her, offering a very small smile. 'Why don't we go back to the shop and see what we can do?'

That was exactly what she needed to hear. The doctor put on his coat and boots and followed her the short distance in the snow. Sarah guided him upstairs and then sat in the kitchen.

He was not long.

'You're right of course,' he said. 'I'm so sorry. Why don't you come back with me and I'll sort everything out?'

'Leave the shop?' Somehow Sarah had the idea that if she left she would not be able to go back there. Whatever would she do?

They locked up, she put the key into her pocket and they walked back to the surgery, but this time they went in through the private side entrance. The doctor's house was bigger than most, even though it was on the main street. It was not attached as the other houses were and behind it were several buildings including stables, a carriage house and five acres of land for the doctor's horses. There was also a cottage where Oswald, who looked after the garden, yard and horses, lived with his old mother and Jimmy lodged there too.

Dr Blair took her through into the kitchen where Ada and Fiona, the two maids, were busy. Ada said nothing. She never spoke to Sarah, Sarah realized now, clearly thinking herself well above a lass who had no family. But Fiona sat her down and made tea and sympathized after the doctor told them what had happened before he went.

Now used to the shock, Sarah didn't listen to what they said but sat there worrying as to her fate. What on earth would she do?

The undertaker and the doctor took away Miss Hutton's body and Sarah returned reluctantly to the shop. She stripped the bed where the old lady had died. It didn't make her feel any better, but it was something to do. She didn't open the shop for she was completely lost and could settle to nothing.

Four days later, when it got as light as it was going to, she realized that something else was wrong. Things had been so difficult since Miss Hutton died that she didn't feel she could handle more problems but as she gazed into the garden from the kitchen window, she thought she could see something unusual moving around.

There were birds and the odd squirrel, but this was bigger. Noiselessly she opened the kitchen door and watched more keenly. There was somebody in the garden. Miss Hutton was lucky to have a garden; many houses had nothing but a backyard. The garden gate was open and somebody small had stepped inside and halted there. It was a half-grown child, a fair-haired girl, and Sarah could tell by her stance that she was afraid.

Sarah left the back door open, approached carefully and then she said, 'Are you all right?' Clearly there was something very much the matter, woe was pitiful on the child's pale and anxious face.

'It is my mother, my mama,' she said in heavily accented English. 'She – she has been so very ill and I think she has died. I had to leave her to find help and it took me so very long to get here and I don't know what to do or how to get back there.'

'Come inside and I will help you.'

The child was very cold, thin and badly dressed and her eyes were dark with fear. Sarah sat her down by the kitchen fire and asked where she had come from and recognized straight away the description of the house on the tops where this girl had left her mother. The place was very familiar to her. She had escaped her hard life to a better one up there, turning to Connie Butler for help. It was the Hilda House, formally known as Blessed St Hilda's Orphanage, and probably where she had first felt happiness.

Sarah was obliged to return to the doctor's house as she thought he would help again. An hour later they were up at the Hilda House. Sarah had not been there in the five years since the Butler family had left. It felt very strange. The doctor would have left the little girl with his servants but she cried so much that in the end they all went together.

The village was just the same, as though time had stood still. The snow was melting and the day was fine. It felt odd but when she saw the Hilda House, she felt a rush of love for the Butler family, remembering how Connie had taken her in when she had run away from the bad treatment of Amos Adams – a minister and a bad man who had brought her in as a small child to work for him.

Sarah had not wanted to go to Newcastle, where Connie's sister and brothers had settled. Connie would have taken her to London, where she and Thomas Neville had gone, but the dale was home and despite the bad memories she loved it well.

Dr Blair drove the pony and trap himself. He was a man of few words. The locals called him 'dour' because of his grave manner but he had proved that he knew what he was doing and the people were confident in his ability to look after them. Sarah was slightly afraid of him but he had been there for her twice in less than a week when she had needed him so she was grateful.

As they got to the front door of the house he said to Sarah, 'Will you stay with the wee one?' and when she nodded he added, 'Don't worry. Archie will keep still.'

It had not occurred to Sarah that the horse wouldn't stay where he was. Once the doctor bid folk and horses to do things, they did them. She knew Archie better than she knew the doctor. She sometimes took carrots for the doctor's horses in the fields behind his house.

He was not long but even so, it being winter, darkness was beginning to fall by the time he came back, saying gently to the girl, 'I'm sorry, lassie, I'm afraid that your mother is no more.'

The girl began to cry.

'There's nothing else we can do today.'

The girl cried softly and hid her face in her hands. 'But I can't go without her,' she sobbed.

'I'm afraid you must. I can't leave you here by yourself.'

'You can stay with me for now,' Sarah offered, rather glad that she did not have to face the shop by herself again, and so he nodded and got into the trap and they went back to Wolsingham.

Sarah didn't like to question the child, even to ask her name would seem like an intrusion.

There were two bedrooms but the memory of finding the old lady dead in hers stayed with Sarah. The girl didn't seem to mind sleeping with her, though she said little.

'Where will I go?' the girl asked when they were lying still in the darkness. *The darkness made people bolder,* Sarah thought, and since it was the same question she had had herself, it did not make things any easier.

'Do you have other family?'

Sarah listened while the child told of her father and brother, of her life in some paradise of a place such as Sarah had never imagined. The girl also told her of the drownings of the men in her family and her father's despair, and Sarah understood that another family would take over the fishing and the house from her father, so they had nowhere to go but forward.

She could not believe that this man had dumped his wife and child in the middle of nowhere, three miles away from the nearest village, when his wife was giving birth and had gone off with his son, leaving his young daughter alone to face an uncertain future – and what a future it had already turned out to be.

When somebody dies just before Christmas, it seems the ultimate insult, Sarah thought, almost indelicate, as though, had they made a little more effort to put off the Grim Reaper, the joy of Christmas would still mean something.

That Christmas there was no merriment at the little dress shop where the two girls stayed alone. Grief stalked them like an unwelcome guest, bringing with it other thoughts which made it all seem doubly bad. These Sarah tried to keep from her mind. What was the point in worrying?

She could not help gazing at the kitchen mantelpiece as though it was about to strike her. In a little pot there, they kept cash that was used for the household bills and shopping. Miss Hutton never even counted it. Why would she? They paid their way with relative ease and even if Sarah had been salting it away, Miss Hutton would never have noticed, but then the trust between the two of them had been complete.

So, when she would normally have gone out and spent money on some little extras as they usually did at Christmas, Sarah could only look at the pot with guilt and distaste, afraid to spend anything for fear of the future.

Neither of them ate much.

She clothed Isabella in the thickest raiment she possessed. The poor child was frozen and continually sat over the kitchen fire wrapped in blankets, huddled against all those negative thoughts which Sarah felt sure her guest had parading through her mind, casting out any positive idea which tried to raise its head.

Miss Hutton had made a fruit cake weeks before and fed it brandy. She had covered it in marzipan and white icing. There were even two small ornaments, Miss Hutton's pride and joy, which came out every year to deck the cake: a robin and a snowman wearing green and red buttons and a black hat. The cake had been finished off with a red and gold sash.

Sarah went over the many times they had had good winters, how they went to the local church and sang Christmas carols, then ate mince pies at the vicarage after the service alongside half the village.

Miss Hutton always made a new velvet dress for Sarah in December for the carol service. This year snow lay thinly, making for wet slushy streets, and a biting wind followed it, so she had no desire to go beyond the doors. The new dress was black velvet with pearl buttons whereas last year's had been blue. Sarah didn't want to dress up and thought she would never happily wear either of the dresses again.

Sarah made a Christmas dinner, since it had already been bought and paid for. There was a leg of pork, sage and onion stuffing, crackling, big tureens of potatoes, and parsnips with honey. The two girls sat at either side of the table and regarded the food with distaste.

*

The funerals had been hastily arranged together since the two women had died only a few days apart. Alongside Easter, this was the vicar's busiest time of year. The girls were comforted as much as they could be by going together and by the vicar's wife organizing some food in the church hall. Luckily at Christmas there is plenty of food available and many women from the village helped provide it. It meant a lot to Sarah that they had respected the old lady so much. She took Isabella to the church hall and introduced her to everyone and many of the women gave both girls a hug. Losing someone you cared for at this time of year was the hardest of all, they agreed. Also, even though Isabella was unknown to them, she was just a bairn and they were duly sympathetic.

The vicar had gleaned Isabella's mother's name from her and the two women were laid alongside one another in the little graveyard beside the parish church. Nobody asked for any money, there would have been no point, for between them they had very little apart from what was in the pot on the mantelpiece and Sarah dared not assume that this was still hers to make use of. She presumed that the village and the vicar, Mr Wilson, had kindly taken care of these things and tried not to think about it.

All Isabella could think was that her mother should be there with her and that, had it not been for the kindness of Sarah and the doctor, she too would have died in that wretched house up on the tops, having had nobody but hunger and cold for her friends.

Sarah and Isabella were both relieved when Christmas and then the funeral were over. Both girls still felt shocked and raw and could not think of anything else. They had not slept properly and had eaten little, and the dark mornings and early nights somehow made it all harder to believe.

When all was done that could be done, Sarah began to panic. She had no idea what would happen now to either of them. She said nothing to Isabella, but it preyed upon her mind like a hunger. She tried to keep up a brave face but the little girl sat in tears over the kitchen fire and cried for her mother and the loss of her way of life, and for how her brother and father had gone off and left her. To Sarah their actions seemed mindlessly callous but there was nothing to be done.

It was almost two weeks after Christmas and the ice and snow were thick on the streets so nobody went out unless they had to.

For some reason the girls were a bit more cheerful that morning. They even ate an egg and some toast each and managed several cups of tea. *Tea was always so comforting,* Sarah thought. She was therefore feeling a little better when she heard the shop bell ring. As that door was also their front door, she went through to open it. She didn't know what to do about the shop or anything else, she thought as she went to answer it. The morning was dark and gloomy and when she opened the door, she saw Mr John East, the local solicitor.

He was looking apologetically at her. She ushered him into the kitchen, which was their dining and living room because the shop and workshop, where they made and mended clothes, took up the other two ground-floor rooms. She introduced him to Isabella and offered him a seat at the kitchen table. There was no easy chair, such a thing would have taken up a great deal of space.

He had with him a briefcase. Sarah gazed at it with instant dislike. It looked so official somehow, especially when he took from it several papers which he shuffled. He looked at them with a frown and then at the two girls.

'I'm afraid I am the bearer of bad news, Miss Charles,' he said. 'Miss Hutton's will contains nothing for you.'

'I didn't expect it would,' Sarah said, no longer sure of herself because she knew it would make her homeless and penniless. 'As I'm sure you are aware, we were not related to one another, but she was kind enough to take me in.'

'Even so,' he said, and then paused in case he might say something detrimental about the recently departed old lady. The pause lengthened. Sarah longed for it to be any other day but this. She was even beginning to look back on Christmas Day with some fondness. Dreadful as it had seemed, it was better than this.

'Will I be able to stay here?' she could not help asking, and the words came out in a rush as though they could be held back no longer, even though she did not expect a good response.

'I'm afraid not.' He studied his papers as if they might tell him something more positive but he looked in vain. 'Miss Hutton's great-nephew John Bartholomew inherits everything. Perhaps you might be able to find employment in the village,' Mr East said.

He meant as a servant. Sarah said nothing. She could remember Miss Hutton's great-nephew. He had turned up for the funeral in a dark, sombre and very expensive suit. She had learned to know good cloth when she saw it. It had to be him because he was the only stranger amongst the mourners. He had not spoken to Sarah, though why he would was anybody's guess, she thought.

When Mr East had departed, the two girls went on sitting over the kitchen fire listening to heavy sleet break the silence as it met the roof.

Four

Alexander Blair had started out his life in Edinburgh, but had come here because, while visiting friends in Durham, he'd met the love of his life. She was called Alice Freeman and her father held the living of St Cuthbert's in the tiny village of Satley in the hills above Lanchester. Her father had wanted her to marry the vicar of All Saints in Lanchester. The young doctor had come a very poor second and even now, when she was long since dead and gone, he felt that her parents still resented him.

Alice and Alexander had lived happily up in Allenheads at the top end of Weardale. She had loved that it was so remote, so scenic. They had a neat little house there and he became a partner.

Having given him two little girls, Alice died giving birth to their only son and the boy had died too. Alexander felt as though he was badly done by, and the people of the surrounding area thought that if a doctor could not look after his own family, he was not capable of looking after them. This was the main reason he had moved to Wolsingham when the previous doctor had gone off to London.

Nobody spoke badly of him in the lower part of the dale, though to be fair he did not listen closely. His two little girls had gone to live with their grandparents at the vicarage in Satley. It was deemed ill that the girls had no mother figure in their lives and to begin with, in the shock of their daughter's demise, they took the children willingly.

That was several years ago now and each time Alexander went to see his daughters he longed for a son. *They must be the least prepossessing children on the planet*, he thought. Doris, the younger child, rarely spoke or looked at anyone and was pale-faced, while Georgina, the elder, was very plain and so unruly that he was glad to leave the vicarage and go home to the peace of his surgery and his fire and his whisky, brooding there over the boy who had never been his and the woman who could not be replaced.

He had become a hunted man. Every mother in the dale saw him as a potential husband for her daughter or, if she was not too old, for herself. Widowed doctors around here were unheard of. It would have been considered a crime that he did not marry even though he had obviously made a complete botch of the health of his own wife and child. But women often died in childbirth. It had been the worst day of his life when he lost Alice and his tiny boy.

His heart was broken but he was comfortable enough at the practice in Wolsingham with his surgery, his cosy sitting room and his servants. Nevertheless, as his daughters grew and went to school, their grandparents were increasingly unhappy about them.

Doris, at nine, was painfully shy and blushed to her hair roots when anybody addressed her. Georgina, the elder at eleven, was what they called a bad child. She was always running away, had a temper and threw her dinner on the floor – not often enough, the doctor reflected, seeing her girth. She kicked her grandfather and shouted at her grandmother and the poor grandparents had begun to complain and say that both girls should be packed off to boarding school.

Getting rid of his children in this way was a tempting thought. Their mother was dead, so they barely remembered her, and now he was considering sending them away as though they were street cats or stray dogs.

He couldn't do it. There had to be another way round it. He ought to marry. He could never love again but he could take on a decent woman who would do her duty by him. He then thought of Alice and how she would have laughed at such ridiculous notions. It was then that he felt guilty about the children. Alice would have been horrified at the idea of sending them away. She had loved them so openly. He tried to think back to what they had been like before she died but it was too hard to bring back memories of what he thought had been the best life he could have lived. It was all gone.

He went on with his work but the complaints of his parents-in-law were getting to him and he also knew that it was unfair to them. Their hearts had been broken when their only child died and they resented being saddled with the children, as his mother-in-law had told him more than once. No wonder the girls misbehaved. Their grandfather had gout. Alexander tried to tell him not to drink so much port after dinner, but he took no notice. Grandmother had arthritis in her hands and feet and was in constant pain, and being an awkward woman, did not believe in pain relief.

The time came when he could no longer ignore the problem. Yet what was he to do?

Five

Harry Leadbetter was seventeen when he came home to Wolsingham that Christmas. He had been in a school just outside Pitlochry for twelve years. He well remembered arriving there in a snowstorm at the age of six and wondering what on earth he had done to be sent so far away, to the bleakest place that he had ever seen.

The school was all grey. The stone walls were grey, the dormitories were painted grey. There were no carpets or even rugs on the floors and the thin, squeaking narrow beds were twelve to a room so that every sigh, fart, giggle and sob could be heard during the bleak, cold nights. The wind swept around the buildings and the ice froze solid on windows, which had been built so high that you couldn't see out of them. Had that been deliberate so that the boys could concentrate? But on what? He never knew.

The rain, which continually poured down, was grey but it was even worse when the winds turned colder and snow fell and drifted among the trees beyond the playing fields and further over towards the town, which was also grey. The snow lightened everything but did not ease chilblains, colds, coughs that rent the night, or the way that the blankets were heavy on your bed because it was either endure that or suffer the cold. The floors were linoleum, so the moment you ventured out of bed your feet turned into ice. Often the snow began in October and did not relent before April.

He supposed that he had at some time grown used to how hard it was and had ceased to think of it. He never went anywhere. In the holidays, when a lot of boys left for their homes, he sat around, disconsolately watching as the maids filled the big trunks with clothing and the porters carried them downstairs to waiting vehicles.

He wasn't the only one who stayed. Various boys had parents who worked abroad as missionaries, ambassadors or engineers so it wasn't that he was by himself. He got used to the loneliness, the way that most of the staff did not come in. The food was actually better when hardly anyone was there, as the cooks went off and a couple of the masters and their families stayed and looked after the boys. There was porridge twice a day, and he was given eggs, bacon and fried bread, plus a little money to spend on fish and chips if one of the masters' wives wasn't cooking that day.

The teachers would talk of their holidays just before they left, of Edinburgh and London, Switzerland and France. They all sounded wonderful to Harry but since he had been and was going nowhere, as time passed he became lethargic and did not want to leave. It was as if he had wrapped the school around him. It was all the comfort he had.

He could not remember sitting close to a fire, as the bigger boys hogged the blaze. In the classrooms the fire was at the front and the masters tended to stand in front of it so unless you were in rows one or two you had no benefit. You were not allowed to wear scarves or hats and gloves in the classrooms but if you didn't want to answer questions, it was preferable to sit at the back and freeze. The only time he was warm was the brief spell during June and July, when sometimes the days were too hot. There were only two seasons here, a winter which seemed endless and a summer which was brief and sti-fling. By August it would rain. Sometimes September provided what they called an Indian summer and after that snow fell and was there for so long that it turned into grey slush when vehicles passed by.

The only way to get out of here was to be good at sport but he had never seen the sense in it. Why would you want to kick a ball around? Why would you want to be in a team and shouted at and mocked? So he made sure he was chosen last and that nothing was expected of him. Cross-country runs were a torture, out there half-naked in inadequate shoes and running for what? He did not know.

So, after years of having his fees paid, the day came one December when the headmaster summoned him into his study and told him that he was to leave.

'Leave?' Harry said blankly.

The headmaster was a cheerful kind of man. He hadn't been there long enough to accept defeat.

'You can't stay here forever, you know. You have enough money for your train fare home.'

His trunk had long since fallen to pieces; he suspected it had not been of any great quality in the first place. His clothes were always too small, as were his boots, so he was now down to nothing but one change of clothing. All the less to take with him.

'Couldn't I stay here and do something useful?' was his last-ditch gasp at trying to get beyond the problem without going anywhere.

The headmaster smiled and shook his head. 'My dear fellow,' he said at length, 'there isn't anything you are able to do. Perhaps it doesn't say much for our school, but we can keep you no longer.'

Harry thought about it and had to agree. He had no skills or uses. He had spent years studying Latin and Greek and had retained little of it, since he could see no need for it. Had he really not picked up anything which could help him now?

It took two days to reach home as the trains varied so much in their comings and goings that he spent a lot of time just sitting about waiting for them. He dozed in railway carriages and on the various platforms, eating a sandwich now and then, which was all he could afford, with weak tea and stale cake.

All the time, he wanted to run back. He was afraid, filled with trepidation, did not know what to expect at the other end of the journey. He could remember little of his home. Dimly, he recalled the big house where he had lived and could clearly remember his mother dying, as well as the small, fair-haired girl who had died before her. He remembered now how his father had reacted, being unable to bear the loss. Had it been easier to send the boy away?

He got as far as Edinburgh via a slow stopping train which he thought he was going to be on for the rest of his life. He changed again at Newcastle and then at Durham. When he finally reached Wolsingham it was full evening and, barring a streetlight or two, completely black. There were no stars.

Being December, it would barely get light during the day, at least it would seem that way to people who had not lived in the Scottish highlands. There, for months in the winter, it was dark and in the summer, on some nights, there was no darkness at all.

He saw the house from the road. His memories of the building were few but he didn't think it had been anything like this. The stone walls which had surrounded the place had fallen into the gardens. Two big rusted iron gates were broken and lay on the ground at either side of the short drive. Beyond, what had been lawns were now fields of grass, unmown or unattended to in many a year.

The house was large and stood stark and solid. It had been built in Georgian times and it didn't look as though anything had happened to it since then.

He walked up to the front door and wasn't sure whether to knock. Did you do that when you had been away for twelve years? He had no idea. It seemed like a ludicrous situation.

He tried the handle. It gave and moments later he was inside the hall. It had a lovely blue and white stained-glass window to one side and the staircase went straight upstairs on the left from a very wide hall. The place was dusty and the corners held big cobwebs. His memories were beginning to come back to him. In his mind he could hear a little girl crying, a mother's voice breaking and a man's tone, deep and angry and despairing.

The hall was silent. There seemed to be nobody and nothing in the house. There was a door on the right and it was open. The room was empty but had tall windows looking out towards the street. In front of him was a huge oak door and when opened it led into a kitchen and then into another big room.

There was someone in this room. An old man was asleep in a battered armchair. *Not just sleeping,* Harry thought. He was drunk and had passed out. An empty whisky bottle stood on the floor with a glass beside it.

Harry looked harder at the man and realized that he was not as old as he had seemed. He looked old because of the dissipation. He could be no more than in his mid-forties but he was a wreck. The man was in fact his father. Harry stood watching him in his drunken stupor and then he made himself lift his gaze to the portrait which hung over the fireplace. He had to make a huge effort to look at it. He knew in an instant that it was his mother, Isabel. She had golden hair and his own bright green eyes, and she looked so pleased to see him that Harry could feel traitorous moisture in his eyes. He blinked hard so that they did not blur, but it was no good. He had to turn away. He remembered the little fair-haired girl who had been so well loved. He could recall his father saying that his mother had died of grief once her three-year-old child was no more.

Harry was beginning to wish that he had not come back. What had been a series of unconnected images was starting to come together to make a complete picture, and he wished he had stayed away because up to now, he had closed it off from himself. She had died of a broken heart? What about her other child? Had she no room for him now her heart had been so irretrievably smashed by the death of her daughter?

That was when he had been sent away. Could his

father not bear the sight of him because he resembled his mother or did he not look sufficiently like her that he might be kept at home?

At that moment the man opened his eyes and stared. His cheeks were an angry crimson with drink and his eyes were bloodshot. His skin had a strange yellow tinge and there were big red bags beneath his eyes.

'Who in the hell are you?' he growled, 'and what are you doing in my house?'

'I'm beginning to wonder myself,' Harry said. 'What in God's name would I come back here for?'

His father frowned and then a look came into his eyes and there was nothing bright about it.

'Oh, it's you,' he said finally and closed his eyes again.

Six

Georgina Blair was never sure whether she remembered her mother or if her memories were just accommodating the longing that she had. She imagined a soft voice, a ready smile and some kind of figure but that was all. Her sister, Doris, remembered nothing. Georgina hated her life. She hated everybody except her sister.

She and Doris were nothing alike. Doris was afraid of everything and she was afraid of nothing. Doris barely spoke and Georgina never shut up. She felt as though if she didn't keep speaking she would disappear completely.

On top of this they rarely saw their father. Did he not like them? Did he not want to see them? But for the fact that he was a doctor they knew little of him. Georgina also remembered the house they had had further up the dale when her father's practice had been there. Now he lived in Wolsingham but she had never been to his house and he came to them looking uncomfortable, as though he couldn't wait to get away. They were stuck here in Satley vicarage with their awful grandparents and the even worse Mrs Prudhoe, who had a school in her front room and was always trying to get them to do things they didn't want to do.

Georgina understood that her grandparents had been her mother's parents. They never let her forget it. They were always talking about how good and fine she had been and how she ought to have married better and how she ought never to have lived in the awful little house by the millstream.

'She could have had anybody,' Grandmother had said, tears rolling down her withered cheeks. 'The vicar at Lanchester, John Irving, adored her. I believe if she had married him she would be alive today. Nothing good ever came from the dale. The folk are ignorant and unschooled and yet he made her go there to live. It was never the same after that. He stole her from us, he hated that she spent time with her beloved parents. I never liked him; the Scots are a strange people, sulky, rude and cold.'

Five days a week, the two girls sat in Mrs Prudhoe's little sitting room with a few other children, none of whom liked one another, and they put up with the woman's droning voice all day.

In the middle of the morning, they were let out into a poky backyard, but the gate was locked and they were told not to go beyond it. Georgina escaped several times by scaling the gate and climbing over the nearby shed but there was nothing to see in the village; she thought it must be the dullest place in the world.

There were no shops; people seemed to stay inside their houses and all of these were tiny places like the one Mrs Prudhoe lived in. The vicarage was the opposite, huge, cold and smelling of fish and cabbage, which they seemed to have every day. It wasn't true, it just appeared so and neither of them liked fish or cabbage.

Their grandmother's cook boiled every vegetable until it turned into mush. They never saw a dab of butter. Fish was fried until the flour fell off in great grey globules and covered in green and white sauce, no doubt to disguise its taste and texture. The potatoes were always half-cooked with nasty little black wormholes in them, as the cook's eyesight was none too hot and she missed such things.

Grandma thought red meat was bad for small girls so they often watched their grandfather make his way through a succulent steak or a brace of lamb chops. On special occasions there was chicken but they were not allowed that either. They were given a lot of thin, barely buttered bread for tea and with that they had tinned fruit in thick syrup. Breakfast was always porridge, bland and bare. At midday when they sat down to eat, it was broth. Georgina did not trust broth. So many indiscernible things floated there. They seemed to her like the dead bluebottles which were always bashing themselves on the closed and dusty windows, and spiders who had dropped down from corner webs in the stables and scurried inside out of the cold. Mice did the same; they came inside in the winter, making her grandmother grumble. But why wouldn't they, Georgina wanted to know.

Their grandmother was cross at first when Georgina and Doris didn't eat this dainty fare but if she persisted Doris would throw up not just fish and cabbage, but everything she had eaten that day. Georgina greatly admired this ability which she lacked. She was unfortunate in other ways. Her insides could not understand why she ate overcooked greens and barley broth, and she spent a lot of time on the outside lavatory, where splinters from the wooden seat tended to stick into her bottom.

Doris seemed to feel the only power she had in her life was what she would eat and what she wouldn't. There was little that she did like other than cake, and when they were allowed cake on Sundays she often stuffed it down so fast that she threw that up too. Doris was tiny and shrunken, as though her life held nothing she cared for except her sister.

They had a bedroom each but they always slept together. It seemed to Georgina the only comfort they had and, even though Doris hardly ever said anything, it was enough her just being there. The vicarage was apparently not big as vicarages went; their grandmother was always complaining about how small and inconvenient it was and how, if the church paid her husband better or promoted him, they would live somewhere civilized.

That was what she called it. The country was not civilized. They heard about it every day. She came from Hexham and waxed lyrical about the beauty of the abbey, the lovely shops and tea rooms, the parks and old buildings. She complained about the maids here because they were village girls and knew nothing about cleaning a house or scrubbing Grandfather's shirt collars, which were always grey with dirt, or so Clara the laundrymaid said when she thought nobody was listening. The girls did not often get to change their clothes and they were given one cold bath a week, which their grandmother seemed to think did them the world of good.

Grandfather and Grandmother were the most important people in the village, so they had no friends, her grandmother said. The people here were parishioners and well below the vicar's status.

Worst of all were Sundays. It was just a round of services, one in the morning and another in the evening, and then there was Sunday school, where they got another dose of Mrs Prudhoe. In between they were meant to sit over their bibles and since Doris could barely read and Georgina couldn't stay still, it was not a success. Their grandfather read to them from a book of sermons. Georgina couldn't see the point of telling people what to do all the time but that was what other people's lives consisted of as far as she could see, and for Doris and herself it seemed worst of all.

They were not even allowed a dog or a cat. The vicar had a horse for his trap but it was a huge animal so they couldn't ride it. Rain fell constantly up there on the tops or it was foggy or both, and it was cold even when the sun was at its best in July. They were not allowed in the garden after they stamped their way through the flower-beds. Eldon, the man who looked after the vegetables, shouted at them when they went near a lettuce. They were not allowed in the greenhouses in case they stole tomatoes.

They were not allowed to sing unless they were in church and there was no piano in the house, so there was no music. Georgina could hear her grandmother wailing and crying often about how the doctor could not be that clever, since his wife had died giving him his only son and the son had died too. Georgina knew that she and her sister were nothing but a disappointment and it seemed all wrong that that was how they were thought of. Surely their grandparents should have liked them the more because they had *not* died and in effect they were all that was left of their mother, but it didn't work out that way. So there were long hours in the schoolroom and long evenings in the sitting room and Georgina had been bored her whole life. Was this all there was to it?

Seven

For two days after Mr East's visit, Sarah had not slept and food made her feel sick; she was too worried about what the future might hold. Then Ada, the doctor's cook, turned up at the shop mid-morning, looking anything but pleased. Ada was a little, plain, middle-aged woman with marmalade-coloured hair that was going grey at her temples and which she tortured into a tight pleat at the back of her head. Sarah knew that Ada didn't like her and she had obviously rehearsed her message.

'Dr Blair says you can come and stay with us until something is sorted,' she said.

Might the doctor find Sarah a job in some dreadful farmhouse down a track where she would sleep in the attic and work from morning till night? And what about Isabella?

'You can't bring much with you, we haven't got room.'

'We haven't much to bring,' Sarah pointed out.

Everything belonged to that man, as she thought of him. She owned nothing but her clothes. She could see that Ada resented having to take her in but they had plenty of room. The house was big and although it was on the main street, it had buildings and fields, at least six bedrooms and huge attics.

'It's very kind of you,' Sarah said.

Ada sniffed and looked away into the distance, as though the kindness had nothing to do with her; she was only the messenger. Sarah had quite a lot of clothes. She hadn't thought about them before now but they could be altered and sold. She was glad that Miss Hutton had made pretty things for her, and as she had grown, they were remade into clothes for younger girls and sold at the shop. She still owned six dresses though and it was more than poor Isabella who owned nothing but the clothes she came in. They were so worn out that Sarah had discarded them and swiftly altered those she had for the younger girl. Also Isabella had very small feet. Luckily Miss Hutton's boots fitted her once she was wearing thick socks. She did not think that Mr Bartholomew would notice the boots were gone. The child could hardly go barefooted up to the doctor's house.

'It's like a home for waifs and strays,' Ada complained to Fiona when she got back to the doctor's house with the two girls in tow. 'There's not enough for all of us to do, you know.' She glared at Sarah as she said this.

That was the problem, she was afraid to lose her place.

Sarah didn't know why she hadn't worked that out from the beginning. Everybody worried about such things and if it happened once in this village, nobody else would take you on, they would think you had been guilty of some grave misdemeanour. She didn't know what to say, she just wished Ada hadn't said it in front of her. Ada so obviously didn't care for other folks' plight, and why should she since everybody knew she came from a large poor family in Rookhope?

Sarah wished they had not had to burden the doctor but although she had thought of the people in the village as her friends, they had avoided her since Miss Hutton died.

Nobody had so much as offered her a meal. Many of them had little to give as they took work where they could and none of it was prosperous. What was she meant to do, go to the workhouse in Stanhope? It had occurred to her that she would have to do that or, if she found a place in some house, that Isabella would have to go there and since she was foreign, things would not go well for her.

Ada showed them into a back room with a big double bed, newly made up.

'You can have your meals in the kitchen,' Ada said. 'You're not to go anywhere else in the house,' and she swept out of the door.

Perhaps Isabella had expected something different.

She stood like someone struck and a lone tear ran down her cheek.

'Don't worry,' Sarah said, doing her best to give comfort where there was none. 'It's just for now. I'll find a job of some sort and we will move on.'

'You will take me with you?' the girl pleaded piteously.

'Of course I will.'

'But I'm not family.'

'You are now.'

Isabella went slowly over to the big window. The view was of the courtyard and the stables and the carriage house and the cottage.

The first meal they were given was bread and dripping with big mugs of black tea. Isabella stared at it in dismay.

'You were nobody until the old woman took you in,' Ada said to Sarah. 'Your mother came from some weird place a long way past the dale and was never married. And you're still nobody, Sally Charles.'

'It's Sarah,' Sarah said between gritted teeth but Ada had flounced from the room. Fiona finished her tea, got up and cleared the dishes. Sarah was more upset than she let on. She remembered various people in her childhood but there was no point in saying anything as she had always known her mother was unmarried, and she had never known who her father might be, so it meant that she was less than nothing.

Isabella was staring at the door. 'I don't think they want us here,' she said.

And isn't that true, Sarah thought, fuming.

There was nothing to do. Sarah had never had nothing to do before and it made her restless. She imagined the kitchen, where the two young women would soon be setting the table for tea as well as working on the doctor's meal, which he usually had after evening surgery or, if he had to go out, whenever he had time to eat it.

She understood better how they felt, though Fiona did not say anything; she just kept her gaze lowered most of the time. They were old maids, years older than Sarah, and they probably resented having a girl like her in the place where they were in charge.

Also, though Sarah would never have said such a thing to anyone, she was much better looking than either of them. Fiona was skinny and had huge ears, which thankfully she mostly covered with her hair. Ada was so nasty that Sarah couldn't think of a single nice thing to say about her but at least Fiona was kind.

Nobody would marry them now they were heading towards their late thirties. This was the best they could expect. They would cook and bake and no doubt sew and knit and clean and see to the house generally, but they had nowhere to go from here. Sarah resolved to be more polite and thanked Fiona profusely when she gave her a bowl, a hot water jug and a towel so that they could wash that evening.

Sarah knew very little about Fiona except that she was from somewhere in Scotland and didn't sound like a Scot but like a rich southerner, which was very odd. Ada's family lived in a house which was one of three terraced houses called Bond Isle, and since their wider family also lived in the other two houses, their money was mostly for other people. Also, it occurred to Sarah that if it was true that Ada's ma had had fifteen children, Ada would naturally be somewhat reluctant to marry, even had some man offered her the chance, which Sarah didn't think had been an option.

She understood now how much she had lost when Miss Hutton died.

That evening, contrary to what Sarah had learned to expect, they were allowed to go and sit over the kitchen fire. There was no fire in the bedroom so though it was comfortable enough, it was cold up there. It also had to be paid for and she had to listen to Ada's rude remarks and put up with her disparaging talk about Sarah's dress-making abilities. She tried to be glad of the fire and of the tea and cake which Fiona had pressed on them.

It was as though Isabella had had her tongue cut out. She didn't speak a word and nibbled at the cake for fear it should never happen again, so she must make the most of it. But also she was unused to the thick stodge they were given that had not been part of her diet in her beautiful island home.

Sarah was becoming aware from what Isabella said that the food she had had in her home was nothing like what people ate here and much better for her, fish and cheese and vegetables, whereas here it was a lot of cakes and pies and potatoes, mostly to keep out the cold.

'Constance Butler was the mainstay though, wasn't she?' Ada said. 'It hasn't been the same since she left and you don't know much about the trade other than what Miss Hutton taught you.'

'I never claimed to be anywhere near as good as Connie,' Sarah said.

'And what about you, little miss?' Ada addressed the child who shrank back in her chair. 'You're from some foreign place, are you? Where is it?'

Isabella said nothing while Ada stared.

'An island in the Atlantic Ocean,' Sarah said.

Ada ignored her and concentrated her gaze on the little girl. 'You don't half talk funny.'

'Spanish is Isabella's first language. I think she does very well.'

'But I heard your ma came from Cow's Hill.'

'St John's Chapel,' Sarah said. Isabella had said so more than once and Sarah knew that the child yearned for some kind of family to belong to. 'The islands are almost four thousand miles away and they are called the Canary Islands. They belong to Spain.'

Sarah had learned quite a lot of things about Isabella's home. She thought that it sounded wonderful.

'You came four thousand miles to here?' Fiona said.

'My mama wanted to come home.' Isabella's voice appeared as she spoke of her beloved parent.

'Mebbe there are family folk there who would want to take you in,' Ada said more cheerfully, thinking that she would not have to put up with these two for long. If the little one could be foisted on to a family and Sarah could find work, the situation would be quite different.

Sarah had thought they would see the doctor either that day or the one following. She wanted to thank him for his kindness, but he was busy. He had two surgeries a day and went visiting the sick day and night. When he was at home he slept or was in the dining room eating or the sitting room relaxing over his own fire.

He was what people here called 'a private man'. He rarely spoke unless he had something vital to say. He was much older than Jimmy who looked after the pharmacy, or Oswald who saw to the horses and the garden. *Maybe as much as forty, like Fiona and Ada,* Sarah thought. He gave them no reason to gossip, had they dared, and after the vicar and the other clergymen, he was the most important man in the dale but for the bigger farmers. He was of no great interest except to those mothers who fancied a medical man as a son-in-law and any of them would have given a lot for such a chance.

Any single man in the dale was seen as an asset but the doctor kept himself to himself and had little to say, which did not appertain to his calling. He went nowhere and had no friends. He did not go to church, which was a great falling off, so the local women had said when he first arrived, but after the shock of having a non-believer as their local doctor wore off, they could find no other fault with him.

The vicar, Mr Wilson, had a good congregation on Sunday mornings and evenings, went around seeing everybody who wanted him to help and did not openly regret that not everybody went to church. He was a kind, amiable man and he and his wife were well thought of.

The doctor was always at home. If he was not called out in the evenings, he read Greek literature, according to Ada, the only one allowed in there other than when both maids waited on him at mealtimes or when the doctor had visitors. She took in his decanter of whisky on Saturday nights and left it. He had a great many books, apparently in varying languages which Ada did not know of.

'I bet the doctor can read and talk Spanish,' she said to Fiona when the two girls had gone upstairs to their room.

At the end of their first week, however, the doctor

called the two girls into the sitting room, sat them down and asked how they were getting on.

Sarah was effusive in her thanks. Isabella didn't know what to say.

'I understand that you think you may have family in St John's Chapel, wee one,' the doctor said kindly. 'I have asked Oswald if he will take you there on the first fine Saturday so that we can find out and I thought that Miss Charles would go with you to help.'

Isabella nodded, eyes full of tears.

'Here.' The doctor got up and from one of his book-shelves he unearthed a book which had illustrations in it. 'It's in English, so Miss Charles may have to help you with the words, but it's got lots of pictures of animals so you might like it.'

Isabella took the book in both hands and thanked him in Spanish and in English which made him smile.

Isabella could not rid herself of the idea that she was in a very long nightmare but that eventually she would wake up and be home, and it would be warm and sunny and she and Nico and her father and mother would be all together again. But as she woke up each day in this cold and dreary place, she learned to understand that it was never going to happen.

She should be grateful for having a bed and she did

try to be cheerful but it wasn't easy when she missed her family so much. Also, the blankets were very heavy on her and although she needed them to keep out the unwelcome bitter weather, she slept fitfully in the cold air and had bad dreams and her hands and feet were always numb from the chill.

She was used to working. She had cooked and baked at home, milked the goats and seen to their feed, gathering special flowers which they favoured. She could catch and gut fish and pluck chickens but now she had nothing to do.

She did not forget that she had been forbidden the rest of the house but the first time that she was given the chance, she went into the courtyard. She saw Oswald brushing one of the horses on a cold sunny day and ventured out and found him smiling at her. She knew nothing of such horses, but it looked enormous and scary with its strange eyes and big feet, nothing like the horses at home, who were fragile looking and elegant.

'We had horses,' she said, 'very clever, white horses who lived in the north of the island.'

'They're called greys, I think,' he said.

She thought this was a strange idea when they were nothing of the sort but it didn't matter and maybe this young man, because he was smiling, might find her something to do.

'Perhaps I could help with that?'

So he showed her how to brush the horse until its coat

shone and then she heard Ada come hurrying across the yard. No doubt she'd been watching from the kitchen window.

'You were told not to bother anybody,' she said.

'She's not bothering me,' Oswald said.

'Much you know.'

'I do know. Go back to your kitchen, woman, and leave the bairn alone.'

'I will tell the doctor of you.'

'Oh, wobble off,' Oswald said.

Isabella didn't follow this conversation well since some of the words were alien to her, but she stared as Ada retreated. Isabella rather admired Oswald for his attitude. Later he invited her in to see his mother. The building was very old and the downstairs had once been kept for the animals, he told her, but that had been a long time ago and it had been made into a cosy house. Inside it was very clean and his mother was doing the brasses, as she called it, so Isabella sat down and helped as the old lady told her what to do.

'You mostly just dip your rag into the polish and then rub it in. You leave it and then clean it off and you get a shine,' she said.

Isabella didn't follow the words very well but she watched and caught on straight away. Getting a shine on a candlestick was very like getting a shine on a horse's coat and she enjoyed both.

Encouraged by Oswald's mother, who had never been further than Northumberland, she ended up telling the old lady all about Tenerife until the woman's eyes were round with surprise and interest.

'You say it's always sunny and warm?'

'Mostly. Never as cold as this and we grow soft fruits and live by the sea. My family are fishermen.'

After Isabella had gone back to the house, Oswald's mother shook her head.

'That poor bairn, having to end up at such a godforsaken hole as this.'

It should be said that Oswald's mother came from Allendale and considered herself well above the rest of the village, since her father had owned his few acres. She had inherited none of it and after her husband died, had been grateful to her son for providing her with a cottage and himself with a steady job. But when she thought back to her early life, it had been just as good as Isabella's. Her family were people to be reckoned with and her mother had worn a silk dress to go to church of a Sunday.

Ada was not prepared for the summons she got from Oswald's mother one January day. His mother rarely came into the house, nor did the maids go into hers, so when Jimmy delivered a note to her from Oswald's mother, she waited until Oswald took the doctor out in the horse and trap and then she went over to the cottage.

Mrs Leighton looked vexed.

'I hardly know what to say,' she said, offering Ada a seat in an old leather armchair which had been her father's and one of the few things of his which she still owned. 'The doctor wants my lad to take those two girls up to St John's Chapel. Now, I've nothing against the foreign bairn, though she strikes me as very odd, but I don't want my Oswald anywhere near that other lass. She had no father.'

The outing was news to Ada but she cursed Oswald for offering to do such a thing and then immediately understood that it was the doctor's kindness which had created the problem.

'I can't say anything to the man but you are his house-keeper,' Mrs Leighton said.

Ada, realizing that she was being flattered by the old lady, nonetheless was pleased to hear herself thus described.

'I just don't think it's right, my lad sitting next to her and nobody but a little lass for company. Folk would talk their tongues numb,' Mrs Leighton said.

Ada didn't know what to do. She was just a paid servant here and she had the feeling that the doctor would be angry if she interfered; she wasn't sure that it was her right to do so. She couldn't risk her place for something so slight, though she would have given a great deal to get rid of Sarah. She didn't want to talk to Oswald, he was as thick as chips and wouldn't have a clue what she was on about, but obviously something must be done.

In the end she called Sarah down into the kitchen while sending Fiona to stay with the little girl and told her that Oswald's mother objected. Could she let Isabella go by herself to St John's Chapel, as she could see no other way?

Sarah was stunned. It had not occurred to her that she would be placing herself in what was called a compromising position, but even more so that it would damage Oswald's reputation if he was seen in her company in such a way. The little she remembered of her family did not include much beyond vague memories and the feeling that she had been unwanted.

But she also thought that if she sat the little girl in the middle of them and it was during the day, nobody could object and she couldn't hide forever.

'You should talk to the doctor if you aren't happy with the arrangement,' she told Ada, holding the woman's gaze. 'He was the one who suggested that I should go.'

'Maybe he doesn't know what you are.'

'It's none of your business and I don't suppose he'd listen to you, any road.'

Sarah regretted slightly that she had argued but it was the only language Ada Southern knew. Besides, she had

Isabella to think of and Isabella would not want to go alone.

How eagerly had she transferred her affections, Sarah thought with some dismay. This child had been discarded and left out and Sarah was the only person she trusted. Isabella had no family left and Sarah saw how the girl followed her with her gaze, was dismayed when Sarah left the room without her. She could understand, for she had had no one of her own before Miss Hutton. She thought that Isabella was terrified to let the older girl out of her sight in case she should prove to be nothing but a dream and so many of her dreams had turned to dust.

Eight

Alex had tried to ignore the letters from his mother-in-law but when they became urgent he felt obliged to go there. He had learned to hate Satley, which he knew was very unfair because it was a pretty little village amidst glorious countryside, but it was the church he disliked most and the graveyard beside it. His beloved wife was buried there and he could not put her from his mind for a single second when he was in the village.

Worse still he didn't want to see his parents-in-law or the children whom he liked less and less each time he saw them. He had to go, he told himself. He did not make it a Sunday or the old man would ask him how often he went to church, and he would have to admit that since his wife had been buried, he could not set foot in a church without wanting to throw up.

So it was Monday. Whether his father-in-law ever did any work, Alex was not sure - no matter what time or day you called, there he was, especially at this time of year, snoring over the fire in his study. Neither did his mother-in-law do anything. There were half a dozen maids – local girls were cheap to employ.

The vicarage was modest in size but it looked bigger because of the shabby furniture, well polished but very old. The house always smelled of rancid fat and burned cakes to him but then it could have just been his imagination. It was not the kind of house he would have wanted to live in. It had few comforts.

He could not keep from his mind pictures of his mother-in-law looking around the house which Alice had been so proud of, and he had thought so fine, with its white rose garden and steps down to the river.

Mrs Freeman said she thought that the house was much too small and its garden was tiny, as though she had expected the doctor to find a better home for his bride.

He had never been good enough for them and felt sure that they regarded him as a foreigner because he was Scottish. He had a feeling they thought he had been brought up as a Presbyterian. He had actually been raised as an atheist, his father detesting any kind of religion. He thought with affection of his eccentric, beloved father and of his sweet and kind mother. They had been dead since he was quite young but he never stopped missing them. The tally of those he had loved and lost sometimes seemed to him to topple over, the tower of it felt so high that it could no longer stand.

He was led through into the drawing room, where his mother- and father-in-law were sitting in armchairs at either side of a meagre fire. It smoked. His mother-in-law greeted him with a thin smile as though he reminded her of her dead child, her only child, and she could hardly bear to see him in her house. He was certain she blamed him for what had happened. Indeed at the time she had shrieked, 'You must be able to save her or what earthly use are you!'

'The children are no longer wanted at the dame school,' was almost the first thing she said to him and before he sat down. 'Mrs Prudhoe – ' (Mrs Prudhoe, a most respectable woman apparently, having been widowed young after her curate husband died, had set up her own school.) ' – says they are unruly. That she cannot manage them any longer. Anthony and I have found a girls' school in York, the Mount, and they will take the two girls as boarders. We have decided that it is the best thing for them.'

She could not have said anything worse, or better, depending on how you looked at it. His first thought was that it would be good for the girls to get away from the old people, a village school and a lot of church services, and that he would worry less about them. But to have his mother-in-law tell him she and her husband had decided what to do left him rather lost. Did she want him to contradict her, thereby enabling her to say that he would have to take them on himself? Or did she hope he would go along with the idea and banish the children for most of the year?

He stood for a few moments, reflecting, and then said that he would go and talk to Mrs Prudhoe. He chose the end of the afternoon and managed to avoid the children altogether by slipping out the back way.

The dame school was in Mrs Prudhoe's front room and from the start he could see how badly off the woman was. There was a yard attached to the property at the back and it was presumably where the children played, but the front of the school was right on the road which wound down into Lanchester.

To his astonishment she was rather younger than he had supposed – he had previously left all communication with her to the grandparents – and she greeted him with a friendly smile and urged him in. The whole place was poor. She was obviously existing on the little she could make from her teaching, which confused him slightly since she seemed to want get rid of his daughters, or was it just that his parents-in-law liked to see it that way? Strangest of all was that she was a very comely woman of about forty with bright blue eyes, dark brown hair and a slim figure.

She sat him down as he explained his mission and she shook her head.

'That is not what I said. I hate to contradict your family—'

He wanted to interrupt and say they were no family of his but of course he couldn't, so he said instead, 'I think they are finding the children too much for them.'

She looked at him as though she wanted to say more and couldn't, or felt as if she shouldn't, but then she changed her mind. 'I'm sorry to be blunt, but they lost their mother when they were young, they rarely see you from what I can gather, because you have such a difficult profession, and it makes the girls wish that things were otherwise.'

This was rather too frank for the doctor, who stared at her.

'I'm sorry,' she said. 'Timothy was always telling me not to speak my mind so readily—'

'Not at all, I would rather have the truth.'

'The truth is that I need your children in order to help keep open the school. I have few pupils and—' Here she stopped, realized what she had said, and looked into the tiny fire in dismay.

'My mother-in-law seems to think they should go away to school.'

'It is a very good school, the Mount in York. It's run by Quakers and I believe the education there is second to none but ... I can't say I think sending small children away, especially when they have little family to start with ... I just couldn't in all conscience say I was in favour of it. They are difficult and disobedient and in quite different ways but what child isn't? I'd rather have them like that than afraid of me.'

Alex didn't know what to say. 'So you think they shouldn't go.'

'If they were my children, I wouldn't send them but what is the alternative?'

Alex thought back to how he had allowed Isabella and Sarah into his house, along with the two maids. If his two daughters came as well, it would soon resemble the Mount if he wasn't careful. Yet what else could he say or do?

He thanked her and then said goodbye to his parents-in-law, saying he would think about what was happening. He thanked them for their goodness and patience and then went back to Wolsingham. After his surgery and his dinner, he drank rather too much whisky as he sat by his fire, until he wanted to shout at somebody for his predicament.

He had the feeling that if he took the girls away from Mrs Prudhoe, she would starve. He couldn't leave them there because his parents-in-law no longer wanted them and neither did he wish them to go to York. He would have to take them himself. It was a terrible shock. He had lost his wife and his son and now these two unruly little girls were to be pushed on to him because he had no other choice.

*

'They're going to send us away,' Georgina told Doris. 'I heard them talking about it.'

Her grandparents had loud voices and the vicarage was big enough to echo. Georgina had thought that things could not get any worse but she was wrong. Potty Prudhoe and her grandparents were bad enough but to be sent away could be so much worse.

She was used to the way that Doris glanced briefly at her but said nothing. Now, however, tears stood in the younger girl's eyes. Georgina had thought about this and had contemplated that going away, no matter where, would perhaps be worse than what they had now. After all, she knew the story of Jane Eyre, for Mrs Prudhoe read it to the school in the afternoons.

It was a wordy, boring book about a dull girl who went to a school where children were starved and lived in horrible long rooms where they all slept together. They were badly dressed and ill-treated. Worst of all was that one of the girls was so neglected she died and Jane was left alone to carry on.

'That is what boarding schools are like,' she told Doris and tears ran down the little girl's face. She had not understood the story until now. 'It would be worse than what we have. We could be down to bread and water and then expire.' Georgina loved the word 'expire'. So much more dramatic than 'die'.

Jane Eyre became a governess in time and got to sit

beside a fire. The fires in the vicarage rarely gave out any heat. Georgina was convinced it was because her grandmother deplored coal fires, calling them dirty and insisted on using green logs, so the gardener, Eldon, complained. Eldon lived in a tiny cottage all alone at the end of the vicarage garden. His life seemed as bad as theirs. He never had any visitors and never went anywhere. His cottage looked to be tumbling down; stones stood in heaps in the garden and the walls were crumbling.

'Them logs ain't no good for the fire,' he kept telling their grandmother. 'They needs to dry out. That's why they hiss and spit and don't give out no heat.'

For a while Georgina amused herself by repeating in his voice that 'them logs don't give out no heat'. It made Doris laugh. It was about the only thing that did. But Georgina had taken to lying in bed at night worrying that they would be sent away to a worse place than this and end up buried in some cold graveyard next to a vicarage – probably the one here as their mother had been – and neither of them would ever get away to anything better.

Nine

Sometimes there are days in the dale in January which are as good as July. The third Saturday of January was just such a day. The snow had long since retreated. Even the sheep looked happier and warmer and snowdrops decorated the gardens with bulbs pushing up green slivers of leaves in the black soil.

Oswald loved the springtime and noted what was happening. Most days, he took Isabella around the place with him and taught her the names of the flowers and of the various birds. She told him about birds they didn't have here, such as the yellow canary bird, which came from her islands, and explained that sometimes there were parrots who belonged to nobody and flew free. Oswald was astonished.

Isabella didn't understand why but from somewhere she was given more liberty. Nobody told her not to go into the courtyard when Oswald was busy.

She went to visit his mother every day and suddenly her life was a lot easier. Also, Oswald's mother baked scones every morning, which were made even better with plum jam, and since Isabella's diet was boring, she took to going there. It made more of her days and also Oswald's mother made up just a little for the loss of her own mother.

Isabella was full of hope about St John's Chapel. As the day for the visit grew nearer, she became excited and recalled the things her mother would talk to her about, and how fondly she had spoken of her home. In fact, if it had been that good, Isabella didn't understand why her mother had left. Presumably she had thought that she was in love. Isabella wondered for how long that illusion had lasted. She couldn't remember her parents ever being happy.

Also, she thought that her mother had forgotten all the hard things about this place, how cold and dark and cheerless it was, how the wind found a dozen ways to blow across and around and through the streets, how it lifted the fleeces on the sheep and ruffled the long winter grass in the fields. It blew soot down the chimneys and smoke into the rooms.

Sarah dressed her in thick clothes and Oswald got the horse ready and then they trotted up the dale. Oswald had contacted his uncle who lived in St John's Chapel and he said that he would meet them and find them something to eat.

Sarah had felt she must go, not just because it made a change but also to upset Ada, to prove that she did not care what anybody said about her. She sat Isabella between herself and Oswald so that the little girl would feel secure and so that she could not be accused of trying to get near him.

Sarah was worried. The child was excited but Sarah was a pessimist and so far she had been right about so many things that it scared her. She didn't believe in happy endings. That was the most important reason for her to go. She would be glad for Isabella if this worked out, if the child had a family to go to, a home, but if it turned out differently somebody would have to pick up the pieces.

Sarah knew St John's Chapel because at one time she'd had family in Daddry Shield, which was the next village. Vague memories of her grandfather came to mind. He had always smelled of tobacco smoke and had ash down the front of his ancient waistcoat. His blue eyes were bagged, watery and red. He did a lot of swearing and spitting and he hated the world and everything it had done to him. He hated her mother and her. She did not remember her father, only the idea that her father had not cared to be married. It would have been a huge shame for her mother.

As they drove through Daddry Shield she remembered that it had seemed a lot bigger when she was a child. But it was nothing beyond a collection of houses clustered around a bridge, beneath which the Wear flowed shallow and brown over stones. Beyond it, further back towards the hills, stood East Blackdene, the prettiest village in the area. It had square fields with stone walls, cobbled paths and tiny houses. She had vague happy memories of things her mother had told her about, of a place called Black Eil, which was apparently somewhere close, but that was all she knew.

The road wound its way through Frosterley and then Stanhope, and on to Eastgate and Westgate. Oswald told Isabella that these had been the entrances to the bishop's hunting park in the old days. When they finally reached St John's Chapel, Isabella was ready to be captivated. She was so glad that the day was bright and now she would see for the first time the place where her mother had been born and brought up.

Isabella had wanted to arm herself against disappointment in case this was not what she thought it would be, but she liked the place from the moment she saw it. It was pretty, was her first thought.

Oswald pointed out the show field on the right and the churchyard, church and vicarage, and then on the left a big square building which was a public house. Then they went into the heart of the village where there was a green and grouped around it were various streets and houses. Isabella was ready to fall in love with the place. She took in every detail.

They got out of the trap and Oswald took her down

to the river and over a wooden bridge, where he pointed out various small black and white birds on stones and fish gliding through the water. Sarah followed and was pleased to see how happy Isabella could be made with so little. She glanced at Oswald and noticed that his cheeks began to redden and he stopped speaking for a few moments. Sarah remembered that Mrs Leighton had not wanted her to go and she could see why now. Oswald liked her. She thought he was being good to Isabella, not only because he had taken to the little girl, but because he wanted to impress Sarah. She half-turned away so that his embarrassment would lessen and tried not to think about Ada's disapproval and Oswald's mother's worries. There was no chance she would have anything to do with him.

Isabella remembered her mother telling her of playing with her friends in the street and that she and her sister Isabel — she named her daughter after her beloved sister — and the other girls thought there were fairies in the water.

Oswald knew various people in the village and took her to the Bluebell Inn on Hood Street, which was the main thoroughfare. There he was greeted affably and introduced the man behind the bar as his Uncle Stanley, who knew everybody.

Uncle Stanley sat the two girls down at a little table near the fire in the bar. They had meat paste sandwiches and shandy (lemonade with a touch of beer in it) which Isabella liked and happily told the men around her so. They all laughed at the idea of a little Spanish lassie in the bar.

Uncle Stanley took Oswald to one side where they could not be overheard and then he said, 'They were an ungovernable lot, the Logans, the bairn's mother's family. The men did nowt but fight; the women drank and wouldn't work. There was blue murder in their house on a Saturday night. Nobody wanted to live anywhere near them. They never had any money and they stole from other folk. The only decent one of them was Marian's sister, Isabel. She married Luke Leadbetter, whose family owned everything and got left with nowt in Wolsingham. She's dead now. It's been a long time since but he's still there and he has a lad. Luke is a drunk like his father and has squandered what his father left him.' Uncle Stanley shook his head over the ways of bad families in the dale.

'I think the little 'un would like to see the house here.'

Uncle Stanley shook his head. 'It's nobbut ruins,' he said.

Oswald went back to the table where his pint of beer and sandwich awaited him but both girls could tell the news was not great. He broke it as gently as he could but the joy left Isabella and she could eat nothing more.

She had begun to think that she might find a home here, she so badly needed one, but it was not going to happen.

Isabella insisted on seeing the house so Oswald took them but Sarah could see why he had not wanted to. It was on the very edge of the village and there was virtually nothing left but a few stones. Around it the grass grew tall and within the rooms which had once been their home. Oswald explained as gently as he could that there was nobody left here who remembered her mother and father.

It was a despondent party that trotted back down the dale to Wolsingham and nobody said anything.

'Her grandfather was a wrong'un from the start,' Oswald later told his mother. 'He fell out with the quarry owners so that they wouldn't have him there and then he took everybody off with him a few years back.'

'And the little un's ma?'

'Ran away, so I gather. A disgrace to the family, running off with a foreigner, I was told.'

Sarah noticed the next day that Oswald was hanging around the back door as though waiting to see somebody. She watched him for a little while. After the trip to St John's Chapel, when he had spent a lot of time blushing and stealing glances at her, she was beginning to think that Oswald had what they called 'a thing' about her. Since she didn't feel like that about Oswald and felt she never could about any man, she tried to pretend he wasn't there, but he was being obvious now, so she decided she must talk to him. Avoiding Ada and Fiona, she went outside. He had gone back to brushing Archie but as she appeared, he took the horse back into its stable. Sarah didn't like to go over, Oswald's ma might see her and get the wrong idea – at least, she hoped it was the wrong idea.

When he came back out, rather red-faced, he said, looking not quite relieved but heading somewhere in that direction, 'I wanted to have a word with you but I couldn't when the bairn was there.'

'What about?' Sarah said, so relieved that it was something they could both help with. Oswald was a respectable lad. He probably didn't want her for his girl and only blushed because he was shy. His mother would want him to do very much better than a girl who had come in through the back door, as they called illegitimacy here in the dale. She felt rather sorry for him. He was a raw, honest dales lad but he had no education and no finesse. He was dull and awkward but she smiled at him now because she knew that he was doing his best for Isabella and would continue to do so.

'My uncle told us that the bairn has other relatives and right here. I couldn't say it in front of her because I didn't know what to do.'

This sounded odd and made Sarah frown.

Oswald didn't say anything at first and then he blurted out, 'The Leadbetters.'

This was not good news. Sarah understood now why Oswald had hesitated. The Leadbetters were a well-known Wolsingham family who had prospered before the old grandfather started hitting the brandy bottle.

'Isabel Logan married Luke Leadbetter.'

The son, Harry Leadbetter, was by this time about eighteen and nobody knew anything about him other than that he lived quietly with his father, spoke to nobody and never looked in anybody's direction. His mother had died when he was very young. Few people remembered her. He had spent most of his life in Scotland at some obscure boarding school.

Also there was nothing left of the fortune made through lead mining and quarrying. It had been frittered away on drink and what the locals called 'debauchery'. Sarah didn't think there were a lot of goings-on like that in the dale, but people saw everything. There had been visits to Newcastle and Hexham; there had been expensive horses and bad gambling. Whatever, it was all gone and there was nothing left but a big, gloomy old house on the edge of town. As far as she knew, nobody ever went there and they had no servants.

It was said that Luke had become a miser and, although there had once been plenty of money, none of it was being spent now and the servants, who were not paid well, declined to give their service. There were rumours that the family carriage had gone to rust and ruin, that the stables were falling down, that the outside buildings were full of rats and that Luke Leadbetter never stirred from his study fire, where he drank considerable amounts of brandy.

The only shopkeeper who went anywhere near was the grocer in Frosterley, who supplied the brandy and apparently other meagre wants, because the Leadbetters lived on very little. The cooks had come and gone and as far as Sarah knew, there was not even a kitchen maid or a boy for the outside of the place.

'We can't let the bairn go there,' she said, horrified.

'I know but I thought I should tell you at least. I didn't know what else could be done. There's no woman in the house and Luke Leadbetter is meant to drop dead of drink any time now, according to talk.'

When Isabella went early to bed that night, Sarah confided to Ada and Fiona that the Leadbetters were Isabella's only family. She didn't want to talk, especially to Ada, but she had nobody else to confide in and she felt the weight of the problem heavy upon her shoulders. The two looked suitably shocked.

'That's worse than having no family,' Ada said. 'The doctor went a couple of times when he first arrived here but he's given up on the drunk.'

Sometimes they glimpsed Harry Leadbetter in the street but he had become an object of pity since he had lately returned home. The local women stayed well away from him. It was not that he was a bad-looking lad – tall and slender with dark hair and green eyes – but nobody wanted anything to do with him. And Harry Leadbetter never talked to people. If he was seen outside the house, he kept himself to himself and never even spoke.

Miss Hutton's shop was going to open up again. Sarah was so pleased she could hardly contain herself, and when she saw activity going on, she hastened to the open doorway and introduced herself very politely to the man who was inside. Something good would happen soon and if she could get some work, she could find a decent place for herself and Isabella, though things had changed. Isabella was enjoying the company of Oswald and his mother so she would likely prefer to stay where she was. Isabella talked to Sarah about the old lady and Oswald so much that Sarah pretended enthusiasm. She knew what Oswald's mother thought about her and that his mother would proclaim war if she thought that Sarah was getting any nearer to her son. Isabella had so few joys though that Sarah could not but encourage her to talk of those few things she took pleasure in, so there was a lot of information about the well-being of the doctor's horses.

Also, as far as Sarah could tell, Oswald's mother had not told the bairn anything bad about her, so she was grateful for that and took to listening about how Oswald's mother's family were a cut above the rest because they hailed from the beauty of Allendale, where all kinds of very respectable and well-meaning folk lived.

The man Sarah faced now, at what had been Miss Hutton's shop and their home, was obviously the manager. He wore a suit and had a kind but pitying look about him as he said hesitantly to her, 'I'm sorry, love, but it's to be a tailors now and we have no job here for you.'

'I lived and worked here and I'm good.'

'No doubt but I'm the tailor and I have all the help I need in my lad. This is no place for a lass like thee.'

Sarah didn't know whether this was meant to be a direct hit at her or just what he would say to any young woman. Whatever her hopes had been, they were now dashed. Despondently, she made her way back to the doctor's house. She had no place anywhere and neither did Isabella. At least they were allowed freer use of the doctor's house now and that was because Isabella ran in and out and there seemed no reason to make Sarah stay in the bedroom, but things were getting worse. Every time she tried to do something in the house Ada got defensive and said it was not her job.

'So what am I meant to do?'

'That is not my problem,' Ada said, sticking her nose in the air.

Mrs Carver, who lived in the next street, came in to do the laundry and then came back to do the ironing. She too did not talk to Sarah, probably for the same reason. Oswald brought in the fuel for the fires and the house was kept spotless by the two diligent women. Ada was a good cook and Fiona made cakes. Jimmy ruled the dispensary and since there were drugs, nobody was allowed anywhere near, nor was anyone allowed in the surgery except for patients.

Worse still, Ada and Fiona sat over the kitchen fire at night darning the doctor's socks and knitting new ones. They even made his shirts and repaired their own clothes, though Sarah did not give them high marks for their mending but dared say nothing. They also knitted cardigans and pullovers, so there was no place for Sarah to distinguish herself.

She was allowed to sit there sometimes but having nothing to do made her miserable. She wished for a book to read but hadn't the courage to ask the doctor if she might take one from the library and even if she did, she knew that Ada would have forbidden her to read in the kitchen.

Ada seemed to think that Isabella should go to school but the child refused and even stamped her foot when Ada tried to insist.

Her eyes flashed. 'I am not going!' she declared and went off to Oswald's mother for sympathy.

'She wouldn't fit in at a school here,' Sarah said.

'That is not the point. She should learn to read and write.'

'She speaks two languages, Ada, which is one more than you or me,' Sarah said. And yet she thought in some ways Ada was right. The child needed to mix with people her own age and she had nobody like that, yet she would not be accepted here. Sarah had heard of outlaws, and in a sense she and Isabella were that.

While the bad weather persisted Sarah found life very difficult but she endured it because the little girl was having such a good time between the house and Oswald's mother's cottage.

Sarah begged wool and needles from Fiona and knitted bed socks and mittens for Isabella. In payment for this, she altered one of her velvet dresses for Fiona. Fiona gazed at herself in the mirror and then couldn't help smiling back at the younger girl behind her.

'It makes me look a lot of things I'm not,' Fiona said.

'It makes you look very pretty,' Sarah said.

'Huh,' Ada said as Fiona turned from the kitchen mirror.

'I could remake one for you if you like,' Sarah said.

'Don't try to get in with me, Sally Charles,' Ada said and she walked out.

After that Sarah dared not ask for more wool. She had planned to make a jumper for Isabella, and also socks since she was good with four needles.

Trouble was not long in arriving and when it did, Isabella retreated to Sarah and declared she would not go back to the cottage.

'Why not?' Sarah asked when they were alone in the cold darkness.

'Mrs Leighton is nasty about you. She thinks Oswald wants to marry you and that you are a very bad girl and she and Oswald have started shouting at each other. She says that I should have nothing to do with you or I will turn into a very bad girl too. You are not bad; you are the only person I really care about. I could have cared about her and Oswald, and I love the yard and the horses but it's all turned wrong because of what she says and it isn't true. You are a wonderful person.'

'Everybody presents a different face to everybody else,' Sarah said, touched and pleased but not wanting to hold back this child who seemed to like everyone given a chance. 'What other people think of me shouldn't affect your friendship with Oswald and his mother. They don't understand and they don't mean anything by it. Don't let it upset you.'

But it did. Isabella had met her first and Sarah knew that because she had helped the child she was therefore more important to her. Though that was lovely, it was not helpful now and was spoiling this child's life when she had already been through so much.

Also, although she didn't want to say so, she knew

now that Oswald cared about her, she could tell in the way that he blushed and turned away, how he avoided her. That he would argue with his mother about her in any way was upsetting. She could never see herself caring about such a young man, never mind marrying him – even if his mother had allowed it, which she never would.

Oswald was kind and caring but he had no ambition and as far as she could tell, no ability beyond what he did already. There was no way, however bad things were, that she would marry him and go to live in the little cottage and bear his children. Nor would she put up with his mother and what she regarded as the small-minded-ness of this town. She wanted to get away but she had not the means to do it. She didn't know for how much longer she could endure such a barren life.

Sarah was now deliberately avoiding Oswald and hoped he was getting the idea, until the morning that he followed her into the kitchen. He had obviously watched carefully because neither Ada nor Fiona were anywhere to be seen.

'I have to talk to you, Sarah,' he said, glancing behind him even though he knew that nobody else was in the yard.

'Is it about Isabella?'

'No.' He was not blushing now, he had moved forward from that and was almost bold, looking straight at her and saying, 'I want you to come for a walk with me on Sunday.'

'Oswald, your mother—'

'I'm tired of hearing what my mother thinks of you. This is my life and I can lead it the way that I want. Mother is only here because I made a home for her. Without me she would be on the street.'

Sarah was a little shocked at this. She didn't think sons should talk of their mothers in that way, no matter what their mothers did.

'I love you, Sarah. I can't go on without you. You mean the whole world to me.'

Sarah didn't know what to say, she was so taken aback, and then for the first time ever she was grateful that she heard Ada's heavy step as she came into the kitchen.

'What on earth do you think you are doing here, Oswald Leighton, get yourself back outside. The only time you are allowed in here is when I ask you to bring in the coal or do a particular job. Out you get, now!'

Abashed, Oswald retreated very quickly. He did not even look at Sarah.

'And as for you, encouraging him—' Ada said but Sarah cut in.

'I never encouraged him and you have no right to say that I did and no reason either. I know you don't like me but I haven't done anything to you and you have no business saying things about me which aren't true.' Then she ran from the room.

Sarah did wonder whether she should go and see Harry Leadbetter and tell him about Isabella's existence but it seemed a pointless thing to do, and since his father was always drunk, she decided to keep the information to herself for now. She could not see it doing any good because Isabella could gain nothing from such a family, so she thought she should leave well alone.

Ten

With spring on the way, Sarah's thoughts went to the Hilda House. She remembered how pretty it had been up there, and as the weather improved she longed to see it again. She didn't mention this to anybody, especially not to Isabella because the child had such bad memories of the place, but the more she thought about it the more she wished she could go there.

Sarah tried to talk to Isabella and say that she was certain Oswald and his mother would miss her, that they had not meant anything bad, and that she ought to go back to the cottage. She thought that Isabella would doubtless have gone there because it was the only place she could go, but Ada had told her that the doctor would not like it. She was only making things worse. The doctor had more important things to do than worry about the small matters within his household, but Isabella didn't like the frequently raised voices, and going to the cottage was spoiled. So the two girls were stuck with one another in their bedroom and the kitchen.

Going up to the Hilda House was a big step forward

but Sarah did not want to be in the doctor's house for any longer than she had to be. She just needed to work out what she might do next, how she could survive without having to put up with the censored life she had here. It was less than half an existence and she became more and more keenly aware of its shortcomings.

There were some fine days in March and that meant they could go outside. It became Sarah's ambition to spend a day at the Hilda House. She didn't think Isabella would want to go with her because of the association with her mother dying but when she talked to the girl, she could see that Isabella was as eager as she was to go somewhere and do something.

'It's quite a long way to walk there and back, will you be able to manage?' Sarah asked.

Isabella assured her that she would. Sarah told the other two women nothing but that she and Isabella had decided to go out for the day and would it be all right if they took with them a bottle of water and a sandwich each.

Ada was so eager to 'see the back of them' as she told Fiona later that morning when the girls had left, that she was happy to provide them with cheese and pickle sandwiches. She wished they would go for good and things could get back to normal here.

'The doctor doesn't seem to understand that having homed Sally Charles and an orphan from some foreign land makes folk talk and some are calling him weird. It's bad enough that he comes from over the border.'

Ada had considered whether to tell the doctor what she thought but the only time he encouraged people to say anything was to talk of their medical conditions, so she didn't dare. The doctor was obviously a man who was used to servants. She liked that in him, it showed he had come from a good background, but it meant he kept his servants in their place and Ada would not have risked her position by trying to tell him how to run his household.

She was just lucky there was no old woman in the house telling her what to do. She would hold on here as long as she could and keep sending most of her wage to Rookhope. As the eldest she had been in service since she was a small girl. Her father toiled in the quarry but there was still never enough money for her to have a little freedom of her own and to be honest, she told herself, that would never happen.

In some ways she was lucky that she hadn't had some lad to ask her to marry him. She didn't want a life of drudgery such as her mother had. Two of her brothers had married and already had three children each. She dreaded the future but she was doing her best and if she could get rid of these two cuckoos in the nest, she would sleep a lot sounder in the bed that she shared with Fiona.

Fiona snored. Ada longed for the chance of having a

room to herself but although there were several empty bedrooms, it would never have occurred to the doctor that Ada would like a room of her own or that she deserved it. She was actually a good cook, having learned at her mother's knee and was certain she deserved better, but there was nothing for cooks to do other than work for other people. So, even though she provided the doctor with perfect meals, he never complimented her on her work. She provided cooked breakfasts, three-course dinners, rare beef which only he and nobody else liked, and fish dishes with finely chopped vegetables and fragrant sauces. Fiona would make rhubarb pie or apple crumble, which were his favourites, but he said nothing and Ada learned to understand that she could expect nothing better. She was invisible as a person. All servants were.

Ada comforted herself with the idea that if she could move on to a bigger household and be the cook and acknowledged for her skills, she would be paid more money. But there were so few opportunities that she would have to content herself with the life she had here, where she held the reins in her hands – at least inside the house.

She had tried telling Oswald what to do in the stables and gardens but since she was mean to him inside, he didn't listen to what she said outside.

'And don't tell my mother lies about me,' he said bravely.

'Lies? What lies are those, Oswald Leighton?'

'That I am making up to Sarah Charles when I shouldn't be.'

'You are. I heard every word you said the other day.'

'It's none of your business. I can court her if I choose. You had better stop it or I will send out rumours about you and that lad from the church.'

'Which lad? There is no lad,' Ada said.

'No, but there will be if you don't learn to shut up.'

Sarah was glad that she had decided to go up to the Hilda House. The sun shone and the trees had new green buds. There were early lambs in the fields, jumping and skipping and running about. There were two steep hills before you reached the top of the dale and could stand looking back at the small square fields and grey stone houses. There was one hill that was not so steep going down into a narrow valley, then up the other side, from where you could see the little town. She felt quite nostalgic when she spied the ragged farmhouse dwelling and the beck which flowed at the bottom of it, the first building of the town.

She had thought she would never want to see it again but even the deserted town had moved on. It was just as shabby as ever and nobody lived there as far as she could tell, but the Hilda House stood tall at the top of the town just before the fell began and when she tried the door it was not locked.

There were sheep in the fields all around and up on the fell when she walked as far as that. More than anywhere else in the world, she loved that place. It seemed a silly thing to be fond of – it was almost barren with nothing but sheep, gorse, barns and byres for miles – but there were farms in various directions and the people who lived there scraped some kind of living.

The air was said to be like champagne, though Sarah had no idea what champagne smelled like. It was fresh and clean and she loved how the wind swept low on a blustery day, wafting in the sheeps' faces. If the weather was bad, the sheep would shelter against the grey stone walls, but most of the time they just ignored it.

The farmers would bring hay out to them, as a lot of the ewes were in lamb and needed more sustenance than what the fell could give them. She had heard somewhere that the land up there could not have been the way that it was without its sheep. Who had told her that? She couldn't remember, just that it was a balance, the way that things were meant to go on.

So life went on here despite the empty houses and the well-scoured streets because of the wild life, and the fact that it brought forth the right grass and the birds which flew low over the tops. The sky was clear blue with the odd white cloud that day and Sarah was pleased to be alive for the first time since she had lost Miss Hutton.

Weeds grew like yellow stars, with spiky green leaves in profusion everywhere and various wild animals had taken up home in many of the buildings. There were few predators – it was a special place where only the toughest survived but that also made it dear to her, for she felt like that herself. She was a survivor and she thought that was what she liked best about Isabella. Somehow she had come through and maybe it was special being up here when other people had failed or deserted it. She would make good, she knew it.

Inside in the kitchen, Isabella looked for the sofa where her mother had breathed her last but the sofa itself was inoffensive. There was other furniture in the various rooms and some of it was in poor shape but she liked the house itself, and since it had so many windows, it was warming up. When Sarah suggested they might come and live there for a while Isabella was quite hopeful.

Now that she was coming to terms with her mother dying and how her father and brother had left, she began to see the house differently and in a much more positive way. She had a sudden liking for this building which she couldn't explain. Maybe in its way, it had helped her to get through, had given her mother somewhere to lie down and die at least. She felt she owed it her affection and was eager to give that now, so she went through the rooms, marvelling at the light.

Sarah discovered that the well still worked when you primed it, which seemed to her like a big step forward, and in the garden, shoots were beginning to appear. But just as she became excited by the idea of living there, her sensible self took over and told her there was no way in which she could. There was no transport, nobody to help, she had no work and no money, but it was spring and it was impossible not to be pleased with that. It was the best time of year when everything was starting up again.

They had their first happy day and Sarah thought that being together had made a difference in their lives. Now they were ready to step forward. Since nobody lived here there could be no harm in coming to enjoy themselves occasionally.

When they got back to the doctor's house at teatime, Isabella ran straight into the yard to tell Oswald and his mother about her day. Sarah was so pleased that the child felt happy and that she had gone back to the cottage to tell his mother what a wonderful day she had had.

'I could go with you sometimes if you like,' Oswald said, his face blazing.

Isabella could see that Sarah was embarrassed because all she managed was, 'That's very kind, Oswald, but it's no trouble to walk on a fine day and we won't be venturing anywhere on wet days.'

Ada stormed out of the house at that point and shouted across the yard. 'Come and get your tea. Don't stand around talking like that.' She then clashed the outside door.

Isabella looked at them in dismay. She had been so excited to talk about her day that she had forgotten how things were until now. Oswald had gone scarlet-faced and was not meeting anybody's eyes. She had caused a fight. Would they start yelling at one another or was it only her mother and father who did that? But of course no more, because he was gone and her mother was in the cemetery.

'Why does Ada keep on saying nasty things to Oswald about you?' Isabella said and she ran upstairs, crying.

Sarah strode into the kitchen accosting Ada who turned around.

'Don't you see that you are spoiling things for the bairn?' she said. 'Try to be nice for her sake. Oswald means nothing to me and he never could, but you could try to be a bit kinder for all our sakes.'

'There's no reason why I should put up with you and Oswald being mucky. We all know what you are – not fit for decent company.'

Sarah could stand no more. She ran upstairs after Isabella and neither of them went down for tea or again that night. Sarah didn't sleep. The following morning Ada loftily told her that the doctor wanted to see her in the sitting room before surgery and when she went in there, he was looking most uncomfortable.

'Sit down, Miss Charles. We seem to have something of a problem here. Ada and Fiona are unhappy.' He sighed as though he wished somebody else would take on his domestic problems because he had more important things to do.

'I didn't mean to cause problems,' Sarah said. 'I do have an idea and I think it could be a solution. Isabella and I could go up and live in the Hilda House.'

The doctor looked blank and Sarah explained. 'But there's nobody else in that village,' he said. ' You wouldn't be safe.'

'I want to try something new and here isn't the right place anymore. Do you think the house on the tops belongs to anybody and that we could be stopped?'

He looked relieved and why wouldn't he? He replied enthusiastically. 'Not so far as I know but how would you live?'

'I don't know yet. I have some frocks I could sell at the market and then I could buy wool and sell other stuff, and maybe one or two shops here would sell me food.'

'It doesn't sound like much of an existence,' the doctor said.

'If it doesn't work, I've lost nothing,' Sarah said. 'I would really like to try it.'

Despite what he'd said, the doctor seemed pleased and after a few moments came up with, 'How about if I get Oswald to take you up there and we give you some things to help you settle in, on the understanding that if you hate it you know you can come back here?'

Sarah was astonished at this offer. She wanted to say no because of the problems with Oswald and how she didn't get on with Ada no matter how hard she tried. But her sensible self told her that she would need heavy foodstuffs and to take her and Isabella's clothes, and there was no way they could do this without help, so she accepted gratefully. This time nobody could say to Oswald that he should not take her. The doctor had said it was going to happen and so it did. But nobody was pleased about the arrangement, even Oswald. He barely spoke to her now he knew that she was leaving, and he walked about the yard with a grim look on his face.

Sarah didn't like to say to the doctor that she was despised in the village. He would not know. He was an incomer. She wanted to talk to Isabella first in case the little girl would rather stay here but Isabella wanted to go with her.

Oswald lit up like half a dozen candles when he was told he would take them up to the house, and she thought that he was desperate enough by now to be grateful for just a little time with her. That sounded awful and she didn't mean to be unkind so she was polite to him without being the least bit encouraging. Even Ada and Fiona were told to help and Sarah smiled just a little because Ada could not complain. She guessed that Mrs Leighton was probably delighted she was moving away from Oswald.

Hastily she altered the dresses she could sell at the market so that she would have a little bit of independence. Also, the atmosphere in the house lifted quite a bit when Ada realized she was getting rid of Sarah. In the end, even though Sarah wanted to sell it, she altered her favourite black velvet dress, letting out what had been generous seams, and said she would give it to Ada before she left.

Ada's cheeks went crimson and she said, hoarsely, 'I don't want any of your stuff, Sally Charles,' and rushed out of the kitchen. For the first time, Sarah understood. Ada and Fiona wished they that they were young again, with different options than they had had at the time.

Sarah stared at the dress, thinking of how much money it would have brought, but she wouldn't go back on her decision. She pitied Ada, and that was a horrible feeling, but the dress was almost magical. That was what Miss

Hutton had said: that it would bring Sarah good luck. Sarah hoped that it would fetch Ada good luck if she could only bring herself to wear it.

Eleven

Fiona McIntyre used to tell people that she had left her home so long ago that she had little recollection of it, but that wasn't true, though by now it was twenty years ago. Her memory did not fail her. Why should it? She could remember very well when she was eighteen and her parents had wanted her married.

They had been so very proud of the fact that she had caught the attention of one of the heirs of the isle, Alastair Beaston. She had been so lucky, everybody said, though her father was a gentleman farmer and they were important on the island too. She had loved her home. She had thought it was the most beautiful place on earth when she was a child. Their house was very old and had several hundred acres. It was just beyond the only big village on the island, which looked out across the sea with its prettily fronted, different-coloured houses – green and pale blue and mauve. When they reflected in the water from the harbour they glistened even brighter and the light seemed to shift across them.

She had wanted to go to school alongside the other

children but her mother thought they were beneath her, so instead she had a governess. The trouble was that the governess, like her parents, kept her away from other children and she had to endure day after day in what had started out as her classroom and became her prison. She was frequently bored and would stare from the window but her governess kept her working hard at arithmetic and grammar and Fiona found it a dull life.

She wished to be free, to run along the beaches, to go fishing in a little blue and white boat. She was never alone and yet she was lonely.

She was considered very pretty until she grew too tall and thin. But she did have dark blue eyes and black hair. And although her mother worried that nobody would take her because of her height, she caught the eye of Beaston, and that was that.

The truth was that Fiona didn't like him. He was a lot shorter than she was, and while that shouldn't have mattered – it certainly didn't seem to do so to him – she hated looking above his head while they danced. Also, he had lost his three front teeth and his hair was already thinning on top. His father had been bald since very young. And worst of all somehow, he had spots on his chin, great big red spots with yellow middles and a hair sprouting from each one. They glowed.

He enjoyed being rich and had many horses. He spoke of them as 'nags'. He talked like an Englishman and had been away most of his life at some English school, which Fiona thought was very strange. His conversation was monologue; he talked and talked at her and never asked her anything about herself, what she cared for, what she wanted, what she had done, whether she was happy. She had the feeling he would marry because he ought to and it was expected and for no other reason.

His parents had fine carriages and many acres, and they went to London for the season – whatever that was. They had at least one other castle as well as the one they had here, which was huge and cold and draughty. When Fiona went there she was always shivering, especially since her mother insisted on her wearing flimsy garments, and the food was brought so far from the kitchen that it was cold before it reached you.

There she was treated with courtesy because she was going to marry Alastair but she made no friends. She began to think that it was her own fault. She never knew what to say to anyone because she had had it drummed into her that she was superior to everyone on the island. Like her mother, she was meant to give orders. She had been taught that she had nothing to do. The housekeeper ran the house – there were dozens of servants – and although Fiona had her own pony, she was not allowed to go anywhere by herself.

Her days were spent at endless tea parties listening to older women talk about their daughters, their marriages and their grandchildren, and her mother was the proudest of all as she boasted about her daughter's coming marriage, which she was so obviously ecstatic about. Fiona was sure that her mother enjoyed the envy of other women.

By that time Fiona had found herself among girls her own age but they resented that she had been chosen to marry the lord of the isle and were never kind to her, so she was lonely there too.

Alastair seemed to want nothing from her. She didn't in truth know why he had chosen her – there were lots of pretty girls on the island, some much better looking than she was, some better off, and he could hardly have found her fascinating. She even overheard Alastair's father tell his son that he was mystified about the boy's choice but Alastair only said that he thought she would do.

'She's too tall to be pretty and her features are long and she has ears like an elephant, but I suppose she will breed well enough when you get in there,' his father said and they both laughed.

Fiona did find out why Alastair did not care and did what he was told. The truth was that he preferred a boy, and although Fiona was rather aghast at this, she thought if Alastair had come to her and been honest and told her, she might still have married him, though it would have been an odd triangle. It might have saved them both a lot of heartache. She did not want to marry but it would have been a reasonable solution as long as he did not tell her what to do.

The trouble was that the boy Alastair preferred was the boy she would have married could she have chosen. His father was a small farmer but he was a merry lad: funny, clever, always kind when they met. He taught her to dance so that she found it easy, and she loved to hear him speak in his lilting voice rather than Alastair's flat nasal London tones, but it was not to be and in the end the idea that the one boy did not love her and the other pretended to love her for what it could get him, put her off.

She could not of course tell her parents about this and neither could she explain the problem. She did try to object but she could see that it was not going to get her anywhere so she made plans to leave. She was horrified at the idea of never seeing the island again but there was no choice. She would be obliged to marry and get herself into such a terrible endless mess of misery that she might never recover.

Luckily she was given an allowance. Her mother questioned her when she stopped buying anything for herself, this being the one freedom she had enjoyed, but she began to stow her money away. Meanwhile, her mother had her wedding clothes made and various pretty dresses so there were tedious hours with dressmakers, lots of talk about her marriage, and sniggers about the many children she was expected to have.

The marriage was to be in May. In April therefore, on a cold, wet day, she left home. The ferry was not far and she dressed plainly so that nobody would recognize her. She wore a dark cloak with a hood, stout boots and the plainest dress she owned and then, knowing when the early ferry would depart, she got on and left the island.

Looking back at the place she had loved so much she could not believe that she had done so. All she had taken was the money and that was in a little bag, safe on her person, around her waist. Many times after that she regretted what she had done until she remembered what her future was going to be.

The trouble was she soon discovered that there was nothing for a single woman who had no skills to do but become a servant, and so that was what she did. She made up a story of dead parents and losing her home and she found lodging as a kitchen maid in the kind of house where she had grown up.

To be fair, it wasn't so bad. Everybody looked down at how humble her place was, but at last she had something to do and though she slept in a big plain room with half a dozen other maids, and worked hard every hour of the day, it was still better than the life she had had and that was a surprise.

Also the cook showed her how to do her kitchen duties and for the first time in her life Fiona was competent at something. She got very excited that she had actually become good at something, even if it was how to pare potatoes and carrots and fashion dumplings from suet, flour and water until her hands grew sticky. Best of all, the cook was adept at puddings and sweet pastries and praised Fiona highly as she took to these abilities right from the start.

With her educated voice and sweet accent, though she had tried hard to modify it, she could so easily have become a lady's maid but she steered clear of such things, concentrated on her work and tried to say as little as possible. Nobody took any notice of her. She was free at last, went to church with the other servants of a Sunday and she liked being among them. She had found a home, humble though it was.

When the cook finally left to go to what she considered a better job, she asked Fiona if she would like to go as well. The cook was tired of so much work and was being taken on at a house in Dumfries which was not nearly as big. They needed a parlour maid as well. So Fiona took that job at a house which overlooked the river and nothing more was asked of her except to do her work. She got paid so she was able to add to her stash of money. Dumfries was a pretty town with many shops and although she was not tempted to buy much she liked looking around and revelled in having choices.

In time she saw that smaller houses were more friendly and eventually she ended up in Weardale at the house of the local doctor. Why she felt that she had come home was beyond her comprehension. There was something about the way that nothing was large and nobody was important that she liked, and she liked also that she and Ada ran the house together. It was a little bit like having a sister, though Ada could be sharp and difficult, but Ada taught her fine sewing and knitting and was accomplished in many ways which Fiona had never seen before and much admired.

Twelve

It didn't occur to the doctor for some weeks after he had met Mrs Prudhoe that he was making excuses to go up on the tops and see her. He was quite embarrassed when he realized. He had thought that he would never love again.

In an awful way it helped somehow that his wife's parents disliked her. Indeed, they were sometimes very disparaging about her, saying that with looks such as hers she ought to have done a lot better than marry a poor curate. Shameful that widowed, she had had to find work and provide a dame school for the local children.

'She's lost her looks, of course. No one would have her now,' said his mother-in-law with some relish, as though beautiful women joined everybody else once they hit forty and their first bloom had gone.

'Her father was a farm labourer,' his father-in-law said. 'And the man she married, Timothy Prudhoe, was nothing but a curate, a most unpleasant individual with less learning than a clergyman should have. I think it was only five years into their marriage when he died.'

Alex told himself that he was being ridiculous, that he was just missing his wife: sleeping with her, holding her, having her there against him, the things she said, the way that she laughed and how she had loved her plain little children, who looked not at all like either of their parents.

The missing of his wife was what urged him to ask Mrs Prudhoe to marry him, despite calling himself a fool a hundred times over. She would do her duty and be a mother to his girls, he comforted himself, and he wouldn't have to bother with them very much, since he would then have three women in his house and the children could go to the local school. He would have somebody in his bed and at his table, and he was content with the idea by the time he proposed to her.

'Here you are again,' his mother-in-law said in alarm when he was at the vicarage for the second time in a week. 'Have you decided what you will do with the girls?'

He debated whether to tell her what he was thinking of doing but then what if Mrs Prudhoe turned him down? He was forty, had two small, difficult children. On the other hand, what was she to do when his girls went? She would be left with no more than nine or ten children, whose parents presumably paid as little as they could for her to take charge of their children during the week all day, which gave them time to work and have some freedom.

Judging by her house and the way that she dressed, Mrs Prudhoe was living on a pittance. She was far too thin, as if often she had not sufficient to eat, and her clothes were almost in tatters, though he could see how neatly she had sewn her apparel to pretend to the world that she was better off than she was. He also worried that she might accept his proposal because it was the only way that she could better herself.

It was unlikely that anyone else would have her in this out-of-the-way place where every decent man was married. Besides, she could read and write, add up, seemed to know reams of poetry and even spoke a little French. Apparently she had had a neighbour who came from the Charente. She was above the local farmers and they would not want a wife who was better educated than themselves. Wives were meant to be looked down on, if only slightly, but certainly not up at. It would upset the order of everything.

It was March, and snowdrops were lifting their heads in clumps in the cold windy churchyard before he ventured to the schoolhouse. The girls were still with their grand-parents, though the arrangement seemed worse every time he called. They were always what their grandmother called 'misbehaving'. Doris hid in cupboards whereas Georgina would jump on the settee. She shrieked with excitement when he arrived, and no matter what anybody said, Doris would not come out of the darkness and

Georgina ran screaming around the house regardless of peace and furniture.

He shut the outside door so that they could not follow him, for he felt certain they would given half a chance. Despite everything, he could not keep from himself the idea that his children hated being there, especially with Doris preferring the dark to dealing with her grandparents.

He walked the short distance to the schoolhouse and there Mrs Prudhoe opened the door to him. She looked surprised, greeted him politely and asked whether there was some kind of problem with the girls. He knew exactly what she was thinking, that the girls were to go away to school. It seemed almost cruel.

She asked him into the parlour and whether he would have tea, but he was too nervous to wait for kettles and ceremony, so when she asked him to sit down he told her straight away that the girls were not going away to school. She tried to hide the relief in her voice but could not. Her lovely grey eyes sparkled with tears.

After that he didn't know how to go on. He had only proposed once before and they had been young and he had felt a lot better than he did now. The thought of Doris hiding and Georgina shrieking around the house and jumping on the furniture spurred him on. He tried not to think that Mrs Prudhoe would be obliged to marry him, even if she thought him a poor speck of a thing, because she had little choice. Neither could he leave the girls where they were in school or in the vicarage. They were his children and he could not fob them off on to anybody else any longer, so he cleared his throat and said that he was planning to take the girls to live with him. It was a start.

The relief faded, her colour went, and now she could see how dark her future was without them. He could see it too. *Could I survive on the little I make?* was her next thought. She twisted her thin fingers in her lap and looked down as though she might never look up again.

'Mrs Prudhoe, I know that I have only seen you as my children's teacher and from time to time at the vicarage, but I have become fond of you. I need a mother for my children and a wife and helpmeet for myself. Would you – might you – consider becoming my own?'

It was the very last thing she had expected, he could see. The colour came and went in her face. He knew that he was not the most eligible man in the dale but to a woman like this he was a godsend, even if she had to do no more than endure him.

She let go of her breath in a sigh. She looked at him as though she had not heard him properly, as though something so good could never happen to a humble schoolteacher, as though she was not the most beautiful woman he had seen in a very long time. She was perhaps unaware of it, or maybe she had had so many difficult things to think about that she did not look in a mirror. She stared at him until the coals in the grate, which made up a tiny fire, fell apart and then she turned and glanced at them in case they should fall forward and further damage the already shabby hearth rug, which was dark with age and burns.

'Marry you?'

'Yes.'

She said nothing and then they began to smile in mutual embarrassment.

'I know it is not an easy thing to do,' Alex said quickly. 'You already know that my children are dreadful, at least they are when they are with their grandparents.'

'They aren't easy,' she said. 'They lost their mother when they needed her most.'

'Their grandparents would be so relieved if you married me.'

That made her smile. 'They don't like me much,' she said. 'It amazed me when they did not object to my little school.'

'I think they were very keen on having the children away from them all day.'

'I am sure,' she said.

'Will you have me then?'

She hesitated.

'I can give you a few days to think about it,' he said.

She said that would be fine and then he left, pausing

at the vicarage only long enough to raise his voice and be heard above the noise his children made. Then he thought how conflicted his parents-in-law would feel. They were getting rid of the responsibility of these difficult children, but if Mrs Prudhoe agreed to marry him and they discovered that their grandchildren were being entrusted to a woman whose father had been a farm labourer, and who had only benefited from education because the vicar in Lanchester had set up a school for the local children, they would undoubtedly be horrified. She had been nobody.

Worried about what he had done, and even more so that she might dislike him so much that she would turn him down, he got on to his horse and went back to Wolsingham.

Thirteen

It appeared to Harry that his father changed after Christmas. He wasn't sure exactly what happened but somehow everything became different. He had grown used over the weeks to his father being almost totally unresponsive. He had tried at first to get his father to eat something or at least go to bed to sleep, but he could see that there was no point. His father had undoubtedly lived like this for years and was too far gone in his own alcoholic world to change anything.

Harry had hoped that it would be different when his father saw him but then he knew so little about his home. His father was all that he had left and a small lift of his heart had occurred when he finally got there but it had dissipated almost immediately.

His father did not move from that chair unless he needed the lavatory or to find another bottle of brandy. Harry tried not to be disappointed. What had he expected? He had never heard from his father in all these years away. Why should it be different now? The other shock was how badly off they were. There was no food in the house, the rooms were freezing cold and it had been years since anybody had taken a duster or a mop to any surface here. Cobwebs festooned the corners. The windows, when he tried to open them, were stuck fast so that he could not let any fresh air inside. He stood open both the back and front doors and opened the doors into all the rooms even when it was wet. He would rather there was wind and rain inside the house than the vile air which was so stale. He learned to hate the brandy fumes and the sound of his father's drunken snores.

There was furniture in all the rooms but it was old and tatty. The curtains were in shreds and dust stood thick upon the surfaces. There was no hot water because the kitchen stove was never lit, but Harry decided that he could achieve a great deal here if he tried.

First of all he discovered coal and logs and sticks and paper in a big building in the backyard. There was a wash house, an empty hen house and several other buildings including stables. In them he found gardening tools, a spade, a bucket, even one of those shallow baskets, which probably had belonged to his mother, that women used to gather flowers in. He tried to remember her doing this but could not. It was frustrating, but at last he was making progress.

He got the stove lit and then he scrubbed the kitchen floor and gradually all the downstairs rooms. He threw out the carpets, which had gone almost completely into holes. He took down the curtains and got rid of them, and was immediately grateful for the extra light which came into the house.

His father kept on waking up, shielding his eyes, and asking what the hell was happening, but Harry went on with what he was doing.

He found soap powder in a cupboard and washed sheets and pillowcases in the kitchen sink on a fine day, hanging them out to dry in the backyard. He gained a lot of satisfaction from watching them blow about like sails and even better was the smell when he brought them back inside, not quite crisp from a sudden frost.

The mattresses he would have liked to get rid of because they were old, but they had had nobody sleeping on them for so long that they weren't grubby or uneven when he tested them, they just needed airing. So he hauled them down the stairs and out into the back garden on the first really warm day.

The property was several acres, he knew, and there was a stream at the bottom of it. So he found a fishing rod and discovered that somewhere along the way somebody had taught him how to cast a line. Had his father done such a thing way back? He did hope so. Anyhow, it worked. And he also discovered a box of exquisite flies, bright in blues and greens, looking almost like the dragonflies they were meant to emulate. Had his father or his grandfather made these when they were decent people?

There was a huge vegetable garden and a lot of greenhouses. There were some vegetables surviving, God knew how, but he was able to cook them lightly and they were okay to eat, though he needed more than that. With the little money he found he went to the closest grocery store and bought flour, yeast, sugar and various pulses, and was glad that one summer, a couple of years ago, the second master's wife, a lovely woman, had spent a lot of time in the holiday teaching him to cook and bake. He didn't think he was going to be any great shakes but he could make bread, broth and various puddings and it was a start. Amongst the books in the kitchen, dirty and up on a high shelf, he found something called the Be-Ro book and he was rather pleased because the recipes he used were successful.

He went down to the cellar. There was no brandy left, which hardly surprised him because what there was his father kept in the kitchen, but there were a lot of other bottles – sherry, port and various kinds of home-made wine, including a very nice fizzy drink which was labelled 'elderflower champagne'. This had never occurred to him. Who had made home-made wines and why, when the family had always had money? The look of the beetroot wine was rich and the orange wine had a bright golden tinge to it. He was not sure that much of it was drinkable but he went through the only-just legible labels and discovered also parsnip and elderberry. Some of the bottles had long since burst, leaving glass everywhere, and there were empty beer bottles rolling on the floor.

Some of it surely must be worth selling. He surprised himself by going to the local grocer at the end of the street, where he had bought basic foodstuffs, and asking if he might buy any of these things. The man, Mr Hauxley, looked suspiciously at him but Harry said he needed money and if Mr Hauxley would just come and look they might be able to come to some agreement.

They did. It didn't make Harry rich but it did mean that he could eat as they exchanged goods for goods. It was such a relief. Harry was able to buy tea, coffee, butter, milk and cheese and it made such a difference.

He also repaired the hen house with wood and a hammer and nails that he found in an outhouse. Then he bought half a dozen chickens from Mr Hauxley and the corn to feed them.

Harry was quite proud of himself, except the chickens didn't seem to know they were meant to stay in one place and began to wreck what flowerbeds were left, so Harry fenced them in and kept them more or less at bay. Also, this meant they didn't lay away as much and it was easier to lock them in at night. The hen coop was old but did its job.

He could not find any money once the obvious places

had been searched, but there must have been some because his father had a supply of brandy. When Harry opened the cupboards in the drawing room there were dozens more bottles. Maybe that was why there was no money. It had all been spent on brandy.

His father woke up suddenly when Harry exclaimed aloud at the lack of money.

'We aren't short of a bob or two,' his father declared and went back to sleep again.

Harry searched in vain, even, though he hated to admit it, looking through his father's pockets and the clothes hanging up in his wardrobe. They had been mostly strewn over the floor but where they lay or hung there was nothing in the pockets.

Occasionally his father went out. Harry did not like to ask where or why but his father could be very crafty and if Harry was not around he would slip out of the front door and evade him. Mr Whitty, the local policeman, would bring him back half drunk and Harry even gave up apologizing because Mr Whitty, unprompted, said kindly, 'Don't worry, we've all got family like him. It isn't your fault.'

That spring two men came to the house and they were obviously friends. Where his father had made friends, Harry'd no idea, and they looked to him like what people called unsuitable, with shabby clothes and dirty hands, but his father ushered them in joyfully. They sat over the fire – which Harry tried to keep up – in the drawing room, drinking brandy, talking loudly and laughing without restraint.

He knew that he ought to be glad his father had found some reason to go out or had somebody to visit him, but these were the very last people Harry would have wanted there. They ignored him, did not speak, looked down at him and called him 'lad' if they had to.

Harry was physically afraid of no one. Boarding school and his life had taken care of that. He well knew how to look after himself against others, but he was in his father's house now and he was not about to cause problems, so when they came or his father went to them, he just kept out of the way. It was easier.

Fourteen

There lived, about a mile from the Hilda House, a farmer's widow called Hilary Nattrass. The small farm was mostly sheep, being too high for the top fields to be much use for anything else, though further down Hilary grew crops. The farm itself had belonged to the Nattrass family for many generations. It was stoutly built of grey stone and had a number of buildings around it. At one time, when Hilary was young, she had been a nun at the Foundling School, such was the name by which the Hilda House had once been known. She had left there to marry but the farm had become an extension of the school and Hilary and her husband had taken in older boys to teach them farming skills.

Hilary's children were scattered. They had gone off to easier places to live in the south and now she was lonely up there by herself. She slightly resented that they had left. Her daughter, Bessie, she knew would leave, as she had always found living up there to be so very difficult, and when the chance had come along she took it. She had met a clergyman, a curate who came to help Mr

Wilson, and when he left to take up his first post she went with him as his wife. They now had a small parish just beyond York. Hilary could not have been better pleased, so glad that her daughter had achieved what she had wanted most of all.

The two boys had hurt her more. Aidan, the elder one, she had expected to take on the farm, but he had been of a scholastic nature. Her boys were the wrong way round: the elder was academically clever, the younger good with his hands. Neither of them had any inclination towards running the farm and Hilary was more injured than she had thought possible.

When she tried to get them to stay they too left. That Aidan was living in Kent was all she knew; she had no address for him. He had effectively barred her from his life and certainly from his future. Hilary knew nothing of this place so very far away but she blamed herself for having asked so much of him. Norman had married a girl whose father ran an inn on the west coast in Devon.

Whatever had she done that they had left like that? Or was it just that the life up here was so hard that they did not want to share it with her? She did not hear from Norman either and when she did have letters from Bessie, she discovered to her disappointment that there were no children. Bessie was having a wonderful time, so she said. Hilary didn't know whether to believe her, but she had no more information and so there was no point in worrying about it since there was nothing she could do.

She knew that she had grandchildren because occasionally she heard news about her family, and since she was by now very old she thought those children would be almost adults. She hoped for a while that at least one of them might choose to visit but they never did and in the end she gave up hoping for it.

She grew lonely up on the tops. She rarely saw anyone other than when she went into Wolsingham to the market and she had managed to keep herself without going far. She had a cow and chickens, made her own bread and cakes, grew her vegetables in a sheltered part of the farm next to the buildings around the front, and had a small orchard which her husband had built, surrounding it with a stone wall to keep out the worst of the winter winds.

That had been many years ago and now the orchard had grown strong and there were plum, pear and apple trees. Hilary shot over her land and wanted for nothing much, except other people and the odd brown trout which she bartered for with the fishmonger in Wolsingham.

Therefore when she heard that the Hilda House was inhabited, she determined to make herself known and discover what her neighbours were like.

*

Sarah opened the front door one day in spring to discover a tall, stoutly built old woman, wisely dressed for the cold wind and carrying a basket in which she had butter, eggs, a bottle of milk, bread, fruit cake and two kittens, one ginger and one black and white.

Sarah regarded her visitor with joy. The food was welcome, she immediately liked the weather-beaten face and big smile, and Isabella fell instantly in love with the two kittens, giving them a saucerful of milk. Hilary looked around her with interest, telling them how she had lived here and how she had left and that the nuns had gone back to Newcastle when the owner of the village died, and since then the orphanage had also failed.

Other nuns had been there for a time but the life had been too hard for them and they also had left. The place had been a home for unmarried mothers for a while but nobody spoke of it so Hilary kept her peace. She remembered Connie and her family after that, and then Sarah vaguely, but she was pleased to see Sarah grown up and the lovely little foreign girl with her.

'It will be nice to have you here.' She beamed, sitting down by the kitchen fire as she was invited to do.

Hilary told them they could have butter, milk and eggs as often as they wanted and that she always had more bread and scones and cake than she could eat, she so delighted in making them. She sold her butter at the market in Wolsingham and there she bought whatever she needed that she could not make, which was in fact very little, just flour, yeast and sugar. She generally got a lift there and back on a farm cart if any were going her way, so if the girls needed anything she might be able to help or they could go with her if they had to.

Hilary did not say so but there was another very good reason for her to be glad of neighbours. She had become convinced that her home was haunted. She thought at first that her mind was going, that having been alone for so long with the cold, dark winters, life had got the better of her. She was not young anymore. She had had nobody to tell and somehow she could not confide in Sarah, who was still very young. Anyway, Sarah would think she was mad. There was no such thing as ghosts and Hilary told herself that she had lived there all these years and never been afraid. Now she was.

She called herself names but then she lay in her bed and shook. Her sheepdog, Bert, shook too, hiding under the pillows, and that was what frightened her most of all – Bert's fear. He would lie with one ear cocked and shiver. He even hid against Hilary. *So much for him being a guard dog*, she thought, with what humour she could summon.

At night the cats were of no comfort. They liked being outside and although she would have welcomed them to her fire they were very independent, sleeping in any of the buildings which were warm or with Daisy the cow, who exuded heat and did not mind them nestling against her.

The cats came for milk and drank water and Hilary did feed them, but mostly they caught rats and mice and poor small birds and devoured them.

In the mornings the sun came late and she was grateful for the light, for what little sun there was and any peace that she could gain.

But then one night she awoke because Bert was whining. When she didn't move he began barking as loudly as he could and she awoke to the smell of burning and smoke. She turned with Bert and ran outside while the stairs still held. There she coughed until she was sick and tears ran down her face.

The cats had fled. She led Daisy out of the barn, which would go up next, she let the chickens out, though they didn't go far from her, and then she just sat and waited, watching her beloved home burn to the ground. There had been no rain for days, so everything was dry and all that she owned was lost.

She stumbled the mile to the Hilda House, with boots on her feet, but no stockings, and her big coat over her nightdress. Bert was beside her, and when Sarah opened the door, she stared. Hilary thought she must have looked like a ghost in her long white nightie and she was so shocked and distressed she couldn't speak.

Fifteen

Ada hated the black dress with the pearl buttons which Sally had given her. She wanted to stamp on it, to throw it outside into the spring morning, but most of all it made her want to cry. She had not in her life seen, never mind owned, such an exquisite thing. She wished she could throw it back into the smug face of Sally Charles.

Unfortunately, Sally had left the hated dress on the bed, which had been clever of her, Ada thought. There could be no confrontation now that she was gone.

Alone with the dress she fingered the material. It was soft and yielding like cat's fur. She wondered who it had first belonged to. Miss Hutton had bought it and taken it to pieces and remade it for Sally, and she could see it had been lovingly done, even though she didn't want to. Now Sally had remade it for a plain old maid, Ada lashed herself.

She hung it up carefully at the back of the wardrobe and tried to forget about it but was amazed when, that Sunday, Fiona dressed after breakfast to go to church and was wearing the blue dress that Sarah had made to fit her.

'You can't wear something like that to church,' Ada protested. 'You'll look silly, all dressed up. Everybody will laugh.'

'Where else am I ever to wear it?' Fiona said. 'Where do I go?'

'People will know how over the top it is,' Ada said. 'It's a house of God, you know, not a circus.'

'I don't think God will mind me dressing up for him,' Fiona said equably.

From somewhere she had found a blue felt hat, Ada suspected from the market, the exact same colour as the dress, but Ada was not going to ask because Sally Charles had given the dress to Fiona.

So Fiona went off to church with her head held high. Ada wanted to stamp after her, she felt such fury. She only possessed three dresses so a new dress was a big occasion but she would not give in. She ignored Fiona and wore her usual least-shabby dress to church as she always did, and the little black hat which she had had for so long that it was falling to pieces and had to be held on her head so firmly that it hurt with the number of hat pins it took.

But Fiona was difficult to ignore. She was like a child at Christmas, singing each hymn very loudly in her enthusiasm so that the vicar, Mr Wilson, shook her hand after the service when he was saying goodbye to his parishioners at the church door. He told her that she had a fine voice and should think about joining the choir.

Ada knew that Fiona had a beautiful voice, but still she resented that nobody had asked her to join the choir and that several of the women who had congregated in the church grounds to gossip congratulated Fiona on her pretty new frock and said how well it suited her.

Sunday was just as busy a day for the two maids as any other day of the week. They had no official time off. The doctor was not a difficult master, he just didn't think about such things. When he had first got here and their beloved Dr Neville had gone off to London, they were inclined to miss him very much.

Also they missed his mother and disliked that there wasn't a mistress in the house. They feared that the new man would be a tyrant. Men so often were. In fact he was the opposite. They were surprised at first but ultimately relented because although he was not given to complimenting the food, he never complained about anything either. He also put up the wages of all his servants once he had been there for six months.

When it was cold he liked having fires in the bedrooms. Oswald, having less to do in the garden in winter, kept the house warm. So Ada and Fiona had a fire in their bedroom. This had never happened to either of them before, except for Fiona when she had lived on her beloved island, and they were much appreciative of it.

Ada was given to watching the fire from her bed before she fell asleep.

The doctor seemed to realize by the time he had been there for a few months that the maids needed time off, and that they must have their days off together if they were not coming home at night, because one maid sleeping in the doctor's house would have raised a great many eyebrows and set tongues wagging.

Fiona had nowhere to go and Ada did not want to go back to the awful house in Rookhope where her huge family lived, but when Fiona begged to be taken because she had nowhere else to see people they decided that they would.

Up to then Oswald, who had relatives in St John's Chapel, had taken Ada up to Rookhope for a few hours at a time. When the doctor decided both maids should go and stay overnight, Ada was horrified that she must take Fiona with her and made excuses at first.

However, the doctor said that he was not averse to a cold supper and on the day they went, Mrs Carver, who came in to do the laundry, would make his meals. She lived just along the road and was paid well so it suited everybody.

They could also take time off in the evenings if they wanted to, the doctor told them. So Fiona politely asked him if she could have part of Thursday evening to herself because she wanted to join the choir. The doctor looked amazed to be asked. He stared at her.

'A choir?' he said.

'Yes, sir. At the church.'

'But of course.' He hesitated and then he said, 'I don't mean you to always be in the house, you know. You can do as much as you like as long as it's respectable and I feel certain you're sure to be that. Do as you please as long as I am fed and have a clean shirt.'

Fiona was delighted and danced around the kitchen, saying what a kind man the doctor was. She saw him in a different light; he had smiled at her and the smile had reached his eyes.

Ada just wished that she had somewhere to go on Thursday evenings too.

Fiona invited her but Ada was too stubborn. She had not been asked, she said, so she sat at home and sulked over the kitchen fire, trying to be superior and above silly things like choirs, and yet she was lonely.

After Fiona went off to choir practice on the third Thursday running, Ada, though she didn't intend to, hurried upstairs and tried on the black dress.

It would be typical for her to be interrupted before she took it off again, she thought, though she wasn't quite sure why. But people called late and early at the doctor's house so you could never be certain of getting through anything.

She put on the dress and looked at herself in the mirror above the dressing table, which was next to the view of the garden. It was a big mirror which was not always an advantage when you considered yourself a little ungainly and plain.

She was glad that they did not sleep at the front of the house as people might have noticed, even though she had closed the curtains and lifted the candle up so that she could see herself better. At first she glared at the woman in the mirror and then she stared. The little plain person had vanished and in her place was a comely figure who, in her view, was almost pretty, with wide blue eyes and red hair. Although the hair was pulled away from her face and pinned up at the back of her neck, and was as simple as it could be, it made her beautiful as she had never been beautiful before.

The material fell in soft folds and here and there was enhanced with pearl buttons. She thought it was the most beautiful dress she had ever seen.

She took it off hastily and threw it on to the bed and then, unable to leave it there to crease, hung it up. She kept turning it around in what was left of the daylight. How much of it was Sally's work and why had she bothered? She must have known that it would get her nowhere. The sleeves fitted but not too tightly, so that they showed off her arms. The waist was high and flattered her figure, and the skirt moved as if it was a dress for dancing. She had never been to a dance. She had no idea how to dance.

She knew nothing of music. There had been no music

in the house in Rookhope, which was one of the reasons she liked going to church so much. She had a love of psalms. They were like poetry set to music and so beautiful that had she not been in church, she would have stood there with her eyes closed as the music wavered around the words. She was always sorry when they reached the end.

Eventually Ada gave in and agreed to Fiona staying overnight at her family's home because she could not think of a way to explain how very dreadful it was. She was sorry the minute that they got there and knew once again that she must never be left like her mother was. She must keep her place, she would do whatever was wanted, but she could never come back here.

Fiona said nothing but Ada could see by the look on the other woman's face how awful the street was. The houses were shabby, and the windowpanes had no paint left on them and were rotten. The children, her nephews and nieces, played in the dirt. They did not go to school. Ada had begged her mother and her sisters-in-law and sisters to give the children some kind of education, saying they would be the better for it, but nobody understood. All the family lived in the same buildings, including two married brothers, one of whom worked in a limestone quarry. The other had never worked at all.

Ada had forgotten how unimportant she was there. She had no money except what she was paid for cooking and cleaning in another man's house. It covered her mother in shame.

The children wore rags. Even though Ada made clothes for them and mended others, the children never received them. Her mother bartered them for more drink and cigarettes for the men. The women were slovenly and did not work and three of the men in the family sat and played cards all day, outside the houses if it was fine and in by the kitchen fire when it was not. All the women of her family were providing a new mouth to feed every year so the place was awash with children of all ages. The women were like unstoppable baby machines. Ada wished that she could somehow halt or delay this but the burden of her family grew ever bigger until she was exhausted trying to keep up with it.

She felt defeated and suddenly, standing there amidst the chaos, she couldn't bear it anymore and wanted to run away. She was so ashamed of the place but so glad that she had brought with her as much food as they could carry. Oswald had to carry it all into the poor falling-down little house where she had been born.

She ran down the road after Oswald, trying to contain her tears so that she could call him back. She didn't want to face her sorrows and complexities any longer than need be.

She caught up with him and said, 'Come back for us early this afternoon.'

She and Oswald did not like one another.

He stared. 'You said you were staying.'

'We aren't.'

'But—'

'We aren't.'

Oswald didn't get it, she could see. Presumably he had been looking forward to spending the night with his aunt and uncle in St John's Chapel.

Ada sacrificed her dislike of him and her pride; in desperation, tears sprang into her eyes, she felt so awful.

'Can you not see how small it is or that it is falling down? My mother has too many mouths to feed. I don't want her to have to feed us so we'll pretend to eat something and then you will come back and get us.'

'The doctor said you were staying until tomorrow.'

Ada looked pleadingly at him. It was the only way to get what she wanted. Then she said, with a genuine break in her voice, 'Oswald, would you want to stay here?'

Oswald stared at the narrow road and the dirty children who played outside, all of them looking a bit like Ada. 'All right then,' he said.

Ada felt relief surge through her and determined to be kinder to Oswald. He would be all right. He liked to go to St John's Chapel, even if he couldn't stay the night. He often got a hot dinner there and a couple of pints from his aunt, and if she wasn't at home his uncle would look after him. Ada envied Oswald his family. It made her embarrassed that he understood why she could not stay with her own family. She couldn't let Fiona endure it and she saw the look of relief on Fiona's face when Ada's mother piteously asked if they would be there overnight, and Ada said that the doctor could not do without them.

She showed her mother all the wonderful food they had brought with them: pies and pasties and cakes, fresh bread, butter, cheese, a cooked ham and even sweets for the little children, which Fiona had contributed. Ada's mother was grateful and tried not to cry, telling them how kind it was of them and how it would make such a lot of difference, but Ada could also feel the relief coming off her mother in waves: relief that they were not staying, that nobody would have to give up a much-needed bed and that she would not have to feed the two middle-aged women.

The hardest thing of all for Ada was that her mother did not like her. She had been the eldest and quickly discarded as her sister Poppy had followed in less than a year. Her father toiled at the quarry and her mother toiled in the house. They were half-starved and yet in her mother's estimation Ada was below her sisters and her sisters-in-law because she had attracted no man. Ada was ashamed of herself. She tried not to be but somehow it was a huge failure not to attract a man. Maybe that was why she liked Fiona so much. Fiona had attracted no man's attention either. Their misery held them together. They were old maids in every respect.

Sixteen

Sarah ushered Mrs Nattrass and Bert into the kitchen and she could see that the woman was very upset. The story unfolded with many tears but Sarah knew that she must act. She needed to collect Daisy and somehow scrape up the hens and the cats but she wasn't sure how to do it.

Hilary dried her tears and they went back to the ruined house. It was still smouldering so both girls were glad they had determined to go back as soon as possible. Isabella was able to lead Daisy away from the place. The hens had to be placed in a couple of sacks before they would cooperate. Sarah was just glad that Hilary did that with aplomb, somehow catching them by their legs but not hurting them. Once in the darkness they settled down.

The cats were easier. They had had no milk and also knew there was something very wrong. They followed, mewing all the way. Daisy was made comfortable in an outbuilding and for now the hens had their own barn. When morning arrived Daisy was milked, rather shakily, by Hilary. It was not the time, Sarah knew, to learn such things, so she couldn't offer to help. Then, the cats got their milk and the hens had some corn.

Sarah knew that Hilary could not put from her mind the way that her house had burned. It was true that the April weather had been warm and dry, but Hilary did not smoke – either in bed or anywhere else, she assured her hostess – and she had, as she always did, banked down the kitchen fire for the night. She had no idea what could have happened. She was so shocked and upset that Sarah did not like to question her but the day after, when Hilary confided about the ghosts, Sarah suspected that something very different to ghosts was happening, but she did not like to say anything.

Hilary was left with nothing and it was a worry to Sarah that she seemed to have to take responsibility for so much, but what else could she do? She tried to think, but she could not ask, who would want Hilary out of there? Her children had not cared for the small hill farm. Who else could benefit from the place burning to the ground?

Somebody, she thought, *made a very good job of the fire as the adjoining buildings also went up in smoke.* There was virtually nothing left but blackened stones.

Sarah went to talk to Mr Whitty, the local policeman, and then to Mr East, the solicitor. Mr Whitty was the most indolent man she had ever met and merely nodded when she told her tale. He also went on about how Hilary was getting older and how she could so easily have burned down the house, but Sarah was convinced that Hilary was too sensible to do anything of the kind. As a woman, Mr Whitty inferred she could do anything stupid. She was almost in her dotage. Sarah was inclined to be ill-tempered about all this but she could not afford to alienate the policeman in the area, so she merely smiled sweetly and told him that she would be very grateful if he could just go and take a look and see if he could discover anything.

Mr East was very helpful and had frowned as he listened to her. So Sarah was glad she had gone to him because she trusted his ideas and knew he would aid her if he could. He said he would have to think about why such a thing would happen and who might benefit from it legally.

Seventeen

Hyacinth Prudhoe thought a great deal about the doctor's proposal of marriage. She had not expected it. So much had gone wrong in her life that she had become pessimistic and thought nothing good would ever happen again. She did not like teaching – she did not really care for children, having never had one of her own that lived – and so it was hard to have to find a bare living in such a tiny place by putting up with other people's children six days a week.

It is almost drudgery, she thought. The people of the village were mostly poor, they had smallholdings, nothing much more, and many were farm labourers on the bigger farms around the village.

She had been married to a curate and they had lived at Thornley, which was above Wolsingham. She had married him from desperation because he was the only man who had ever asked her and because she had to marry. Her mother wanted her married quickly because she was the only good-looking girl in the family and clergymen were looked up to.

The curate lived for five years after they were married and it was even harder being married to him than if she had still been at home with her mother.

They had a tiny, shabby house and his stipend was so low that they could barely survive. Nightly he took her to him in their cold, damp bed and there she was obliged to pretend that she did not mind. She had two miscarriages and then there was nothing else and she was grateful. After that, for the short time while he was ill, he bothered her no more in bed but lay there while she did everything in the house. Then the bishop decided that since he could not do his work another clergyman must do it, and he must be paid out of Mr Prudhoe's stipend, so after that they could barely afford bread. The other curate was an unpleasant man and when her husband was very ill and she did not like to leave him, he chided her for forgetting her church. When her husband died she was turned out.

Mr Wilson, the kind vicar in Wolsingham, found her a tiny house in Satley and suggested she might set up a small school there, so she did. It was the best she could expect and she had been thankful at the time, but her skills as a teacher were not great and few people could afford to pay for their children's schooling. She told herself she would have done anything to escape but she was surprised when the doctor asked her to marry him.

She would have given a great deal not to have needed

to marry again. It had been bad enough the first time. But the small amount of money she got from her teaching dried up almost totally as people could not pay and took their children from her, or said they would pay and then didn't.

The promisers were the worst. She couldn't help liking best those people who sent their children regardless of not paying. Sometimes she was given a few vegetables but even that stopped as the winter marched on, and although it was now getting a little bit lighter and brighter she could afford nothing

She would have to marry the doctor. He was a man of means with a good position and it could not be any worse than existing here like this. She knew that she had been beautiful, so perhaps the doctor could see something that she could not, but mostly she thought that in his way he was as desperate as she. He needed a mother for his difficult children and she longed to get away from the displeasure of the local vicar and his wife, who made her life even harder than it already was.

With a little more effort she could have hated them. They had never even offered her a cup of tea in their home. They would be glad to see the back of her but she could not help taking pleasure in the fact that they didn't like her and the doctor would elevate her to become his wife, and she would replace their daughter in his life.

She only wished that she could overhear how they would accept the facts when he divulged them.

No longer would she have to go to church twice on Sundays and teach the Sunday school. Saturday was spent doing everything she had no time for the rest of the week – she mended and cleaned, made nourishing soup and baked so that she would have something for the days to come. At night she lay in her tiny room and wondered if this would go on until she died and how on earth she would bear it.

For the first few days after the doctor proposed to her she went around in a state of light bliss, and then she thought about his children and how he would expect her to sleep with him and put up with the disgusting things men did to women. She thought then that there must be another way out but there was not. She gave herself a headache every day that week trying to think of some other way out of her difficulties but could see nothing. She was trapped.

She was so skinny, so undernourished, that she wondered he saw anything attractive in her at all, but he too needed someone.

So she braced herself and sent him a message saying that she would be glad to marry him, even though she looked in the mirror at her tiny, wan face and shrunken cheeks and dull eyes and lank hair and wondered why this had happened. She must move forward. It was not that the doctor was old or bent or smelled or was stupid, it was just that she did not like what she saw. She could tell that he had adored his wife and that the dead woman held his heart. The parents spent an hour at their daughter's grave every day putting fresh flowers in a vase and she had the feeling that while they were there they prayed. They had a right to; they had lost their only child and they blamed the doctor. She had overheard them saying so more than once.

They thought he was dour and sour and they hated his accent and his mean Scots ways. Alice should never have married him, they said, she could have done much better. And he had killed her, he had not known how to save her, so what use was such a doctor to anyone?

Sadly, for so many reasons, she sat down and wrote that she would be happy to marry him. It was a lie but what else could she do?

Nobody mentioned love. One day Alex thought he loved her, the next he felt guilty because he was sure he had asked her only because he couldn't think what to do with his children, but it was too late now. He had asked and she had answered.

His next job was to go and see her but he felt that first he should tell his parents-in-law what he was going to do. He was unhappy about it all. He told himself that he was just missing his wife. Perhaps that was what encouraged him to fall in love in such a strange fashion, blowing hot and cold on the situation when it was too late to take any of his words back. He called himself a fool a dozen times a day. He comforted himself that she would be a mother to his girls and they had never needed one more than they did now.

'Here you are again,' his mother-in-law said. 'I didn't realize that we were so fascinating. Have you decided what you will do with the girls?' Her voice sounded dreary and tired. She and her husband had had enough, Alex knew.

'I'm taking them to live with me and they will go to the school in Wolsingham. If you could get their belongings together I could take them this week.'

His parents-in-law did not look happy and yet they did not want the responsibility. This was the only solution which would work, he said stoutly to himself.

'However will you manage?' his mother-in-law said scathingly. 'And what a fate for your poor servants.'

That was another job he had put off. He could put this off no longer. He found comfort in the rug beneath his feet.

'Mrs Prudhoe has agreed to marry me.'

He had tried to pretend to himself that it would be momentarily hard for him to tell his parents-in-law that he was to marry again, but the moment that the words were out of his mouth he could see that they were appalled.

Phyllis Freeman's face drained of colour. His father-in-law's countenance grew dark and so did his eyes, all indications of anger.

'But – but you can't,' Phyllis told him and she stumbled over the words. 'Alice has just—' She was going to say 'just died', he could tell. It was untrue – his wife had died four years ago – but to her mother she would never be dead, he could see that now. This woman did not think it would be respectable for him to ever marry again.

'You won't lose the children,' he said, perhaps too hastily. 'I will bring them to church on Sundays and you can have them for overnight stays.'

Phyllis stared, wordless, and a lone tear ran down her withered cheek. Then he saw that they had lost their only child and that the sight of her unruly children was not as painful to them as the idea that he would besmirch her memory by taking another woman to him – and such a woman.

'My God, Alex,' his father-in-law said, forgetting formality. 'You cannot marry that woman. She's common. She has no background and, truth to tell, less education than I thought when I met her. My grandchildren could never live in the same house.'

He had prayed they would be glad to be relieved of

the responsibility of his children. He had got this very wrong.

'I was hoping that you would marry us,' he ventured and immediately knew it for a mistake.

Anthony got to his feet. 'Never!' he declared and strode out of the sitting room like a man who had never heard the word 'gout'. Alex thought about how Anthony had presided over his only child's marriage to the doctor not so long ago.

His wife put a delicate white handkerchief to her nose and sniffed disparagingly.

The question remained of who would tell the children. Alex had thought the grandparents might do it, but he could see now that that was not going to happen. In any case they must be told immediately that they were to go and live at the surgery and that it was to be in the next few days.

He could hardly do this at the vicarage because no doubt the grandparents would become even more upset. He privately told one of the maids, Clara, when they met in the hall, that the children would be leaving and she agreed to pack up their belongings. He tried not to see how relieved she was to be getting rid of them. Then he decided to tell them by asking Mrs Prudhoe if he could do this by himself with them at her school.

It was only when she had managed to give him some space that he made himself talk to them, and since it was a fine day he took them into the vicarage garden. It was next to the graveyard and since Alice had died grave-yards had taken on a whole new disagreeable meaning. Georgina wanted to go and jump on the gravestones but he said he needed to talk to them and she lingered. Doris sat wistfully on a garden chair and studied her bitten dirty nails.

'I've got something to tell you,' he said. 'Two things in fact.' He tried to smile but wasn't very successful. He had neglected his children as men so often did. He felt guilty that his wife had died, that the longed-for son had died with her, and that he barely knew his daughters. But it could not be helped and he was doing this for their benefit.

Georgina's dark eyes were hostile but when he asked her to sit down beside her sister she did so. She turned from him and looked across at the fields behind the vil-lage as though she longed to run off to them and never come back. Alex half wished he didn't understand how she felt. It was bad enough already, without him wor-rying even further about his children.

'You are going to come and live in Wolsingham at the surgery house with me,' he said, taking deep breaths in order to get out the words required. He had rehearsed them so many times and now they sounded inadequate, so wrong.

Nobody said anything for a few moments. Nobody

reacted and then Georgina looked him straight in the eyes and said, 'Why?'

He was astonished. He didn't think she had looked at him since her mother had died.

'Well because you can go to school there.'

'We aren't allowed to go to the village school here and it can't be so very different. Grandmother says the children at village schools are common and stink and we must have nothing to do with them.'

'I think they thought that Mrs Prudhoe was a better teacher than the gentleman who runs the school here.'

'She isn't,' Georgina said roundly. 'They go for nature walks and they can have time off when their mothers and fathers need them. We are stuck in that tiny, stupid yard. It's boring. All of it.'

Alex was having a bad time here, he acknowledged to himself.

'Grandfather and Grandmother don't like us, do they? That's why we have to go,' Georgina said.

'They are very old to look after children.'

'I thought plenty of old people did.'

This was true.

'You can go to a bigger school.' This was the only thing he could think of and even to him it sounded lame.

'Why?'

There it was again.

'I thought you might like it.'

'Why?'

'Well, there will be other children to play with.'

'Grandmother won't let us play with other children. It's because their parents are servants and a lot of them have dirty houses. Grandfather says the school in Wolsingham is not fit for us, so why are we going there now?'

Alex tried to keep his face neutral. He had not thought any of this would be easy but he hadn't understood that it would be so hard. He plunged and it was like he could feel the cold water in the river drench him. He breathed carefully. 'You need a mama and I am going to get married again.'

There was no reaction at all. He was mystified.

'We had a mother,' Georgina said, after what was possibly the longest silence in history. 'Grandfather says she is in heaven. I don't believe in heaven. I don't believe in angels either. If there is a heaven, why do we have planets and stars?'

He sidestepped this difficult issue. 'I'm going to marry your teacher, Mrs Prudhoe.'

That was when Doris looked at him and there was no mistaking the horror in her eyes. *She is not a comely child*, he thought, wishing things were otherwise. She was pale-faced, as though she never stepped outside. Her eyes were small and too close together, her hair was loose when it ought to have been tied up with ribbons, and her dress was much too big for her meagre form. She looked like a waif. He glanced at his other daughter. She was so different. She was glaring at him now as though she could not believe him to be so stupid, but she had suspected it all along. Her dress was too small. Her cheeks grew red now with temper and her eyes blazed as she took in the words he had just said.

'Potty Prudhoe?' Georgina said, her face so full of astonishment that he badly wanted to look away but knew that he mustn't. There was a long pause and he could think of nothing to fill it. 'Grandmother says she's common and Grandfather says only frogs speak French so Potty Prudhoe must be a frog.'

He couldn't resist. 'That's not very kind,' he said.

'Kind?' Georgina reacted as though she had never heard the word before. She tore her gaze away and once more regarded the fields beyond the village. He suspected that she was about to cry and needed to get her quivering lips and suddenly liquid eyes under better control.

'You are to come to me at the end of the week and you will like it. I have horses and a big garden and there are the maids, Ada and Fiona, and there is Jimmy who looks after the surgery, and Oswald who does the garden, and Oswald's mother who lives in the cottage with Oswald and Jimmy.'

This time there was no 'why' asked, so he hurried on.

'I am marrying Mrs Prudhoe in the summer when the school term ends so she won't be running the school here any longer, but I thought you should get used to the surgery house and the school in Wolsingham first.'

He looked at one and then at the other, but nobody said anything. He could not decide whether the silence was worse than what Georgina had said. He felt sick as he waited for either of them to say anything, but they sat there regarding their grubby, scrubbed-toed shoes with such concentration that he said, 'I have to go now,' and he went. He felt almost as awful as he had the day Alice had died. How could she have gone and left him to such a fate as this?

The two children watched him as he left the vicarage garden and it was only as he disappeared from sight that Doris said, 'Do you think it will be worse than living here with Grandfather and Grandmother, having Mrs Prudhoe telling us what to do all the time?'

Georgina could think of nothing to say.

'We will have to put up with Potty Prudhoe every day,' Doris said.

'We could run away,' Georgina said.

'Where to?'

They couldn't think of anywhere, so in the end they went back into the house and watched Clara pack their belongings. Life at the vicarage had gone downhill and Georgina had been convinced it couldn't get any worse. Their grandmother cried all the time and their grandfather had stopped speaking to them as though this was all their fault, yet it did not occur to him that the fault was his daughter's. She was the one who had died because she had to have a son for some reason. Georgina could remember her parents talking about what a joy it would be if the third child could be a son. Daughters were not enough apparently, you had to have sons. Georgina couldn't understand why. It seemed so little to die for.

When the week ended – and it was one of the longest weeks the two girls had ever endured – the horse and trap came for them and they met Oswald. They hadn't seen him before so Georgina was half inclined to ask him for some money and a lift to the nearest railway station, except that she couldn't think of anywhere they might go. Their grandparents said nothing. They did not even come out to wave them goodbye or say when they would next see them. Georgina wondered if they were ever going to come to the vicarage again, but the thought didn't dismay her.

Alice had died and yet it was as if Alice had never died. She lived on here like a ghost, never getting any older, never being here but always in her parents' minds and never speaking her children's names or hugging them close. Georgina didn't remember being hugged; all she remembered was Potty Prudhoe's ghastly school and how she liked to be called Madame. '*Cochon*,' Georgina said under her breath.

Eighteen

It was Easter Saturday when they arrived at their father's. Both Georgina and Doris hated Easter. You had to eat fish, which they loathed, and you were supposed to feel really bad because Jesus had died, though Georgina could never understand why she had to care since Jesus had been dead for two thousand years or so.

Their grandfather had always been very busy that week with so many services. They'd had to go to church with him almost every day and on Good Friday everybody cried or pretended to cry. Even Potty Prudhoe managed a few tears somehow, Georgina remembered, and all those plodding hymns. 'There is a Green Hill Far Away' made her want to burst into tears but that had nothing to do with Jesus. It made her think of her home in Allenheads, the pretty house by the River Allen where her mother had hugged her and told her she was the most beautiful child on earth. It didn't matter that her mother said the same to Doris. Her lovely, lovely mother.

Georgina didn't believe Jesus had anything to do with anything or her mother would never have died and gone off and left such a mess and so many people suffering. The only good thing about living in Satley, and all she would mind leaving behind, was that on dark nights the stars were very clear. She had found a book on astronomy in her grandfather's library and of all the things in the world she longed for a telescope.

God was not up there and she didn't believe that she would ever see her mother again.

So leaving her grandparents meant fewer church services and, unless her father went to church a lot, which she couldn't imagine he did, life at the surgery house might not be so bad, at least until he married Potty Prudhoe. She was trying not to think about that.

The surgery house was about the same size as the vicarage but it felt strange and since they didn't know anybody there they had nothing to say.

They were given a pretty room between them that overlooked the street, which made it easy to see other people, children and dogs go by. One of the maids – Georgina couldn't tell which one, they both looked like old scarecrows – unpacked their belongings, hanging up their dresses, putting their shoes neatly at the bottom of the wardrobe, placing their nightdresses and underclothing in the drawers and even finding a bookcase for the books they had brought, most of which Georgina had stolen from her grandfather's library. She had chosen these carefully. A set of green encyclopedias, and all four books on astronomy – though she thought it was strange that a man of God should be interested in such things. Maybe her grandfather just wanted to look modern because it was obvious to her that a lot of the books she had taken had never been opened.

She had also taken history and geography books. Had there been any stories she would have grabbed them too, but her grandfather did not approve of what he called fiction. That was one thing about Potty Prudhoe, at least she read them stories, even though they were not the kind of stories Georgina cared for. They seemed to be filled with unfortunate women who became governesses or married the wrong men who went mad, blind or died of overeating, and then the women died on train tracks or by poisoning themselves so that they expired slowly and in agony. Georgina longed for a happy ending but then life was anything but happy. Worst of all was a book by a man called Thomas Hardy in which all the children died at the end. It was horrible and came between her and her sleep on bad nights when the wind howled around the vicarage and seemed to her to moan. How on earth did this Thomas Hardy sleep when he wrote such dismal books?

She liked the room they had been given. It was cosy and the fire was laid ready to be lit should it turn cold. There was a bed each and there were pretty curtains and matching bedspreads. The maid talked to them and they discovered that she was called Fiona. She was not very pretty but she was very smiley and spoke softly to them in her very strange but rather nice sing-song voice.

They both liked the tea that they were given even though it was in the kitchen. Their grandmother had told them that ladies knew nothing about kitchens but they didn't care. There were lots of beef sandwiches cut into diamond shapes, and small cakes with butter icing.

The maids, Ada and Fiona, introduced themselves and asked what they seemed to think were polite questions, but Doris and Georgina had been taught that you didn't talk to the help and said nothing.

Better still, they weren't sent to bed as early as they had been before. Their grandparents had liked the sitting room to themselves and sent the children to bed at seven. Fiona, who seemed to have forgotten they were there, remembered at half past eight and took them upstairs and helped them into their nightclothes.

'It is such an important day tomorrow,' Fiona said as she tucked them up into bed. 'Your father is having people to dinner and Ada and I go to church on Easter Day.'

'Do we have to go?' It was the first thing that Georgina had said to her.

Fiona stared. 'Don't you usually?'

'Our grandfather is the vicar at Satley,' Georgina said, rolling her eyes. 'We spend half our lives there.'

'Well, I suppose if you don't have to we could ask Oswald's mother to have you there. Would that be better?'

Georgina, having not met Oswald's mother, had no comment to make but it sounded like the easier option.

'Shall I read you a bedtime story?' Fiona said. She had not had much to do with children before and these two were interesting.

Georgina stared, wide-eyed. 'You can read?'

'Of course I can read.'

'But you're a servant.'

Fiona had to laugh. 'I can read, write and add up and I'm very good at telling stories I make up.'

'That would be lovely,' Doris said, getting down lower into the bed. They had never had a bedtime story before.

Fiona, both girls later acknowledged, was a very good storyteller. She lay down beside them and closed her eyes so they did the same, and then she made up stories about two wonderful girls and all the exciting adventures they got up to. Georgina couldn't help reflecting that their father had not been altogether wrong. This was not as bad as she had thought it would be.

Their father had put in no appearance. Georgina had assumed they were to see more of him and that this was one of the reasons he wanted them with him. But he was important and had to look after people who were ill, and people were always ill so he was always out.

The two girls were left with Oswald's mother that Sunday. There had been a slight discussion about this, with Ada saying that they ought to go to church, and Fiona saying she couldn't see why since the doctor didn't, and Ada talking about the grandparents and the church. But in the end, since neither girl said anything, they were quite glad when Oswald's mother agreed to have them. The two maids were thankful to go off to church without the encumbrance of two sulky little girls whom everybody would stare at because they had not seen the doctor's children before.

Oswald's mother turned out to be what was locally known as a godsend, Georgina and Doris thought. She played cards with them and dominoes. They had never been allowed such things before and were very taken with the whole idea of winning and losing. She also had something called a compendium of games which they were allowed to look through and after that they played snakes and ladders and draughts. Mr Oswald's Mother – that was how they thought of her, and with affection – gave them sweets. They were never allowed sweets either, and she gave them something called mint humbugs as well as toffee and fudge and even boiled sweets, as though she had been saving them up for just such an occasion. It was the happiest Sunday morning they could ever remember.

Ada put on the black velvet dress. Nobody said anything about the dress and Ada was very self-conscious, but she enjoyed the feel of the material and the way that the skirt moved when she walked. As they trod the short walk to the church it began to snow big, square flakes. It was so pretty that it made them feel cheerful and Easter Sunday was the most joyful day of the year. Christ had risen, the bells rang out and the church was festive.

When they got back to the house Fiona went to collect the girls and Mrs Leighton said she had never met such well-behaved children. They just sat still on the settee and never said a word out of place was what she told the maid.

To Fiona and Ada's surprise there was an unexpected visitor for Easter Sunday dinner. The doctor had earlier than morning called them into the sitting room and told them that he was going to marry Mrs Prudhoe.

No wonder the two children had been pleased not to go to church, Ada later told Fiona. He really was going to marry that stick of a woman with a thin mouth and no smile.

All the joy went out of the day. They knew very little

about her but having a new mistress in the house would change everything.

'Worst of all,' Ada said in a whisper when they were by themselves in the kitchen, 'she's older than me. And she comes from some hovel down the road towards Lanchester. I have family who lived near her.'

'She ran the school and you know what that means,' Fiona said. 'Bossy.'

Georgina and Doris were given jelly and blancmange and chocolate cake in the kitchen, and Ada and Fiona scuttled backwards and forwards with food and drink between there and the dining room, where eight people were seated. Mrs Prudhoe was being introduced as the doctor's intended wife.

'A bit of notice would have been nice,' Ada said.

The two maids were now used to having the children in the kitchen and since the girls said nothing, they were inclined to forget and talk in front of them.

And then Ada remembered. 'She was your teacher, wasn't she?'

'We hate her,' Georgina said.

'We call her Potty Prudhoe,' Doris ventured and this was the first speech they had heard from her. 'Grandfather says she is a frog because only frogs speak French.'

The two maids didn't look at one another because they badly wanted to laugh.

Ada was first to become sober. 'The big question is, will you have more cake or more jelly and blancmange?'

Georgina considered.

'Both,' she said finally.

At first when Fiona heard that the doctor was to marry the schoolteacher from Satley she didn't think she minded. At least not much. Ada was worried that the new mistress would interfere and was horrified at how common the woman was, but it occurred to Fiona when they went to bed that night, worn out from their day, that she did not want the doctor to marry.

She was surprised. For some reason she hadn't minded that he didn't marry. She couldn't imagine anybody wanting to marry again after the other partner had died, and he had two children, though as far as she could tell he wasn't interested in them. She wondered why. They were just children like any other, grubby and quarrelsome, and in some ways so very interesting to her. She had never felt like that before either. She had not felt that way about Ada's nephews and nieces but then she didn't know them well.

She had very much enjoyed making up a story for the doctor's children and she had lied when she said that she had done that before. Somehow, though, she knew that she could tell stories. She had no idea why but she had begun to love the children.

She didn't sleep. The fire was not on and, though it was unnecessary because it was Easter, it had snowed earlier and the movement of the flames would have been nice; she liked the comfort it gave and how it changed and would never be the same again. She liked how things never happened twice: each sunrise, each sunset, each day was just passing through like a travelling salesman.

Worst of all, she discovered that she disliked the woman the doctor would marry. She didn't know her but that didn't matter. She could see that she would never like any woman the doctor married. It wasn't that she wanted to marry him herself but she liked the way she and Ada had him to themselves somehow, as the only women in the house.

When she had lain awake for a couple of hours she heard Ada saying to her softly, 'What's the matter, Fi?' Sometimes Ada could be so caring, so gentle. Was she the only person who benefited from this?

'I don't want the doctor to marry.'

'I know what you mean,' Ada said and Fiona turned over, facing her friend in the dark. 'We've had the house to ourselves for such a long time, we know what he wants and how to provide it, and now it's all going to be turned upside down and for what? We could look after the children perfectly well without him going mad and bringing another woman into the house.'

'Do you think it will be bad?' Fiona ventured.

'I think it will be awful,' Ada said.

It would, Fiona silently agreed.

To say that Hyacinth Prudhoe had been nervous about going to the doctor's for Easter Day dinner and meeting his family and friends would be a gross understatement. She hadn't slept. Part of her wanted to hide behind the sofa and pretend that she was out when he called for her. She panicked in every possible way.

She had nothing to wear, she didn't know what to say, she had never seen his children in their domestic capacity. She almost refused, nearly wrote to him and said that she had changed her mind about marrying him. Then she looked about her at her few things, the darned gloves which were her only pair, her thin dress which was her best and had been patched, her shoes which were almost worn through, so she could feel the pavement beneath the soles of her feet. She looked in the mirror and saw the lack of nourishment, how her cheeks had almost fallen in, how her eyes were dull. She tried to be ill so that she could not go and yet she knew that this would be her last opportunity to pull herself up out of poverty, and so she clung to the idea that it would be much better than what she had now.

The doctor came in his own trap to take her to Wolsingham. He was no longer as she had envisaged him; she saw how nervous he was, how he did not look at her or understand what to say. They made the journey down the banks into the little town in silence and when he helped her from the trap by the lightest touch of his fingers, she almost fell and disgraced herself because there was no excuse. She stumbled and her face went into flames. She dared not look at him, so smart in a good suit he was almost, what was the word? Dapper. The doctor was dapper and she looked even poorer beside him. She was humiliated and longed for the tiny fire and the silence of her damp little house.

He led her inside. Her first impression was that it was very clean and neat. Fires burned in the hall and in the sitting room. There were lots of books on the bookshelves and easy chairs; that was reassuring.

He called to the girls to come and see her.

'Come and meet your new mama,' he said in the hall. They came in and her heart sank even lower. Neither girl looked at her. 'You will not be able to think of Mrs Prudhoe as your teacher any longer.'

Georgina seemed to find the view of the garden fascinating and Doris stood on one leg and then the other, twisting her fingers and looking as though she would cry.

Then he ushered in the servants and she knew that they knew she had come from no better a background than any maid. They looked straight at her, not quite in disrespect, but as though they knew where she had come from and they were undeceived. Outwardly they made their little curtsies and went back to their kitchen.

Then there was the church service to get through. It was not her church but she knew Mr and Mrs Wilson because she had met them when they came to visit the church at Satley and have tea with the Freemans, and they had helped find her the little school she had learned to despise. They both greeted her kindly and congratulated her on her good fortune.

It was a joyful day to be in church and also it staved off the horrors of the dinner to come. The doctor had invited Mr and Mrs Wilson and several other people from the village so it was yet another ordeal. The bile rose into her throat and she almost choked. What should she talk about? What was a safe topic?

Mr Wilson adroitly steered the conversation towards the wedding day, which would be in July. He asked her if she cared for particular hymns and said how pleased he was that they would be married in his church. She could have kissed him for his tact and kindness, while Mrs Wilson, who sat next to her, kept up a flow of conversation which showed how much the vicar's wife she was. When Mrs Prudhoe became one of them, she said, they would be glad of her help at the church. Would she like to teach at the Sunday school? Mrs Wilson told of how there were various meetings for the women of the village. Mrs Prudhoe could be of great help if she chose to but Mrs Wilson was tactful and did not push this. Were they going away for a few days after the wedding, she asked. Mrs Prudhoe had no idea, they had not talked of it.

Somehow she got through the meal and the afternoon. She had never been as glad to get back to her shabby little house. There she burst into tears. The fire had gone out and she could not even find the strength to revive it. Worst of all, somehow, it began to snow. She shivered. She must learn to be grateful for her opportunities, she told herself, she must endeavour to accustom herself to what after all would be a much better life.

When everybody had gone the children went into the garden to see if Oswald was about and whether he might take them to visit the horses, so for once the maids were not overheard.

Ada watched from the kitchen window. 'She couldn't even afford a decent dress to wear for Easter Sunday and on such an important day for the doctor,' she said, slamming plates into the sink. 'What a shabby woman.'

'We need to talk to Sarah,' Fiona said.

Ada stared for a second and then she thought what a good idea it was.

Ada had taken to thinking less badly of the other girl

since she had worn the black dress, but she did not want to call a truce.

Fiona looked at her in understanding. 'I know you don't like her and I'm not that keen on her myself, but she has been very kind. Every time I wear my dress I feel good so maybe she would make a dress for Mrs Prudhoe and it would help things.'

'Sally Charles isn't a magician,' Ada said huffily, 'but the poor woman does need something new to be married in or she will let us all down.' And since they liked to think of her as 'that poor woman', they both giggled, which changed the mood a little bit. The trouble was that they knew they were well off and could not leave to go anywhere better so they must be polite to the new mistress, however common she was, and it would look the better for all of them if she was married in a decent frock.

When the doctor returned from Satley he thanked them for the dinner and the day and said that he hoped they would be respectful to their new mistress.

Ada put up her chin and said nothing but it was Fiona who said helpfully, 'Sarah Charles makes lovely dresses. Perhaps Mrs Prudhoe would like a wedding gown.'

This had obviously not occurred to the doctor. He frowned for a moment and then said, 'Yes, I imagine she would.'

'Though of course, with it being her second marriage, she wouldn't be wearing white,' Ada said.

They giggled again when they got back to the kitchen but there was a sad note in it all. The house would never be the same again. They were just sorry that things were in such a bad state with his parents-in-law. Otherwise they did not think the doctor would have taken a second wife. He had seemed content as he was.

'I had heard that that the girls were very badly behaved but so far they've been no bother,' Ada said. 'I think it's that the old people were his first wife's parents and couldn't come to terms with anything after she died.'

They thought the chance of the doctor and his second wife going off to the continent like posh folk did after their weddings was slight; she would have to put up with Wolsingham and all that it entailed.

Nineteen

When the Easter holidays ended the children were supposed to go to school. Both of them refused and Ada
didn't know what to do. They were not her children so
she could hardly make them go, persuasion didn't work
and she loathed telling on them to the doctor; it made
her feel like a snitch.

'A what?' Ada said when Fiona introduced this word.

'Betraying your comrades,' Fiona said with a flourish.

'Hardly comrades, poor little souls. It's understandable
that they are difficult. They've had far too many changes
and now that dreadful woman is going to take over. I've
a good mind to hand in my notice.'

Ada tilted up her chin as she spoke but they both knew
it was an empty threat. They were stuck with the new
mistress as much as the children were.

The trouble was that both maids felt responsible for
the children because they seemingly had nobody. They
had thought that the doctor might spend more time with
the children now that they were living with him, but he
went on as he had before, eating by himself, drinking in

the library or smoking in the garden. It was as if nothing had changed. Ada and Fiona had endless discussions about this and about how it might be worse when that woman came here as Mrs Blair.

They could not make the children go to school, they felt it was not their place, and although Fiona had coaxed them as far as the school gates and into the classroom, twice they ran away, once back to the surgery house and the other time into the village streets. People would talk, Ada said, and say that the doctor's children were a dreadful nuisance and ungovernable.

In the end the mild-mannered teacher, Mr Gloucester, came to the house, sat down at the kitchen table, as though he did it every day, and talked to the girls. He did not even try to persuade them to go to school, but instead left coloured pencils and paper, and various children's books, and told them that if they did want to go he would be happy to see them there, but if they didn't he would come to them as long as they didn't mind.

This rather unnerved Georgina. She had never met anybody like this before, willing to engage on her terms. She looked suspiciously at the old man.

'Do you believe in God?' she queried.

'Yes, of course.'

'Then how do you explain the planets and the stars?'

And that was Mr Gloucester's hidden weapon. He knew a good deal about planets and stars and told

Georgina a lot of things she had longed to know, then promised to bring her a book.

'Do you have a telescope?' she asked, thrilled.

'I have a friend, Mr Paddy, who lives up on the tops, who has one. The best view is up there on the fells. No lights, and on a clear night on the way to Consett, which is very high up, you can see all kinds of stars. Would you like to go and see it?'

Georgina clapped her hands in glee. The maids were astonished at such animation.

There was going to be a full moon very shortly, Mr Gloucester said, and he promised to take the girls up to the observatory on the tops and show them the wonders of the sky.

'What a good man you are,' Ada told him as Mr Gloucester said goodbye and left the house. After that Georgina couldn't wait to get to school and what she did, Doris automatically followed.

Doris had said nothing about going to see the observatory but that afternoon she tugged on Fiona's skirt and said softly, 'Do I have to go?'

'You don't have to do anything you don't want to do,' Fiona told her and on impulse she lifted the little girl into her arms and Doris put her hands around her neck. It was the first time Fiona had felt that she might like a child of her own. She couldn't understand why the doctor didn't show affection towards his children; they were so ready for him to love them and yet somehow he could not manage it. She wondered whether he was afraid, or perhaps embarrassed, or that he just had no idea what to do. She had the feeling that a great many fathers were the same and left such things to their wives, but these children had no mother and they already disliked the woman their father was to marry.

Holding his younger daughter close against her, Fiona wished that she could have married the doctor. She knew it was stupid but now she did wish that she could be a mother to his children. She imagined the dream. She and Ada would go on just as before really, at least she hoped so – and then she knew that that was a silly idea. Worse still, Ada came back from taking in the clothes from the line as she stood there with Doris in her arms, and Ada did not miss the way that Fiona's face showed her affection for the little girl.

When Fiona came downstairs much later after telling the girls a new bedtime story, Ada looked sharply at her.

'It's never going to happen,' she said.

'What's never going to happen?'

'You and the doctor.'

Fiona stared at her. 'I've never—'

'Yes, you have. It's written all over your face that you have fallen in love with his children. It's not the same thing as loving the man, Fi, you must know it.' She was going to go on but they were so friendly Ada put aside what she had been going to say and instead said, gently, 'I wouldn't care but you would have made a much better mistress than she ever could. You're much more of a lady.'

Fiona burst into tears. She was shocked and so grateful and yet she knew also that it could never be. Like a child denied sweets, she now wanted the doctor as she had never wanted him before.

'Don't say such things, Ada,' she begged, slumping down on to the kitchen settle where they so often sat when it was late.

'I've always thought you were a cut above everybody else.'

'I'm not.'

'Oh, Fi, you can't hide things like that. At first I just thought you fancied him because he was Scots, as though you would ever do owt so daft. But I can see it. You like his bairns. You have turned them from brats into people.'

'I haven't,' Fiona sobbed.

'They adore you, Fi. You're a lady, the sort of person who is always kind to everybody, and though you never talk about your family, and I know you like to keep the mystery to yourself, I do sort of understand.'

Fiona couldn't stop crying. Yes, she loved these two small beings who needed affection so very much, yet the man himself was unlike any she had met before. But then she had never loved any man before now and the timing was just so awful.

'I know,' she said, blowing her nose with vigour, 'I liked it when there was just the three of us here, but since the children came everything has altered. The hardest thing is that he doesn't see them and it seems to me that if he had the right wife he could be made to.'

'I don't think that happens,' Ada said. 'It shows how inexperienced you are, and so am I, when it comes to men. They don't change. I think he broke his heart over his wife but was he any different before? If he had been a softer-hearted man it would never have come to this. I think he's marrying her because he feels so guilty about his children, and she's marrying him because she can't afford not to. Did you notice the way that she wolfed down her dinner even though she was nervous? In her shoes I wouldn't have got down a mouthful. The whole thing is going to blow up in their faces. I'm not my mother's daughter for nothing, I can see how other people get themselves stuck in marriage. My brothers have awful wives and there they are, bonded for life in grubby little Rookhope.'

'I am trying to be sensible but you're right. I haven't been in love before so I'm not sure how much is caught up in the children, and how much is the idea that I could give him a much better life than she ever will,' Fiona said. 'I envy her and I'm going to have to watch them get married and live with them married and go on watching from the sidelines, because I know now that I'm too old to attract any man. I just wish I had the courage to leave it all behind and start afresh somewhere else.'

'Oh Fi, I'm not sure I could stand that,' Ada said.

'Well you won't have to, because I'm staying here,' Fiona said. She blew her nose a second time and got up to go to the table, where she sat down with her darning as though she would right the wrongs of the world by mending socks.

Twenty

Harry heard from Mr Hauxley that Mrs Nattrass's house had burned down. It was a great mystery in the area. Mrs Nattrass had gone there from the foundling school many years ago and had lived the rest of her life without incident until now. It could not be that she had anything for anyone to rob her of. And if so, that was no reason to burn down the house. Was somebody trying to frighten her?

Mr Hauxley and the whole area were perplexed and felt sorry for the poor woman. The local policeman, Mr Whitty, was of the opinion that it was all about nothing and the silly woman had done it herself, but Mr Hauxley and a good many other people were ill-satisfied at this unlikely explanation, so the story kept on doing the rounds.

Various men in the village said that, had they known something was going wrong up on the tops, they would have gone there and intervened, but since this was use-less now, nobody did anything.

Harry didn't know Mrs Nattrass and was not very

interested. He was more concerned that the cellar at his home was emptying into Mr Hauxley's storerooms until there was not very much left to sell. Once they had established that it had not been Mr Hauxley who had sold his father brandy they got on quite well.

Apparently the grocer from Frosterley had done the dirty deed, but since it had been long before Harry arrived home, he could hardly go accusing anybody — and, after all, that was what grocers were for. It wasn't for them to ask why people wanted their goods; they had to be grateful that they could sell them. Although there was still a lot of brandy in the house, it disappeared at such a rate that it would not be long before it was all gone. Then Harry would have words with the grocer from Frosterley and tell him that there was no money left for such luxuries, though of course it was not a luxury to his father — it was the direst of necessities.

The two men who were seemingly his father's only friends had been to the house several times by now and it worried Harry. His father had been nowhere to meet them in a long time and to him they looked suspicious, but perhaps that was only his mind. He had taken to hovering in the hall, listening to the laughter and the rough words. On the last occasion he had been more worried than ever. They had brushed past him at the door as though they belonged there and knew the way, and he did not like their manners. Harry made himself go into the drawing room and was in time to see coins disappearing into two small bags on the coffee table. He had to admit to himself that he had done this deliberately and wasn't sure whether he wished he'd stayed in the hall or was pleased that he'd uncovered something that wasn't right.

His father glared at him and Harry took in the glare and left the room, but he was angry. His father obviously had money but Harry didn't know where he kept it. It was his father's own money, of course, but his father would never have agreed to spend it on anything Harry thought important. Why was he doing this now? Had his father discovered a new source of brandy? Were the men there not as friends, but for business?

After that meeting the spring progressed into early summer and his father seemed to be in a much better temper. Although he was no more sober than he had ever been, he no longer cursed Harry, so things became slightly easier.

Harry tried to take advantage of his father's humour and asked for money but his father got up and threw things across the room at him, including a couple of vases that were no doubt not worth anything, but only came to hand. After that Harry kept out of the room most of the time.

'It's gone!' his father said. 'The money is all gone and to good purpose.'

Harry was very unhappy. His father was impossible and there was no one to talk to. He could do nothing other than see to the place, because although he was sure he could have held down an office job easily, he felt that his father could not be left alone. He couldn't be trusted to not get lost or fall into the river. Daily, Harry imagined terrible fates for his father's demise. He wished that he didn't care but the truth was that his dreadful father was all he had left. Harry was only glad that fires were not needed anymore. He had dreams of his father burning the place down and both of them losing their lives. His father often awoke crying for his wife and lost daughter, and sometimes he did not remember who he was or where he was. Often he went back into those days when he had been happy, when they had all been happy, when Harry's mother was alive and his little sister was there too.

It was not a very clear memory for Harry. He wasn't sure whether he actually remembered it or just hoped that he did. He had been in Scotland for so long, for most of his life, and it seemed to him that nothing would improve. He even wished his father would not drink himself to death and that was a surprise. The man had never been any good to him and yet Harry knew nobody else and there was something about his father which meant Harry could not give up on this desperately unhappy man.

The doctor no longer came to the Leadbetter house. Harry couldn't afford to pay him and Harry's father had not benefited from the man's earlier visits. It was becoming very lonely. At one time Harry had gone to church and Mr Wilson would come to the house, but again his father ranted and raved if he knew that the vicar was anywhere close and Harry was embarrassed. The vicar had retreated while encouraging him to go to church, but he had stopped. Nobody spoke to him but Mr and Mrs Wilson; people had stared, and it felt even more lonely than when he was at home.

Harry had tended what he could of the gardens so that they had fruit and vegetables. Most of the glasshouses suffered also from no repairs. Several of them had blown down in the wind and there was glass everywhere. The one big greenhouse which stood still held glass. He blocked up the gaps with cardboard and managed to get the door open and closed so he could grow fruit and various salad stuffs in there. He could still shoot over the land they owned and fish in the nearby river, and he chopped up the trees which blew down in the gales or died because they were old, piling up the wood and keeping it under a large tarpaulin to dry out for the coldest winter days. But it was a hard way to live. He had nothing but books and these were his only real life.

Harry set to tidying outside as best he could. He liked being there and could not help but think cynically of all those freezing runs when he had been at school in Scotland. Was that why he was so hardy? People here complained about the weather but it was nothing compared to those nine hideous years when he saw no one he liked and did not visit his home.

On some days now his father didn't know Harry's name. Just when Harry thought that things couldn't get any worse, his father's mind took on a different tone. His eyes gleamed, he laughed a great deal and also, to Harry's dismay, he began to wander the house at night as though he could not tell darkness from day. He would mutter about how they would get rich and things would be better than they had ever been.

Harry didn't drink brandy but he did like a glass or two of decent claret and the cellar was full of it. Mr Hauxley said that he had no sale for claret. He did take the port and sherry, and gin and vodka, and some strange bottles of liquor from various countries which Harry knew nothing of. Mr Hauxley seemed happy to pay good money for it, and since this enabled Harry to buy various foodstuffs, as well as tools and materials for repairs in the house, he was grateful for it.

At first he worried that he would go the same way as

his father and grandfather but he never had more than two or three glasses. He liked the summer best, when he could leave open the huge library doors and sit there with a book, gazing out at the ruins of what had been his family home.

There was little he could do but try to keep it in order. It had been built in 1820 and was showing every sign of needing huge maintenance. When Harry opened the big French doors as spring arrived, he thought that one day they would fall into the garden and break into a thousand splinters. In his dreams he was covered in glass from the greenhouses and from the double doors. The doors were forever breaking and he was eternally picking up the pieces, his hands bleeding where they were cut from glass and splinters.

But then he had renewed hope when he awoke each morning and remembered that he was no longer in a freezing cold dormitory in Scotland. He had come home, and he resolved to search for a solution to fix his crumbling house.

Twenty-one

Isabella grew very lonely up on the tops with no other child for company. She missed her brother more than she had thought possible. It was all very well being with Sarah and Mrs Nattrass, but neither of them were family and it was a hard way of life, even though she got to take the kittens to bed with her.

Her only relief was that they very often – if the weather was clement – went down into Wolsingham to the weekly market. She longed to see other children but she could not go to school. There was not one anywhere near the tops and the children she did see when she was in Wolsingham were with their mothers or playing in the street, and she did not want to ask if she could join in. She particularly liked the ring games which she'd played at home. That home was indeed a very long way from here. She doubted she would ever get back to it.

Sarah did what she called her bartering and Isabella knew how important it was, so she didn't mind that. Also, it got them away from the Hilda House which she was beginning to loathe. It was so cold and draughty and big that at night it seemed to her to echo, and since Mrs Nattrass had talked of ghosts, Isabella was afraid to leave the room where they had a light and venture into the hall or up the stairs. And even though the nights were light, she did not want to go outside.

When it was late she could hear the sounds of various animals and she often had the horrible thought that they were inside and coming to get her in her bed. She refused to go upstairs before the others and even then she didn't sleep well. She seemed to be afraid of everything, whereas before they had left Tenerife nothing had scared her. With her family and friends and all the good things life could provide, she had felt safe.

She found Hilary bossy, though she had the feeling that the old lady didn't mean it, it was just that she had lost almost everything she possessed and she got very low in mood. Sarah seemed to spend all her time attempting to cheer them up, with very little result, so it was good when they could escape down to Wolsingham. Very often Hilary did not go with them now and to her shame Isabella preferred it.

The little money the initial sale of her dresses had brought in meant that Sarah had bought materials which she thought would sell to the shops or on the market. A lot of women were good at needlework and knitting. Some made their own quilts for the beds and they all made and mended their family garments, so Sarah had to offer them something they would not make for themselves.

She could not knit thick clothes because the better weather was here, so Isabella suggested they should take up lacemaking, a skill that she had brought with her. It was meticulous work but the needles and materials were cheap and women loved a lace collar or cuffs. It was all the luxury many of them might long for.

The two girls also made thin summer shawls and lighter babywear. Smaller garments were more difficult to make, especially the tiny embroidered caps and hats. Isabella did a good run in cotton summer bonnets, which were so pretty that she began to make bigger ones for the older girls to wear, and she started off something of a trend. It was all reassuring and meant they could eat.

One day in May, Isabella noticed on the edge of the market a very untidy man. There were tramps about. Sometimes they came to the Hilda House and Sarah would give them a little food or soup, which she could ill afford. Isabella had the feeling that they told their friends food could be had up there but she had never seen anybody quite as shabby or untidy as the man on the edge of the market. He was tall but stooped and had a long, dark beard, messy, lank hair and wild eyes, she thought, and it scared her.

He was not close to anybody but it seemed that he was staring at her, so she moved near to Sarah and they bumped into each other. Sarah seemed unaware and went on talking to the woman who ran the material stall. They had begun discussing whether Sarah might make a dress or two for better-off folk who could afford to buy such things.

The woman had stalls on other markets. She went to Frosterley and Stanhope, and the better-off farmers' wives might long for a professionally made dress for special occasions so that they could flaunt their money in front of poorer folk. In the evenings while the light held Sarah would make various sketches of such things and in the end, when she did get the odd commission, she produced patterns.

The woman in the market went halves with her. She provided the material and Sarah made the dresses, but it was slow going, Isabella thought, and meant a lot of hard work.

The man went on staring at her and then he drew near.

'Isabel,' he said softly, and his watery eyes lit up. A lone tear made its journey down his whiskered face. Sarah felt the girl stiffen and all of a sudden Isabella became a small child and turned and clung to her.

The odd man drew nearer, calling out what was almost Isabella's name like it was a love song, and when he got closer his rheumy eyes cleared and then he beheld her with joy and called her 'my little lassie, my own little lassie'.

Isabella cried out with fear and hid her face against Sarah, which was hardly surprising, Sarah thought. She was astonished and upset and had no idea what was going on. Sarah stared at the man. He was big and not that old but he was unwell. His gaze had fixed itself on the child and he put out his arms for her.

Sarah stepped back. Had Isabella been able to get any nearer she would have, so Sarah turned her back to him, the better to shield the child, while Isabella whimpered like a lost puppy. Sarah put a reassuring hand on Isabella's head and told her that everything would be all right.

The man must at one time have been fit and able, Sarah decided as she held in her mind that picture of him, but he was bent over and still huge to her. His clothes were shabby and his hands were gnarled. His whole demeanour gave off not a threat but more of a yearning and then he started to cry ever harder, as though he didn't do it often and had given in to whatever memories assailed him. Somehow that was the worst of all.

Mr Whitty appeared from behind Sarah. She heard him and turned around, and for the first time ever thought what a reassuring voice he had. She was glad to see him. He was not exactly the most capable man in the world but he was the one she wanted to see most at that point. She thought he would roughly bid the man to go home, instead of which, to her surprise and partial reassurance, he took the man by the elbow. Isabella began to emerge from Sarah's embrace and they saw Mr Whitty talk to him softly and urge him away. Several men took hold of him, but gently.

Sarah didn't know what to do or say as Mr Whitty melted again into the crowded marketplace. After that she tried to go on as usual but the child was so upset that long before they usually went back up to the Hilda House, they left for home and were glad to do so.

She tried to reassure Isabella that it was just a mistake.

The child was not impressed. 'He said my name.'

'Lots of people are called similar names. It has so many variations that half the dale answers to it,' Sarah said, but she was not convinced.

She couldn't rest and the following day, it being warm and bright, she left Isabella with Hilary and made her way back to Wolsingham to tackle Mr Whitty about the incident. Isabella shrank back when Sarah said she was going there and stayed on the kitchen settle with the cats.

Sarah was also worried about Hilary. Since the fire she had lost all her oomph, which was hardly surprising, but worst of all she seemed tired all the time. She had taught Sarah to milk Daisy and it was easy to feed the hens and collect the eggs, which Isabella loved doing, especially since the hens were out during the day and seemed to lay wherever they happened to be.

Hilary was of no help now and it was hardly surprising. She had lost everything but her animals and seemed ten years older. Nevertheless, she would keep an eye on Isabella. It was like Isabella had gained a grandmother. Hilary would tell her stories and play silly games so they were good company for one another, though Hilary never seemed to forget her loss for a moment.

Mr Whitty obviously didn't want to talk to Sarah and she could see that he would have made himself scarce, had he had any warning of her arrival. Unfortunately his wife ushered her into his office. He attempted to hide the dismay on his face and that was when Sarah knew she had done the right thing. Something other than what she understood was going on here.

He was obliged to offer her a chair across from where he sat behind his empty desk.

'I am very busy,' he said. 'What can I do for you?'

Sarah took no notice of that. She was aware that Mr Whitty was not a fan of hers but, she insisted, she had not walked three miles each way to be fobbed off with pleasantries. Mr Whitty could see that he was being bested.

'You seemed to know the man yesterday?' she said.

He tried to look blankly at her. It almost made her smile.

'What man?' he said.

Sarah was not going to have that and looked sternly at him. He had the grace not to meet her eyes.

'You know very well. The one who came up to Isabella and called her by her name.'

'The place was full of old men. It's always like that on market day. They have nothing else to do but drink their fill and smoke their pipes and talk all the afternoon.'

'He didn't seem that old. You had him taken away. Isabella is scared now and I would very much like to know who he is and what he meant.'

'She's best off up there on the tops,' Mr Whitty said vaguely.

'There's no reason why she should be frightened into not coming down here where there is a bit more life,' Sarah said.

He said nothing.

'If you don't tell me I shall ask everybody in the village until I find out. There were a good many people who surely would be able to identify him and the stallholders know everybody,' she persisted.

'All right,' Mr Whitty said. 'It was Luke Leadbetter. He's completely harmless. I'm sure he didn't mean anything.'

Sarah stared. Perhaps this should have occurred to her but she knew nothing of them other than that Isabella was related to them.

'You've heard of him,' Mr Whitty said. 'You and the bairn had best stay away from him. He's all right now but he could turn strange. They're a bad lot, the Leadbetters, cruel masters, greedy and grasping and no good. And drunken sots. Half the dale went off to the new world because of the way that the Leadbetter family treated them. The grandfather was the worst of the lot. Drank himself to death and this one's going the same way. No doubt Harry Leadbetter is just as bad but luckily he keeps himself to himself. Just stay away and everything will be all right.'

Sarah was horrified and confused. This was the family Isabella's aunt had married into. She walked slowly home, not knowing what to do. Should she go on pretending to Isabella that it was nothing to worry about? But as soon as she got back she saw that it was too late.

Isabella was scared and uncertain and hardly moved. She was tearful, tired and wouldn't eat, and then when she was hungry and overtired she cried herself to sleep like a child half her age. Sarah didn't blame her. It was all so much for a child to endure.

Isabella sensed that everything had changed yet again and was exhausted. She felt as though a weight had descended on her on top of everything she had been through and a gloom came down on her despite the warming weather. The brighter days did not seem to penetrate her moods. Sarah and Hilary did their best to keep her jolly, but Sarah knew that Hilary was feeling anything but jolly herself. Very often now she would walk across to the ruined farm and perhaps in her mind see it as it had been when she had been happy there with her husband and her children, when everything was the way she wanted it.

Twenty-two

'I want to see the lawyer,' Harry's father told him one June afternoon when Harry was in the garden and reasonably happy. His father had been inactive for the last few days. He did that when he was trying to think and, although it was a temporary respite, it made Harry's life so much easier than when his father roamed the grounds and sometimes now the streets.

After being brought back that last time he had not gone out again, but it was difficult trying to watch him. Now that they had this interval Harry cultivated his vegetables and tended his tomatoes, cucumbers and lettuces in the greenhouse. He was satisfied with his crop.

His father was sitting on an old wooden seat in the shade of a tree and Harry's heart sank when his father spoke.

'What lawyer?' Harry said, choosing to be awkward.

'Are you a parrot, echoing me?' his father said. 'East of course. I want him here.'

'Why?'

'That's not your business, lad.'

'And what will we pay him with?'

'I can pay him,' his father said loftily. 'Go and do what I say.'

Harry disliked the gleam in his father's eyes, but he didn't think it was madness so he went and saw Mr East and asked him to call on his father.

In the end, Sarah went to the Leadbetter house. She couldn't think what else to do, and she had to do something. There was nobody else to do it. She was nervous and didn't know what to say. She feared the older man would come to the door and she didn't know the younger one, so she hesitated at the gates. It was not as bad as she had thought it would be. The whole place was shabby but the gardens were weeded and neat. She hesitated at the front door, then changed her mind and headed around to the back and into a courtyard.

There she could hear a man's voice, educated and young. As she approached the greenhouses she saw that there was somebody in one of them. It had to be Harry Leadbetter. She had never met him before now, just caught glimpses of him in the village, but he went to few places and their paths rarely crossed.

Harry was nothing like she had thought. He was nowhere near as old as she had imagined, not that much older than she was. He sensed her and smiled. The first thing she saw as she got close was that he had exactly the same green eyes as Isabella. He was talking to a small spaniel who was looking up at him with admiration, such as dogs ever did to people who took them in.

'Hello,' Sarah ventured.

'Hello.' He came towards her. 'I was talking to Ernie.' He indicated the dog. 'Just walked in here one afternoon and stayed.'

Sarah was amazed at this friendly tone and rather happy about it. She had not expected good manners. Also, she had been told that although Harry was a nice-looking lad, he came from too bad a family for anybody to speak to him. He seemed unaffected by all that had happened to him, though, and his voice was soft and Scottish. It wouldn't take much more for her to think him attractive.

'I'm Sarah Charles. I would like to talk to you if you have no objection.'

He hesitated and then agreed. 'Yes, of course. Do come into the house.'

He led the way to the back door and through the kitchen. It was all basic and very shabby but spotlessly clean. He showed her into a big library where the doors opened out into the front garden. Since it was a fine day, sunshine poured into the room. He offered her a seat and waited until she sat down before sitting himself.

'I don't like to say it but it's about your father.'

He didn't seem surprised but was obviously dismayed. 'I thought it might be. Has he been bothering you? He forgets where and who he is and although I do try to keep an eye on him, he does sometimes give me the slip. What did he do?'

Harry Leadbetter looked so intently at her that Sarah felt able to tell him. She had not thought of him as well-bred, well-spoken and approachable, but he was.

'I am living up on the tops in the place that was the Foundling School for Girls and later Blessed St Hilda's Orphanage. I was staying at the doctor's house but he said he thought we could go there – we being me and the little girl from Spain, Isabella. Your father saw her in the market place the other day and thought he recognized her. He got very upset, not with her, but somehow it affected him. She was the one who became upset with him.'

'I'm so sorry. I'm sure he didn't mean anything. He is harmless, he just can't cope with things. Why did he think he knew her?'

Sarah took a deep breath. 'Because he did.'

There was a long silence. Even the cats who sat by his feet noticed it and stalked out, flourishing their long, cream-coloured plumed tails as they left.

'You are related,' Sarah said. 'Her mother was a Logan from St John's Chapel. She married a Spaniard and they lived in the Canary Islands. Her daughter is called Isabella after your mother.'

Harry Leadbetter stared and then his face lit up. 'My mother has been dead for a long time. My father adored her and they had a little girl who died when she was very small; she was named after her mother. He thought he had found her? Oh, how awful for you and for her and for him too. Does she look like us?'

'She's the very spit of you,' Sarah said, and his emerald eyes gleamed as though she had just given him the best present he had ever received. 'She has your eyes but she has golden hair.'

'I had golden hair when I was a child,' he said. 'No wonder my father thought he knew her, and in his state of mind she was his child brought to life again. Come and see this.'

He took her into the next room and there above the fireplace was a portrait in oils of a woman very like Isabella.

'That's it exactly,' Sarah said.

'My mother died a long time ago and he took to brandy like his father before him. He boasts that she was engaged to be married to his elder brother, James, and he took her away from James just a week before the wedding. I don't know whether it's true. When he drinks, the ghosts become real and he mourns both his wife and lost child.'

'He called Isabella "my little lass",' Sarah said.

'I'm sorry he frightened her. This house has become a

prison to him so he longs to get out, and then his mind puts up shutters as well because he can't remember things and he gets everything jumbled up. Some days he's perfectly lucid and to be frank I worry more when he's like that. I'm sure he plans and schemes but it rarely comes to anything because his moods shift constantly. He shouts and swears at me but as far as I know he has never hurt anyone. He can't go around frightening the little girl, though. I will make sure it doesn't happen again.'

Sarah couldn't think of what to say. The room must have been beautiful once and it was swept and clean, but the windows were rotten and uncurtained and the huge marble fireplace had seen no fire, she imagined, in years. There was no rug and Harry's footsteps echoed on the bare floorboards. There was nothing but the painting.

She wondered whether it hurt him to see his mother's portrait and if he stayed out of there on purpose because the portrait kept her memory alive. Sarah had not understood how lifelike good oil paintings could be, and in this one it looked as if the woman was about to step out of it, her eyes were so green and alive.

When they got back into the library, he said, 'How often do you come into the village? I will try to make sure he doesn't bother you.'

'That's very kind of you. We usually come to the market. I buy and sell clothes and lace goods to help us make ends meet,' she said.

She couldn't think of what more to say – the memories here haunted her – but most of all she was disturbed by the idea of him to talking to his dog as though it was his only real contact. Even now the little spaniel sat at his feet and he caressed one of its long silky ears. Sarah was almost glad that he had some companion and she liked him all the better for his loving treatment of the dog.

That same week Mr East came to the Leadbetter house. Luckily, or unluckily, depending on how you looked at it, Harry thought, his father was clear-headed, so Harry took Mr East through into the library where his father sat in a large armchair. His father looked hard at him until Harry went out, closing the door behind him but wondering and worrying about what was to happen now.

Mr East was deeply surprised. He thought brandy had taken Luke Leadbetter and he was now off his head but it appeared not today.

'Sit down then,' Luke said. 'I have something in particular to say to you.'

'So I imagined,' Mr East said drily but below his breath.

Luke looked carefully at the door as if to make sure that he could not be overheard.

'I'm thinking of acquiring a few acres up on the tops,' he said.

'A particular piece of land?' Mr East prompted when he did not go on.

'Obviously. I would hardly be venturing up there willy-nilly. It's the old Nattrass farm.'

Mr East knew that place, the Nattrasses had farmed there for hundreds of years. Poor Mrs Nattrass had been forced to go to the Hilda House for refuge and stay with Sarah Charles and the strange little foreign girl when it had burned down not long since.

'Really?' was all he could think to say.

'I want you to offer the old girl a small amount for it. It's nothing but a few acres, I gather, but I thought I might build up there. The views must be splendid.'

Mr East could hardly believe his ears. This house was failing the man but apparently he had money to start again and in one of the most godforsaken places in the area, where the wind whistled past your face and the snow almost came that far. Was the man mad? He revised his ideas. Mr Leadbetter definitely had problems. How on earth would he pay for such a thing and why, when he was so obviously on his last legs?

'How many acres did you think to purchase?' Mr East asked.

'I gather there are about twenty. It can't be worth much. I understand that the old woman has gone to live with neighbours, so I thought that you could go up there and talk to her and see how little she would take for it. It cannot be worth much, no good for anything but sheep.'

Mr East could not help but think that Mr Leadbetter was not losing his mind at all, unless this was a totally unrealistic idea like fairies and ghosts and spirits. Perhaps Luke Leadbetter had sovereigns hidden away under the floorboards. People were inclined to do such things.

Mr East went home and found himself perplexed about the whole matter. Usually he could eat his dinner and put such things from his mind, but tonight he could not. He had a very good life. His two children were grown up and had children of their own. They both lived in Durham and he saw his young grandchildren at regular intervals. He also had a wife whom he had adored from the minute he set eyes on her. She understood when he was thinking hard about what he should do and knew that he would likely tell her everything, because he had relied on her advice for thirty years when it came to business situations.

They sat outside in the garden with their coffee after dinner. He explained and she listened, wrinkling her brow, but when the story was finished all she said was, 'What if you get through all the negotiations and then Mr Leadbetter has no money?'

'I suppose I will have to take him on trust.'

'And more to the point, what if Mrs Nattrass doesn't want to sell her farm?'

'If she has no money there's not much she can do to put it right. It would cost a lot to do anything and perhaps her memories would cause problems.'

'I should think almost burning to death in her bed is enough to cause anybody problems,' said Mrs East, who had a lot of imagination but no doubt was accurate here, her husband thought.

Mr East decided that the best thing to do was to go and see Mrs Nattrass and put the offer which Mr Leadbetter had made to her.

It's perhaps the best time of year up on the tops, he thought, but none of this seemed to have affected Mrs Nattrass. She looked upset and it was hardly surprising after what had happened. She might be glad of the chance to leave the ruined farm, as he thought there was no way in which she would be able to rebuild it. Seated at the big kitchen table she said nothing for a few minutes after he put the proposition to her.

Then she said, 'I don't want to sell it.'

He would have liked to ask her why not, what was she going to do with it now, but of course that would have been unethical.

'Who wants to buy it?' was Sarah's first question.

Mr East wasn't sure he was obliged to answer this but he saw that she would do whatever she had to to find out, and everybody always knew everything in a small town like Wolsingham, so he told them.

Her eyes widened. 'Mr Leadbetter? But he has no money. His house is falling down and he's drunken and strange and . . . ' There Sarah ran out of ideas.

'He says that he wants to build a house up here.'

'Whatever for?'

'I don't know,' Mr East said, 'but he told me to put the proposition to Mrs Nattrass and so of course I am obliged to do it.'

'What made you think it was for sale?' Hilary said.

'Everybody knows what happened and you can't go on living there. Perhaps somebody else could buy it and build anew.'

'It sounds an unlikely story,' Hilary said.

When Mr East had gone the two women went outside and sat in the afternoon sunshine.

'You're worried about it,' Sarah said.

'I don't understand what Luke Leadbetter is trying to do.'

'He's lost his mind, I'm sure his son thinks so. I did go to see him about Isabella after Mr Leadbetter behaved so strangely in the market square, but Harry promised me it wouldn't happen again so I left it.'

Hilary stared at her.

'He's a very strange man. He must have heard that the house had burned down and thought it would be worth less.'

'If he had wanted to buy it he could have just offered before.'

'Would you have sold it then and at a low price?' Sarah asked.

'I will never sell it.'

'Then perhaps he miscalculated.'

'It could have been his son. All the Leadbetters are rotten to the core,' Hilary said.

Sarah hadn't mentioned that she had very much liked Harry Leadbetter and found no fault in him. She said nothing but it got her thinking.

Most of the village people thought the Leadbetters were all alike, so perhaps she had been mistaken in Harry Leadbetter and he had set the house on fire because his father had some strange idea that he wanted it. After all, no matter what the man was like, he was still Harry's father and families always came first to everybody.

Twenty-three

Once the idea had got into Sarah's head she couldn't free her mind from it. Perhaps Harry Leadbetter thought that if his father got something he wanted, it might improve his behaviour. Why he would want to build a house there, she had no idea, but Harry might do it out of misguided love. She didn't know him well, had met him only once, but he had stayed in her mind: the way that he talked to and treated his dog, the light and kind look in his eyes. Every time she thought about him it made her happy and she wanted to get to know him better. But then, if he was like all the other Leadbetters, why shouldn't he be capable of doing such a thing without remorse?

As a family the Leadbetters had hurt a huge number of people. Hilary was devastated by what had happened and, but for Sarah, she would have been homeless. Sarah did not pretend to herself that Hilary was happy there with her and knew the older woman longed for the home she had called hers for so long.

Isabella was hurt too. She was no longer the confident child she had become after all of Sarah's efforts, so on the next market day – and that was another sore point, Isabella no longer wanted to go with her – Sarah strode across the street determined to ask Harry Leadbetter exactly what was going on.

She didn't bother going to the front door as she thought, it being a fine, warm day, Harry would be in the garden around the back. She slowed her steps just in case he wasn't there and she would have to retreat to the front door, but she heard a barking and the little spaniel ran right across the lawns to her, wagging its tail madly until she got down and stroked its ears.

Harry came to her, smiling just a little. 'Miss Charles, good day. How are you?'

'Worried,' Sarah said flatly, 'and upset.'

She stopped there and Harry called the dog to heel, which was exactly what she wanted him to do. The little dog hesitated and then went to him obediently, his tail no longer wagging.

Sarah was beginning to doubt herself now. Harry was so clear-eyed but she knew that might be nothing but a front.

'What is it?' he said. 'It can't be my father. I haven't let him out of my sight.'

'Mrs Nattrass's house burned down.'

'Ages ago. Yes, I know.'

'And presumably you know also that your father wants to buy it?'

'Does he?' Harry sounded puzzled and taken aback.

'Mr East came to see us and your father has said he will buy the farm.'

She had silenced him. Sarah made herself say, 'You did it, didn't you? All the time behaving like butter wouldn't melt in your mouth, but you burned the farm down because you knew that your father had set his heart on it. He hasn't much money so you made it possible. You could after all sell this place, though it's falling apart, and move up there, and he would be away from other people and it might make him happier. It would certainly make things a lot easier for both of you.'

The silence seemed to get deeper the longer it went on.

'Mr East shouldn't have said that my father wanted the farm,' Harry said, which was hardly the point. 'I thought solicitors were meant to be discreet.'

'Was there a good reason why he shouldn't have?'

'If it's true, then he was betraying my father's confidence.'

'Perhaps it wasn't said in confidence.'

'I think these things always are,' Harry said.

'But he does want the place?'

'I don't know. I can't imagine why he would. It's just a nondescript smallholding in the middle of nowhere. This is a family home and has been our house for a very long time. In any case it doesn't belong to my father, it belongs to his elder brother, so he's in no position to sell it. As far I'm aware he hasn't a penny. Mr East came here, yes, but I don't know what it was about and for you to think that I would do such an underhand thing is appalling—'

'He's your father.'

'—Or that my father would. He may seem strange to you but I don't think burning buildings comes into his repertoire,' Harry said, sarcastic and light-voiced.

'I shall go and tell Mr Whitty.'

'No!'

She wanted to leave but she couldn't. It wasn't that Harry got hold of her or tried to stop her in any way. Even his voice was reluctant as he took a step back.

'If Mr Whitty believed my father could do such a thing he would have him put away. You know what that would mean. Anyway, he couldn't have done it. He can't walk very far. Half the day he doesn't know who he is or who I am.' Harry's voice broke and he turned away. 'Have you any idea what those places are like? It would kill him.'

'The fire almost killed Mrs Nattrass.'

'But it didn't and it's nothing to do with us.' He turned back to her, green eyes swimming. 'How could you have thought that I would endanger an old lady's life so that I could give my father what he wants?'

'I don't see why you shouldn't,' Sarah said and she strode off, almost breaking down herself before she reached the street. She didn't go to see Mr Whitty. She tried to make herself but she couldn't. Hilary wasn't hurt, at least not physically, and Sarah heard again and again the awful things she had said to Harry. She had made him cry and had seen how much he loved his dreadful father. That was a horrible thing to do.

She went back up to the Hilda House, sobbing all the way.

Harry couldn't believe that he had cried. Not only had he never cried before – not when his mother died, not when he had been sent away to school and left there, deserted by his father, not when he was beaten up at school or when the teachers had hit him, or when he had been lonely and left out and completely desolated – but he had cried in front of a girl.

He was mortified. It was the only thing he could think of. What made it worse was that his father was having a particularly good day and came to Harry saying softly, 'Is there something wrong?'

Harry was obliged to shake his head and say that there was nothing. He loved his father when Luke was like this. It didn't happen often – his father was always swearing and throwing crockery at him very inaccurately – but still his father knew that there was something the matter in Harry's world and that was comforting. His father could not have done such a thing and for that girl, that lass, his dales' voice told him, that bit of a lass to think either of them would. The only people Harry had ever deliberately hurt were when he got into fights at school and had to get out of them. He had learned to land as many punches as you could as fast and hard as you were able, until they could only take him if there were three of them, and not even then sometimes.

And now. It took him two days to calm down and even then he silently called her names. After that he lay awake and thought about why Mr East had come to see his father. That made him angry. He did not hesitate then. He went to Mr East's office and when the woman on the desk told him that Mr East was busy, he went straight into the man's room. Two men were on their feet. He knew Mr East by sight. He also knew Mr Whitty, who had brought his father back when he had escaped and got lost.

The woman had followed him in apologizing but Mr East said that it was fine and she went out. Mr Whitty merely nodded before he left.

When the door was shut Harry said, 'You went and told Mrs Nattrass that my father wanted to buy her house.'

Mr East looked at him. 'She asked.'

'And you told her?'

'Why wouldn't I tell her?'

'Presumably if he did want to buy the house he told you in confidence.'

'I didn't take it like that. Why?'

'Because I've had Sarah Charles accusing me of burning down Mrs Nattrass's house!' Harry said.

Mr East stared and then he said softly, 'Do sit down. Please, Harry.'

Harry sat, fuming.

'This is a very small community. If your father did want to buy somebody's house it stands to reason that names would be exchanged, surely?'

'Not through you.'

'Then who? I was trying to sell for her and buy for your father. Quite simple, I think.'

'So he does want to buy it?'

'I imagined you knew.'

'With what? We have no money. There's no money in the house, I've searched everywhere. I'm selling things from the house so that we can eat.'

'He could have money in Darling's bank. You wouldn't necessarily know.'

Harry laughed. He actually laughed. 'Mr East, if my father had any money he would spend it on brandy.'

'He shouldn't be drinking brandy.'

'I don't think that's any of your business. And next time my father wants to buy a house he won't be coming to you.'

'Since I'm the only solicitor in the dale that might cause difficulties,' Mr East said.

Harry wanted to smash him in the face.

When Harry went to bed that night his mind recalled clearly the two men who had come several times to the house. Had money been exchanged then or was he just imagining it? He had hovered outside the door, all to no avail since the doors were thick oak, but he did think the sound of chinking coins had prevailed, though when he barged in, he saw little. Did his father have money, and if he did, why would he spend it in such a way? Why would he pay people to burn the house down?

The following day he taxed his father with this but Luke looked blankly at him. His condition was worsening so that even if he had done such a thing he had obviously forgotten it. Harry tried to put it out of his mind and to put Sarah Charles from his mind too. He almost hated her.

It was the following week on a particularly warm day when Hilary and Isabella trekked over to see the burned-down house. Hilary thought she would never get past the fact that it had burned but she could not live without sight of it for any length of time. They sat with their feet in the little stream which ran down from the top of the hill and it was cool bliss in such weather.

Isabella could not stay still for long and in the end she went up to the top of the hill, came back down and then walked around the edges of the farm while Hilary sat there in the shade with a big straw hat on her head.

Isabella came back carrying something. She wasn't sure what it was, just a small piece of some kind of metal stuck into a big piece of stone. They pored over it for some time, carrying it back to Sarah at the end of the afternoon.

She stared at it for a long time.

'Perhaps this is the answer to why Mr Leadbetter wants to buy the farm,' Isabella said. 'Gold.'

'It isn't worth anything much; it's fool's gold and everybody around here would recognize it,' Hilary said.

'What if he doesn't know that?' Sarah said.

'But he would.' Hilary frowned and the frown deepened.

'Maybe he would have known had he been better, but he could have been deceived. If he thought it was gold, he could have got somebody to burn down the house so that he could buy the land and be able to mine it,' Sarah said.

'Luke Leadbetter paid them to start a fire and make the house burn down, knowing that I would not sell it because it was my home?' Hilary stared. 'I've heard of silver mining up in the dale but there has never been gold around here. We call coal black gold and that's the closest we get.'

'Terrible to think he could be so misguided.'

Hilary wanted to go and see Mr Whitty and Sarah was half inclined to let her, even to go with her, but she remembered what Harry had said and how he had reacted. To him his father was like a misguided child and though part of her wanted to have Luke Leadbetter locked up, the cost to all of them would be irretrievable.

She wanted to say to Hilary that they ought to see Mr Whitty together but Harry had been right, and if Luke Leadbetter had believed tales of riches it was just that he was not all that he should be. In the end Hilary agreed and Sarah kissed her because she thought it was a very generous gesture.

'Even if the house was as it had been, I'm not sure I could go back now,' Hilary admitted. 'You're so kind and it's a long time since somebody your age bothered about an old stick like me.'

Sarah told her she was nothing like an old stick, more like an oak tree, and that made her smile, but a tear ran down her weathered cheek at the thought of somebody destroying the little she had.

'There's nobody left to want the place anyroad,' Hilary said roughly so that she wouldn't cry.

Sarah told herself over and over again that there was no need for her to bother any further with Harry Leadbetter, but she thought that he ought to know the truth, and so she made herself go as soon as she had gathered enough courage. She went alone the following market day. It rained. She felt sick and couldn't concentrate on what she was trying to do. This time she banged hard on the front door. When it was finally answered and Harry saw who his guest was, he stood back a little and he said, 'More accusations?'

'I just want to . . . I just . . .' Sarah ran out of words and tried not to run away. She half hoped he would close the door in her face but he just stood there and waited. It was horrible making herself stand still with that look on his face. She tried to look away and couldn't. Hastily she pulled the rock out of her pocket and offered it to him. 'Do you know what that is?'

'Obviously. Everybody in the dale knows fool's gold when he sees it.'

'I don't think your father did. I'm sure at one time he would have recognized it but I think he thought he was going to make a fortune and so, in whatever mindset he had then, he encouraged somebody to burn down Mrs Nattrass's house.'

'You never give up, do you?'

Sarah said nothing else and so they stood like that for some time, which seemed long to her, but still he held open the door and then he said, 'You'd better come in,' and she did.

He took her through into the room where his mother's portrait dominated the walls and where his father was asleep on a sofa which she thought had not been there the last time she saw that room. Had Harry got the sofa so that his father could sleep more comfortably? Also there were two battered armchairs set around it as though almost in protection, and today, because of the rain, a log fire burned slowly in the grate. Sarah thought the wood smelled of apples; it was strangely comforting.

Luke Leadbetter was curled up almost like a child.

'There he is,' Harry said, flatly. 'The man who burned down the house.'

They stood for a few moments and then he led the way into the kitchen and closed the doors behind them.

Harry hesitated for a few seconds and then he looked straight at her and said reluctantly, 'They came here several times, two men, and I didn't like them. They were rough characters, rude, pushing past me in the doorway and, after the first time, going into where my father has always sat. It got to the point where I started worrying about what they were doing here and whether they could harm us, so I listened outside the door and then I deliberately opened it. I caught a glimpse of and heard the chink of money. I don't know who they are or where the money came from; he must have had it hidden somewhere he thought I wouldn't look. This is a big place.'

'I'm sorry,' Sarah said. He was obviously ashamed that such a thing had happened but she was glad that he had been honest enough to confess it, even though his father was involved. She couldn't look at Harry.

'It sounds to me like a plausible explanation,' she said while Harry looked down. She could see the disappointment on his face that his father had been involved in something so awful.

He didn't speak for several minutes and then he seemed to accept that what he had thought and said was true. 'There's nothing for you to be sorry about,' Harry said. 'It was him. I don't know what happened and I have tried to tackle him about it but he's ill. He's very ill. If you want to go to Mr Whitty then you must, and I will tell the truth, because it's only right and I'm very sorry for Mrs Nattrass and for the little girl he frightened.' He had pleaded for his father last time and wouldn't do it again, she could see.

Sarah had already made up her mind about seeing Mr Whitty and knew she wanted to bear responsibility for such consequences. She was trying to make up to Hilary for what had been done to her. Perhaps that had to be enough.

'I shan't go to him,' she said at last, and she left the rock on the kitchen table.

Twenty-four

Sarah walked to Satley to talk to Mrs Prudhoe as Fiona and Ada had said they had spoken to the doctor and the woman would need a wedding dress, and also perhaps others for her new life.

It was a Saturday morning when she went. Mrs Prudhoe was still running her school so Sarah thought that Saturday would be the right time to call. Presumably Mrs Prudhoe, like half the world, went to church on Sundays, possibly more than once if she needed to keep in with the vicar and his wife. Sarah imagined, though, that she would not be welcomed in Satley Church any longer now that she was marrying their daughter's widower.

It was a lovely early summer's day but Mrs Prudhoe wore deep black. It was thin and worn and had been mended several times. This woman had no money and wore what she had and went on wearing it until she could afford better. No doubt she would be happy and grateful that the doctor had offered new clothes for the wedding.

Mrs Prudhoe sat her down and listened as Sarah

explained her mission and then she said, not looking up, 'I can't afford a new dress, Miss Charlton. I can't afford anything.'

She looked pleadingly at Sarah, who instantly understood. She was surprised that it had not occurred to Dr Blair sooner that his bride could hardly go to the altar in her shabby widow's weeds, which were so obviously all she had.

Sarah thought quickly. 'Perhaps we could make a bargain,' she said. 'If you go to the altar in a beautiful dress I will get a lot of custom out of it.'

Mrs Prudhoe stared at her.

'I need the work and it's summer. I could make a dress that would make other women think they could carry it off equally well. If you don't mind me saying so, you are the right person to do so. You will be easy to dress with your looks. I could make similar dresses in cheaper material to sell and we would all benefit.'

Mrs Prudhoe had evidently never heard of such a thing. She frowned, and then the natural woman in her came through and she said, 'Perhaps I could pay you back in some way?'

'You could let me make other dresses for you as the doctor's wife,' Sarah said.

Mrs Prudhoe blushed from pleasure and embarrassment and they began to talk about it. Sarah got out her sketch book and they sat at the kitchen table. Mrs Prudhoe even made tea from her carefully hoarded stash and there they spent the afternoon.

Twenty-five

Luke Leadbetter had a letter at about this time. He read it twice over, screwing up his eyes, which he claimed were not good, and then announced, 'My brother is coming home. He wants the house.'

He thrust the letter at Harry. Harry read the missive twice and started to say all manner of stupid things, that it was their home, that generations of Leadbetters had lived there, though it wasn't true, not in that house if you were being pedantic. It was, however, the only home he had ever known, though so much of his life had been spent in Pitlochry that he was not certain it counted.

Surely enough, two weeks later at about three o'clock in the afternoon there was a banging on the front door and Harry opened it to a well-dressed man of about fifty. He was evidently wealthy, Harry could glimpse a motorcar. He had never seen such a thing outside of cities and couldn't help staring. The man was smiling.

'Good afternoon. I'm James Leadbetter. I hope that I'm expected.'

Harry showed him in and his uncle looked around him as though it was a palace.

'Yes, I remember the old place very well now. I went off, you see, to make my fortune.'

'And you did?'

'I certainly did,' the man said and grinned. Harry wasn't sure he liked that grin.

'Made and lost it several times. You are my nephew, Harry, I take it?'

They shook hands and Harry showed him into the drawing room where his father sat just like somebody normal. Harry knew the effort it took and how his father had dreaded the meeting ever since the letter had arrived.

'Luke?' the man said, and Harry's father turned a ghastly pale colour. Harry thought he would pass out.

' You don't look well,' James said.

'What the hell do you want?' Luke growled.

Harry got himself out of the room as quickly as he could. He had no idea what would happen now but it couldn't be good.

'I want my house back,' his uncle said.

In the end his uncle left. Harry saw him as he drove away in his beautiful car. Harry went back into the drawing room where his father sat hunched over the fire.

'He wants us out now. He wants the house and it is his,' his father acknowledged, looking down as though to make himself try to believe it.

Harry had no idea what to do next. He had recently given up his watch, the only valuable thing he had left, which had been his mother's gift to him, and then the silver cross that he wore around his neck, which had been hers. He had planned to shoot pheasants and partridges in the autumn and fish their stretch of the river even more often, but by then of course they would be gone. How he would pay for brandy in the autumn he had no idea, but his father sobbed constantly when he did not drink and Harry couldn't bear it.

Harry wandered disconsolately around the house and the garden like a lost soul and tried to come to terms with what had happened. He had no idea what he would do now. In a matter of days he and his father would be on the street.

Twenty-six

It seemed to Ada and Fiona that the doctor paid no more attention to the two little girls than he ever had. He didn't read them a story or tuck them into bed. He didn't sit with them while they ate. It was, the two maids decided, just as though he didn't know they were there.

The children had become, Ada said, little treasures. They seemed to like school now. They rarely spoke of their father but they were good friends with Oswald and his mother and spent a lot of time in the stable yard, at Mrs Leighton's cottage, and in the garden now that the weather was warm. Nevertheless, a cloud hung about them and Oswald wanted to know what it was.

'Don't be silly, Oswald,' Ada said, becoming vexed with him. 'They've lived with their grandparents all these years, they hardly know their father and they are getting a new mother who used to be their teacher. It's an awful lot to have to put up with when you're so young. Worst of all they don't like her. They didn't like her as a teacher, so how much less will they like her replacing the mother they lost?'

Oswald obviously had no idea what she was talking about and merely shook his head and went back to tending the plants.

Fiona and Ada were both lonely that summer and confided to one another how hard it was when the evenings never darkened. The nights seemed to mock them. They were convinced that lovers walked by the river and down the lanes, happy together, but these people were twenty years younger than them. They felt left out, left behind, invisible, and did not pretend that things were going to get any better. They knew now that they would be servants all their lives and in the end would be too old to work. What would happen to them then? They had no future. Women of their age were married with grown children, some were already grandmothers. They had their husbands, their homes, somewhere to be and they were somebody. They were not old maids as Fiona and Ada were in every sense of the word. The two women became frustrated and discontented, and after that just plain unhappy.

Sarah called in after she had gained the making of Mrs Prudhoe's new dress. They had never liked her, though they'd warmed slightly to her after she'd remade the velvet dresses for them.

'I don't see why that awful woman can marry the doctor,' Fiona said with some bitterness. Ada looked away and Sarah realized that they both envied the other woman who had no better a background than they did.

Ada glanced at her friend. 'Fiona is stuck on the doctor.'

'I am not,' Fiona said, and Sarah couldn't help smiling at this childish exchange. Fiona blushed and Ada smiled.

In the end, Ada got up and said she would put the kettle on and Sarah took the offer gladly and said, 'I could make new dresses for you.'

They both looked at her.

It was Fiona who looked at her friend and she said, 'That's a good idea.'

'Don't be silly, Fi,' Ada said. 'What would we use for money?'

'I've got some money.'

'You can't have much left, you've given most of your wages to my mother for the family.'

'I've still got enough for new dresses for us both.'

'I couldn't take it.'

Fiona looked at Sarah. 'She gives every penny she makes to her mother for the family.'

'Fi—'

'You do. But I've still got some and why shouldn't we have a new dress each? It would cheer us up.'

Sarah described what she could do and how they could go to the market and look at cloth, which she could buy cheaply. So, after a quick cup of tea, off they went, both secretly thrilled at the idea. Not a second-hand dress but a new one, a dress which Sarah could make for each of

them of light cloth, and they could choose the colour
and material and the kind of style they wanted.

Sarah did enjoy taking the two old maids to the market
and letting them finger the stuff that they longed for.
She was glad to bring such pleasure to their faces and
even Ada was polite.

Fiona had dark hair and brown eyes. Sarah found
materials which would flatter her looks – pale colours,
not quite lemon and not quite orange and not quite
white. Ada was red-haired and blue-eyed and although
she might have shied away from bright colours, with her
creamy skin, red and pink materials could make her hair
look like fire.

Ada tried not to let Fiona pay for it all, saying that she
could never wear such things. In the end she was persuaded and the flush of her cheeks told Sarah how very
pleased she was with the purchases, and how grateful
she was to Sarah and to her friend for making one of her
dreams come true.

'I never thought any of them would,' she confided to
Fiona later. 'I'd given up on them all.'

'You mustn't, and now look, when everybody else
is sweltering in their dark dresses, we will be going to
church in our summer finery.'

Ada was half inclined to think that it wasn't very polite
but on the first Sunday that they wore their new dresses
to church, Mrs Wilson came over to them and said that

she appreciated they had made such efforts to brighten the church, and on the very day that the clouds had gathered and it was as dark as November.

The vicar brought coffee for them with his own hands and said how they graced his church with their singing. They were happy even though they knew it for flattery and thought Mr and Mrs Wilson the best of people. Folk went to church there because Mr Wilson improved their days. He never accused them of sin or wrongdoing or told anybody how they should behave. Mrs Wilson took the children off and told them all the best Bible stories in the Sunday school, such as Joseph's coat of many colours and how the one lamb was received back into the flock after it had strayed. It had been brought home and there was rejoicing.

In church, the old blind organist gave it everything he had, and even though he was out of step with the congregation many times, nobody minded, for they were singing all the hymns they knew so well and had learned at their mothers' knees.

After that particular Sunday, young women who could afford new dresses or those who had mothers who could buy such things for them, talked to Sarah when she came down to the market. Before long there were a lot of pretty dresses for the Sunday services and Sarah had more money.

She made sure that she only charged what they could

afford. As long as she kept going she could make a small profit, but she also liked how she brightened the faces of so many women in the dale. Sometimes she would make dresses for those who could not afford to pay a lot because a new dress meant everything to most women she had known – it could lighten their lives and moods and their ideas.

Twenty-seven

Hyacinth Prudhoe did not sleep at all the night before her wedding. The night seemed endless. In vain did she tell herself that this was the only sensible decision and all her life she had been sensible. She was staying with the Wilsons, as she was to be married in the Wolsingham church the following morning.

She did not pretend to herself that she could keep on in the drab life she was leading, and she knew that to many women Alexander Blair would seem like a miracle, but having had a bad first marriage she could not convince herself that this one would be any better. Yet what else could she do?

She could not even eat the food which Mrs Wilson had so generously provided. She had felt sick for days now and could not get down anything but water, no matter how hard she tried.

'You must eat, my dear,' Mrs Wilson said in vain.

She had tried to tell Hyacinth that Georgina and Doris would make excellent bridesmaids and she had actually shuddered at the thought. She said that she did not approve of children at weddings and needed no one to attend her. Mrs Wilson thought this was most unusual but left it at that. The woman should have the wedding she wanted, even though other folk might look askance.

So Mrs Wilson was the only one to dress her in her wedding finery and she admired the dress with enthusiasm. Hyacinth looked at herself in the mirror and all she saw was a stupid, middle-aged woman trying and failing to look like a young bride.

The dress was beautiful, it was true, but she was not. Her face was pale, her cheeks almost sunken, her lips were bloodless and her eyes were dull. She had even lost weight since the dress had been last fitted and it hung like a small blue and cream tent.

Mr Wilson's gardener had picked cream roses from the garden and had fashioned them into a posy for her to carry when she walked down the aisle to meet her husband at the altar. On her head she wore a very small net with another rose. She thought it made her look stupid.

The whole village had turned out for the doctor's wedding and in her heart she knew that they thought she was not good enough for him. He was marrying down socially and the whole area was aware of how common she was. Her cheeks burned as she went into the church on the arm of Mr Wilson's brother, who was staying for the event.

She remembered very little of the service. It all seemed

to be over so quickly and yet she had taken an irrevocable step. There was nothing else she could have done, she told herself. She could no longer half-starve in that ghastly little house in Satley where the vicar Mr Freeman and his wife despised her. They had not wanted to see their son-in-law become another woman's husband and she had not expected them to.

She tried and failed to smile until she made herself. Her hand shook when the signing of the register took place and she did not even look at her new husband. She could not bear to think that she was now a piece of his property; that was how it felt.

Alex had awoken in the middle of the night on the eve of his wedding, after bad dreams. He was sweating so hard that he could feel the drops trickling down his back. He felt sure that he was making a mistake. He felt guilty that his parents-in-law were not speaking to him and had refused to go anywhere near the church in Wolsingham. Mrs Prudhoe had proudly proclaimed that she did not need to go away after the wedding, she would be perfectly happy in her new house with her new family. He wasn't happy with this, but somehow to take her away at this point felt all wrong. She would have enough to cope with without visiting new places when they knew one another so little, at least that was how it felt.

He had had visions of leaving the children with their grandparents for a few days so he could at least take his bride as far as York, but it was not to be. He couldn't imagine why he had thought this a good idea. It was exploding in his face like a Catherine wheel.

He had nobody to invite to the wedding. Mr Wilson said it didn't matter, he was quite sure the whole village would turn out for it and Mrs Prudhoe said that she had nobody either. Fiona and Ada put on a big help-yourself meal at the surgery house, using every table they possessed so that people could move around and talk to one another.

Ada was miffed. She had wanted to go to the wedding but there were a lot of last-minute things to do and the doctor seemed to have given out casual invitations, which Ada had never heard of before. So they made a lot of cakes and scones and sandwiches and pies. There was a table laden with plates and cutlery and another where there were cups and saucers, and then on the sideboard there were various bottles and glasses.

Hardest of all, the children were not allowed to go to the wedding. Oswald's mother had refused to go and she took the two girls into her cottage. They sat side by side all the time that the wedding went on and didn't move or murmur. What good children they were, Mrs Leighton told Ada with some satisfaction.

The wedding didn't last long. The bridal party came

home after about an hour and a half, soaked as they had walked the short distance from the church, and soon the rooms were full of noise, people eating and drinking and talking. Finally the rain stopped and the sun came out, so halfway through the afternoon they wandered off into the garden.

'Messing up my clean floors with their wet shoes,' Ada complained as she made yet more tea.

Fiona and Ada were already worried about the new Mrs Blair. She had come with very little luggage and nothing else beyond a few educational books and the kind of clothes, Ada said, that even her mother would have thrown away.

The maids had hoped that the doctor's former parents-in-law would take the little girls and that the married couple would go away for a couple of weeks and they could take it easy, but it wasn't like that. They were all to stay in Wolsingham.

When Georgina and Doris came back from Mrs Leighton's, Fiona was brave enough to ask them whether they had had a nice time. Georgina looked sideways at the question, her latest alternative to raising her eyes to the heavens, to show grown-ups when they were being particularly obnoxious.

For a moment nobody spoke.

'Did you get to brush Archie?'

'No, of course not,' Georgina said. 'Archie was out all

morning picking up people to go to the church and then bringing everybody here. We were the only ones who weren't allowed to go.'

'Not really,' Ada said softly.

'Fancy,' Georgina went on, warming to the topic which had held her mind all day, 'not letting your own children in at your wedding. They'll be saying babies aren't allowed at christenings next and then where will we be?'

'Where are you going?' Fiona said as both girls made for the door.

'To bed.'

'But it's only five o 'clock.'

'We are not going to risk meeting Potty Prudhoe in the hall,' Georgina said. 'At the moment she is in the parlour with our father so we shall go now.'

'It's not the parlour,' Ada said, having told them that they must call it the drawing room because that was what the new mistress wanted it called, but it was too late. The girls had left the room.

Ada and Fiona heard the clatter of the stair rods as the two girls trod heavily up the stairs and then the clash of the bedroom door.

Alex felt as strange as he had ever done in his life. Once the wedding guests had drifted off home he was suddenly left in the drawing room with his new wife. All he wanted to do was run away. Was he dreaming? Could he be having a nightmare? What on earth had he done?

He glanced across at the skinny middle-aged woman who also was standing, as though she was about to leave. He thought she looked ridiculous in her blue and cream dress. It was too big and hung off her like it belonged to someone else. Had she lost more weight recently? There had been nothing of her to start with. He tried to think whether she had eaten anything that day and then couldn't remember what he had eaten either.

'Won't you sit down, my dear?' he offered, just for something to say. She promptly sat down in his own favourite chair, the most comfortable one in the room.

'Perhaps you would like some tea?'

'I'm awash with it,' she said, and didn't look at him. Was she regretting this too – and already?

'Perhaps a glass of sherry?'

'I don't like alcohol. My family is Presbyterian.'

That made Alex shudder. Scottish church tended to be even more repressive than English church, he was just glad that he had such a good man for the vicar here. Mr Wilson was the most practical man of God he had ever met.

Ignoring his wife's disapproving look he went over to the oak sideboard, poured a substantial amount of whisky into a squat cut-glass and diluted it with just a tiny amount of water.

'Sláinte!' he would normally have said, because whisky was a joy, but there was not much joy in drinking it sitting in his least comfortable chair well away from both garden and fire, though today the fire was unlit. That was a shame because even though it was summer and the sun had finally come out, the rain had made everything feel cold and damp. He shivered.

As the silence became prolonged he asked if she would like to take a walk in the garden. The sun was bright and in a daft way it reminded him of his home in Edinburgh, which had been on Charlotte Square and had gardens. The roses would glitter there after rain when he had been a little boy. It had been a beautiful house and he had had a lovely childhood, both parents adored him. Now the house belonged to somebody else and his parents had died long since. He did own a property in Edinburgh but it had belonged to his aunt, who had willed it to him two years ago when she died. He had never seen it. He didn't want to go back to Edinburgh, he had too many sad memories there. He had always missed his mother and father, and now his late wife was at the top of the list and his son.

Hyacinth declined the walk in the garden. No doubt she was thinking about her dress, which was already stained inches above the hem where the rain had caught at it as they walked home. Oswald had not been there to take them back to the house but neither had said anything. Oswald was not the brightest lad and also, by then, the rain had almost stopped and he and Archie had had a heavy day.

'Perhaps we should have gone away,' Alex said, slightly exasperated.

'I don't want to go away, Alexander. It's difficult enough for me having a new life and trying to get used to it.'

Nobody had called him Alexander since he had left school. It sounded so formal, so strange.

'Surely it can't be as difficult as what you were used to in Satley.'

'We shall have to wait and see,' she said.

He hardly dared say her first name, in case he spluttered over it. It was the stupidest name that he had ever heard. He hadn't realized women really were called Hyacinth.

'Does your name have a diminutive?' he said, trying to smile and get past it that way.

'No. My mother called me after her mother, who was Cynthia. She had French connections.'

'How lovely,' Alex said, and he realized that his glass was empty and he badly needed a refill.

It was early when they went to bed but he couldn't think of anything else to say or do.

His bedroom was the biggest in the house but somehow seemed much smaller with this woman in it. No woman had been in there except for Ada and Fiona coming to sort out the room or bring him early morning tea. He was already thinking of how quiet it had been. How restful. It looked out over the gardens, which since it was July were in all their splendour. The lawns were green with recent rain, the flowerbeds thick with scented stocks in pink and cream, tall purple irises, sweet peas tied up against the far wall, cornflowers and lilies. The smell was heavenly.

As he closed the door she turned to him and looked at him possibly for the first time that day and she said, 'I would like a room of my own for a little privacy, you know.'

This had not occurred to him. He and Alice had one room, one bed and love.

'Yes of course, Hyacinth,' he said. 'Whatever you want you shall have.'

'Thank you. That's very kind.'

They undressed turned away from one another; a screen had been put there, undoubtedly Ada's idea, which he very much liked. Then his new wife got into bed enveloped in an enormous nightgown with a white nightcap, which covered her head. She turned away from him, pulling the bedclothes tightly to her chin, her fingers clinging to the top sheet. He thought she looked like a scared child, almost quaking with terror. Neither of them slept though they pretended to.

The following day was Sunday. Somehow, Alex thought with a sigh, they must try to get through it.

It turned out to be one of the longest days of his life. For once nobody needed him. Usually everybody chose Sunday to require the doctor. He found it funny, in a ridiculous way. Surely to God somebody in Wolsingham or round about it needed the doctor to hurry around and stop them from departing this earth?

The doctor and his new wife went to church, of course, which broke up the day and to his horror for some reason the two girls went with them. Fiona delivered them into the drawing room with their hair neat and their hats tied under their chins and their brightly cleaned shoes. They trailed behind the two adults as they walked and said nothing.

Hyacinth did not of course wear her wedding gown, and he was somewhat horrified to see the gown she actually put on. It was thin and black and had been mended several times. It was even bigger on her than her wedding dress had been. He vaguely remembered it from the Easter Day meal but somehow such things had not mattered then as they did now.

He didn't take much notice of other people's clothes. As for himself, the tailor called on him and took his measurements and brought his clothes to be fitted. He had always had all his clothes and shoes made for him and was used to throwing them away when they needed mending, though his two maids had been horrified at this waste and either put them back into the wardrobe or gave them away because he rarely wore any of them again. *Half the men in Wolsingham were going round in the doctor's discarded suits*, Ada thought, with some satisfaction. Her father even went to the quarry in one of the more disreputable ones, and his sons and sons-in-law were equally well-kitted out the few times they chose to be.

Hyacinth steeled herself to tell Fiona that she was to make up the room across the hall for the doctor. Fiona merely curtsied a bob and went off to the kitchen to tell Ada, only to have Ada say, 'Does she not realize that I'm the head maid here and she ought to have asked me? Anyroad, that room's titchy. Are you sure she said it was *his* things that were to be moved?' And then they looked at each other and giggled.

As the second day of the marriage was a Sunday, the maids had not had time to take the master's clothes and belongings into the other bedroom, so the newly married couple had to endure another night in the same room in the same bed and neither of them liked it.

The candles out, he reached for her very gently, which prompted a soft, 'Please don't, Alexander.'

He stared at her back in the darkness. 'But—'

'I must tell you that . . . that I had two miscarriages . . . that I lost two children during my first marriage and . . . and was told that there must be no more attempts at such things. So if you don't mind I would rather not.' She moved to the very edge of the bed, leaving him so stunned that he couldn't think for a few minutes. Then he felt as though she had deceived him. But what choice had she had? He almost wanted to laugh against himself. What choice had either of them had? He had met no woman before her who seemed right for the role. Half of him was sorry for her but he felt betrayed and there was resentment also.

He was seeing her in a new light. Not only did she not want him to touch her but now he was repulsed. He had fallen into some kind of trap but then so perhaps had she.

The following day the doctor's clothes and belongings were moved into the much smaller bedroom across the hall by Fiona, who lovingly stroked his coats and silently bemoaned his fate.

It was Monday, and for him it had not come soon enough. He had something to do. He didn't mind if half the village was ill; it was easier to deal with that than his wife at home. At least here he was safe. She would not come into the surgery part of the house, nobody did except Jimmy, and even the maids were very careful when they cleaned, and that was only when he was gone from home.

He breakfasted early, had nothing but a sandwich at midday because he had his rounds to do. He wished the evening would never come, and was glad of a full evening surgery.

After that he went back into the main part of house. The girls were nowhere to be seen and his wife was sitting by the window with some kind of plain sewing in her hands. She did not look up or speak. Dinner was held in silence. After it, they sat with the drawing-room windows open to the evening and that was when she said, 'I'm very concerned about the girls' education. I know we decided not to send them away but I have been delving into Mr Gloucester's past, and indeed his present, and he is not the man to have the schooling of two young girls.'

'I don't understand what you mean.'

'I mean that he has strange ideas about religion. Do you know what he thinks about heaven?'

Alex wanted to laugh but couldn't. 'What?'

'He thinks there is no heaven, according to Georgina. Would you really like a man of his calibre to teach your children? Do you know that Georgina says that she doesn't believe in heaven and that Mr Gloucester knows all about the planets and the stars, and that he believes there are other galaxies where other people live?'

'So do lots of educated men,' Alex said.

'Not in that way. He is very strange. He has an odd relationship with some Irishman who lives alone in a house up on the fell. What goes on there I can only surmise but I don't think it's anything healthy for young girls to see. Georgina has been there several times. She comes back in strange moods according to your servants. It doesn't seem healthy, young girls and old men.'

'What about Frosterley school?'

'I don't think it's much better.'

'We could have a governess?'

'Georgina is well beyond the reach of any ordinary schoolmistress and they are both beyond what I could teach them though now I know it was less than they should have had at the time.'

'I don't want to send them away.' He didn't say that that was one of the reasons he had married her, so that his children could find stability and comfort

'Neither do I, Alexander, but the problem needs solving somehow – and soon. You could speak to Georgina yourself and she would tell you, quite unknowingly, about all this and if there is no other option there is plenty of time to approach the Mount and make arrangements for them to go in September. It's a school with a top reputation. The best outside of London some people say.'

Part of Alex had always thought this was a good idea, but instead he had married her, to keep his children close and for her to look after them. It seemed now that Hyacinth had no intention of doing so and there was little point in arguing with her.

He was hardly ever there. She would be the one who did all the parenting. Except that she wouldn't, he could see that clearly now. She did not want to be a real wife to him and she did not want to be a real mother to his children. She was making no secret of the fact that she didn't really like them, her lips twisted when she talked of them and she spoke quickly, as though she needed to get beyond what had to be said. There was a small part of him that didn't blame her. She had married him purely because she was hungry and had no future. Many women had married for less, he knew, but it did not make things any easier.

Ada and Fiona decided to make the best of things. They would try to make the new mistress comfortable because if they didn't, there would be a bad atmosphere in the house. They determined that they would help her as much as they could. It was a sacrifice in one way but well worth it, they decided.

The truth was that Hyacinth was afraid of her servants. Not Oswald, who did as he was told, or Jimmy, whom she hardly ever saw, but the two maids she didn't like.

She knew some members of Ada's family who lived near her old home, so Ada knew that her new mistress came from the same humble beginnings as she had done, and no doubt she had told Fiona all about it.

Neither of them was pretty. Hyacinth won completely in the looks stakes. Ada was little with ample bosom and hips; Fiona was tall and skinny with sallow skin. Fiona carried herself well, but she gave herself airs – that was what they called it – as though she wanted to be a lady. But she was nothing of the kind and never would be, Hyacinth thought.

They didn't like her, of course they didn't. Why would they? She could not make friends of them. The doctor had elevated her far above them, but also she had been married before, and to a clergyman, which took her way out of their sphere. Still, she didn't understand why she was afraid. The trouble was she had never been sufficiently well off to have servants so she didn't know anything about them or what to expect.

Ada came to her on the first Monday morning, bobbing briefly and saying, 'Would you like to sort out the menus for the week, Mrs Blair? I've done it on my own since the doctor got here, there being no mistress before now, because the doctor wouldn't know a fish from his elbow, but I thought you might have other ideas.'

She stood there waiting. Hyacinth could think of nothing to say.

Ada prompted her. 'The doctor likes to have a pudding every night. Is there any sort that you favour?'

A pudding a night, Hyacinth thought. She would end up looking like Ada if she went on like that.

'And he's very fond of his cakes and pastries,' Ada said.

Hyacinth was horrified. She had imagined a delicate diet, lightly steamed fish, rare beef thinly cut, tiny carrots fresh from the garden. It was summer after all and she had already noticed that the doctor was prone to a slight corpulence. He was not tall enough to put on any weight. Short and portly he would be soon and she could not bear the idea of any man with his stomach sticking out.

She shook her head. 'We won't be having any of those things,' she said. 'Very bad for you, all that sugar and butter and flour.'

Ada stared.

'Nothing sweet,' Hyacinth said. 'He doesn't need it and no cheese or butter. And the same for the girls.'

'They love jelly and blancmange and my special chocolate cake,' Ada said.

'Well they would, wouldn't they? You only have to look at Georgina to see that her diet is dreadful. And only one potato for the doctor and one for me. None for the children. Vegetables are what they should have, lightly steamed. The garden is full of them, small, fresh vegetables.'

'They don't like vegetables,' Ada protested.

'Then they must learn to. And please take the decanters away. It's vulgar having them in the drawing room.'

The doctor had always called it the sitting room and in Ada's world it was the parlour if you were lucky enough to have a house big enough, she couldn't help reflecting. But she was in no position to have an opinion on such matters and Mrs Blair had undoubtedly already instructed him.

'No butter anywhere,' Ada reported to a shocked Fiona when she went back into the kitchen. 'I feel like crying. All my wonderful baking and cooking. I'll show her. She can have boiled fish and hard, cooked mushy veg and not a dab of butter or a decent sauce in sight.'

'What about the girls?' Fiona said.

'She never comes into the kitchen so she won't know what they eat,' Ada said with a smile.

Alex thought of talking to his wife about the food but convinced himself that it was just a phase. They had only just got married and maybe she needed time to adjust – maybe they all did – so he didn't say anything. But the house had already changed so much that both Ada and Fiona were thinking of what else they might do with their lives. Mrs Blair had put little bells in all the rooms and summoned them that way. She forbade cakes and puddings, other than semolina, which Ada detested making or eating. Then it was cheese, which she said made the whole house smell. Even though Ada never let the cheese get beyond the kitchen, she was accused of breaking the rules. She said nothing and didn't even slam the kitchen door.

Mrs Blair changed the butcher's order so that Fiona was ashamed to take in the meat when it arrived. They had always had the best of everything, now it was cow's liver, which could be tough no matter how carefully Ada cooked it, and tripe, which Mrs Blair liked simmered in milk. The vegetables seemed to have cottoned on to what was happening and grew so big that even chopping carrots made Fiona's wrists ache, and they were hard even when cooked to hell, Ada said.

Mrs Carver, who came in weekly to launder the clothes and do the ironing, also had problems, because the washing soda had to be the kind Mrs Blair had decided they would use, and it turned her hands red and itchy.

The mistress wanted fires in every room, which meant a lot more work than her servants were used to. Hyacinth drank endless cups of tea, made so weakly that Ada declared it was a waste of time putting any tea in the pot. Then it was milk. The mistress took her tea black and expected everybody else to. The children were to be given nothing but thinly buttered bread for tea and allowed to drink nothing but water. Secretly, the children ate and drank whatever they wanted. It was the doctor who suffered. The two maids had no idea what to do or where to go but the situation got worse. Ada said that she just wished one of the mushed vegetables would choke the mistress.

It was not that Hyacinth was mean, it was just that she had set ideas and put them into practice.

The decision was made to send the girls to York. It was mid-summer, so there was no time to lose. Hyacinth convinced herself that she'd done the best she could for the children. She ordered big trunks for them to take to York with every item of clothing, several pairs of stout shoes and the best games equipment. She even bought three different nightdresses for them covered in blue flowers.

Sarah came to the house and there were fittings so that Mrs Blair could look like the doctor's wife, and these times she seemed to enjoy, even though Sarah was given tea in the kitchen after the business of the afternoon was done.

Instead of giving the girls her time, Hyacinth gave them things. She bought books they did not read and toys they never played with. Georgina looked with disgust at the doll and pram Hyacinth had bought as a surprise. Georgina knew that her stepmother was trying to help, it was just that she didn't understand them.

'Could I have a chemistry set?' she enquired.

Hyacinth was horrified. 'And blow us all up?' she said.

'Jimmy could help.'

'Jimmy is not coming in this part of the house and you are not to go there. You know that your father wouldn't approve.'

Georgina had the sinking feeling that her stepmother was right.

Also, they both had very straight hair, which Hyacinth determined to better, so she sent them to bed with rags twisting their hair, and they couldn't sleep for the lumps.

Georgina asked for a pony and got it, only to discover that the pony, which her father had on loan from a local farmer, did not like being ridden and did its best to get rid of her. Doris was too afraid to even go into the field. In the end, Georgina took refuge in books, but even that was no escape. Her stepmother would pursue her and advise her on what to read and what was unsuitable and showed her how to darn and knit and sew and Georgina found it very boring. Doris would run into the kitchen and hide in Fiona's skirts. They both liked Fiona because she was so kind and Doris loved her cuddles. They also liked having their meals in the kitchen. Seeing what their father and stepmother were getting, they were very pleased that they didn't have to try and eat grey fish and tiny bullet peas.

Twenty-eight

When Sarah heard that James Leadbetter was putting Harry
and his father on to the street she was horrified. She knew
that nobody would take them in, they were too badly liked
for that. The weather was fine at the moment, it was true,
but it wouldn't last, it never did, so when she went down
to the market and saw Harry in the front garden, she went
to him and asked him if he would like to stay at the Hilda
House. He looked astonished and rather uncomfortable.

'I can't do that,' he said. 'Mrs Nattrass wouldn't like it.'

'I've already talked it over with her and she has agreed.
When are you leaving?'

'Saturday.'

'I'll get Oswald to bring you up to the house and you
can bring whatever animals you have.'

Harry didn't know what to say.

'You want me to what?' Oswald said when Sarah
approached him.

'I did ask the doctor.'

*

'You should play chess,' Hilary had said drily when they talked this over.

'I feel obliged to give them a home, since I more or less accused Harry Leadbetter of being involved in burning down your farm. I knew it would be hard for you but I can't let them live on the street when we have so much space here.'

'I've got nothing against Harry Leadbetter,' Hilary said, 'but if he's a decent man he will be the first Leadbetter who ever was. After what his father did, though, I just wish I didn't have to live in the same house but I will try to understand.'

Sarah also talked to Isabella and saw the child's eyes grow wide with fear. Sarah explained that Harry was all right but his father was very ill in his head and that was why he went on like he did. She would never leave Isabella in the same room as him on her own, she promised. Sarah was ashamed of how she talked a good deal about Harry's spaniel. They had only Bert and he was so decidedly Hilary's dog that she thought Isabella would be able to share Harry's dog with him. Harry probably also knew how to play games like football and cricket since he had spent so much time at school.

'Yes, but he's nearly as old as you,' Isabella protested. 'I want somebody my age to live with us.'

Sarah had thought about the whole thing and knew that Miss Hutton would not have had Harry or his father on the street. She had taken in Sarah and Sarah was determined that she would help those she could. Sometimes she thought she could see the old lady smiling with approval over the things she did.

She had the feeling that Luke Leadbetter would be a disaster to begin with. She would not give him money for drink and Harry wouldn't be making any money. However, they had not got that far yet; they would have to see.

'I don't think I'm going to be very much help,' Harry had said to her.

'You clean your house and tend your garden. Hilary is too old to do much, and I'm sewing all the time. You will be a big help,' Sarah had told him

'You fancy him, don't you?' Oswald said.

'Please, Oswald, don't be silly,' Sarah said, but afterwards admitted to herself that it was true. Harry was a gentleman. She hadn't met many of those. It did help that she thought he was very good-looking, but the best thing about Harry was that if she had been in the same predicament, she knew that he would have helped her. He was so kind.

'I'm not being silly,' Oswald said, but he pouted like a schoolchild.

*

James looked at the portrait of Isabel on the day that Harry and Luke left. There was a part of him that wanted to pull it down, smash it to pieces, slash it with a knife or throw it on to a fire, but he couldn't do it. It had been painted when they were betrothed to be married. Before his brother had taken her from him.

James had tried to hate her for preferring his younger brother, who was less intelligent, not nearly as charming, and definitely no better looking. What was it she had seen in Luke that she did not see in him? Perhaps a laxness that some women admired. He was given to laughter, billiards and public houses. Why women married men like that James could not imagine. Was a good husband one who drank himself stupid and couldn't get up in the mornings for the pain in his head? That was the trouble with Luke. Women liked him, he seemed to be carefree and he enjoyed having a good time. Whether he went on having a good time after he married Isabel, James had never known. He hoped not. The Logans had always been a nasty family but he had seen no sign of anything in her other than good nature, and Harry was a much better man than his father, so he must have got it from his mother.

Could Isabel not have told him sooner than the week they were to be married? She had humiliated him and so in hopeless despair he had left, but somehow he had never stopped loving her, as though determined nobody else should have his heart.

And then she had died. He had not known for a long while, it was only when he met a man from the dale in Chicago that he found out she had been dead for two years. Luke was devastated and had sent his son away. The little girl was dead too. *So Luke has got his just desserts and more,* James thought. He was sorry and yet triumphant.

He had hated Luke for a while afterwards, but then it stopped and he could not hate his brother anymore. They had both lost her and Luke had lost his child. James tried not to feel sorry for him but it was no good.

If he was being honest he had always wanted to get away. Luke loved the dale as he never had. He was like a dog on a short chain and desperate for new sights, countries and adventures. He had wanted to taste freedom. Luke felt free wherever he was.

James had gone to America and right from the start he had fallen in love with the place. Everywhere he went, from New York to San Francisco, and lots of places in between, seemed better than the one before. He found that he had a generous heart and was kind and good and gave freely to those who had nothing. He had made fortunes in industry. The one thing he did not have was a replacement for Isabel. She had held his heart forever.

But he worked, laboured physically and mentally every single day so that he could keep on moving forward. The more time and money he invested, the more he made, and it was not until recently that he had felt the urge to go home.

He had not forgotten about Luke's son but had envisaged him being just like Luke. The trouble was that Harry was not like Luke. Harry was like a son of his – good, kind, caring – and James could see that Harry loved this drunken slob and he was envious. He had tried to harden his heart against Luke but found it impossible, yet still he could not stand the idea of Luke in his house.

When they left he saw how carefully Harry lifted the little spaniel into his arms, placing the lovely cream cats in an open bag on his shoulder. From there they peeped out at James as if in disdain. The spaniel gazed into Harry's eyes and Harry smiled. Luke was drunk of course. He seemed not to know what was going on but let Oswald put him into the trap.

When they had gone James was lonely. He hired skilled workmen to replace the doors and windows, had the rooms redecorated and new curtains hung. He had the gardens changed so that there were lots of flowers, new fruit trees as well as old, and had the vegetable patches made bigger and the greenhouses replaced. He had an orangery built. He had always wanted one so he could grow citrus fruit, pineapples, tomatoes and other salads. He had all the buildings brought up to date and then he began to throw lavish Saturday garden parties, to which everybody in the village was invited.

And all the time, Isabel looked down at him until he wanted to curse her.

His life was empty. He had not noticed until he'd reached home. He didn't understand what he was trying to do here. He had long since outgrown this place; it meant little to him now. He had ceased to care for it. Luke was chained here and yet he liked his chains and they could be loosened and fall off if Luke could ever give up the drink. James felt sorry for him. He felt sorry for both of them.

So when he realized that Sarah had taken them in he called her a wretched, clever girl, and he was angry. But he also admired her. How smart she was, and how young.

The only thing Hilary said was that she was worried about how Isabella would react to the drunken man who had frightened her.

'They are all the family Isabella has left,' Sarah said. 'I must try.'

She was worried about Luke's behaviour too. They would see. On the other hand she was also aware of the new Mr Leadbetter and all his money. Did he know of Isabella? Why should he? If he did get to know that Isabella lived up at the Hilda House he might want to see her, or even ask for her to live with him, but Sarah decided that a likeness to the woman he had loved was not a big enough reason for any man to want a child. It was not as if she was his daughter.

Sarah did talk to Isabella more than once about Harry's father once she had decided to offer them a home. She wanted Isabella to accept the idea that nobody should be left homeless, and nobody knew it better than this brave child. *That was the whole concept of the Hilda House*, Sarah thought.

When Oswald deposited the two men, the little spaniel and the two cats, who were still residing in Harry's knapsack outside, Sarah, who had been waiting for them, came straight away to greet them. The elder man gazed at her and then all around as though looking for somewhere to escape to. She thought he might run, but he didn't.

The cats, when Harry lowered the knapsack to the ground, climbed out quite unconcernedly as though they had known that everything would be all right. Since they were some special kind of feline with cream long-haired bodies and dark-shaded tails and legs, they went off to lord it among the other cats. Harry had no idea where these two had come from, they had just shown up in the yard one morning, with a dead mouse each as a peace offering on his doorstep, so he could not turn them away.

The little spaniel, Ernie, clung so close to Harry's legs that Harry was obliged to pick him up so that they could go inside. When he saw Bert he hid his face against Harry's shoulder, though Bert pretended not to know that anything was happening. Sarah wished that she could do something similar. She was already half regretting what she had done. Everything would change.

'Thank you so much for taking us in, Miss Charles,' Harry said as his father went on gazing around him as if they were visiting another planet.

Harry couldn't feel comfortable even though Sarah was welcoming. Hilary scowled at them and stayed in another room as often as she could, and it seemed to him that Isabella was always hiding around pieces of furniture. He tried to keep his father out of the way but it was difficult because the only way Luke would settle was with a bottle of brandy and his own company, after which he would sleep for hours, snoring. When he was awake and not drinking he drifted from room to room like somebody lost and Harry couldn't settle either, as he was so eager to keep his father away from the little girl.

Ernie was the one who settled in first. He stood gazing at Bert, who shadowed Hilary, and so Ernie started hovering around the older woman until Hilary, who could never resist an animal and could see how much Ernie wanted to be accepted, lifted the little dog into her arms. Hilary allowed that nobody could have resisted him. Bert was too idle to be jealous and although he sighed a couple of times he let Ernie sleep close beside him at Hilary's feet.

*

It was hard for them all. Harry had wanted not to bring drink for his father but the shock of leaving would be hard enough, so he had brought as much brandy as one suitcase would carry. Luke went off by himself and, taking a bottle from the suitcase, hid upstairs in one of the back bedrooms, which did not belong to anyone. All he wanted was to be left in peace and to forget that he had been thrown out of the only home he could remember. Self-pity got the better of him and he cried and the level in the bottle sank steadily. Just three hours after arriving at the Hilda House he had passed out on the unmade bed and was dreaming of better things.

Harry was determined to make himself useful and agreeable. Once his father had disappeared into the rest of the house to drink, he went out into the garden where Hilary was toiling.

'May I help?'

She ignored him.

'Mrs Nattrass, I hope you don't think I had anything to do with the destruction of your house, I would never do such a thing,' he said.

Hilary didn't reply. Harry found a hoe and began on the weeding. The garden did need a lot of attention and it appeared to him that it was too much for Hilary. She did need help because Sarah was always stitching, sewing, cutting out patterns or tacking material, and there was also the food to see to and the cleaning and washing. It was a very big house. Harry began to attack the weeds with skill. He also, and without asking anybody, cleaned the house. He had few cooking skills so he left the intricate bits to Hilary, but she became used to having him in the kitchen and he would chop and peel and do whatever she asked him.

Although she said nothing, Hilary could not help but be pleased.

Also Harry was good with animals. Hilary had no idea where the skill had come from but he was always the first to help when a dog got a thorn in its paw or was unwell. He seemed to know what to do. One day, Bert had picked up some kind of poison and Harry knew this before Hilary worked it out, so he got a lot of salt water down the dog until Bert threw up, and threw up, until he was exhausted. Then he slept and was well again.

Hilary was too embarrassed to thank Harry because she thought he had saved the dog's life, but Bert, not being one to let a friend down when he had been helped, began to follow Harry around the garden. Harry would clean small carrots and feed them to Bert. Bert had never eaten vegetables before but now he began stealing shallots, though Hilary complained that it gave him the runs.

Harry found netting in one of the old buildings and placed it carefully over the huge bed of strawberries Hilary had been nursing. She was pleased that it kept the birds off.

Hilary showed Sarah and Harry how to bottle and preserve what they could not eat and how to use isinglass to preserve the eggs. They made jams from gooseberries, blackcurrants, strawberries and raspberries and, as the few fruit trees started to drop fruit that wasn't ripe when a good wind took the apples and pears away, they made chutney. Hilary also showed them how to make compote, adding sugar to take the sourness away. Hilary was good at making pies, tarts and crumbles. With so many mouths to feed she made light summer soups and Isabella remembered some of the recipes her mother had taught her. She made a light dough, which she arranged with cheese and baked. She also had many recipes for fish they had never known before, so they ate well that summer.

Harry went fishing in his uncle's ponds and the stream below the house. He had humbled himself to go and ask for permission, because the fish meant a great deal to them.

He was surprised when his uncle took him into what was now the library. He tried not to look at the portrait of his mother. The room was furnished. The bookcases were filled and there were easy chairs and rugs and the whole house smelled of good cooking. Harry could not help involuntarily remarking, 'This is what the room should have looked like.'

His uncle, who had said very little up to that point,

remarked grumpily that it never had, not that he could ever remember.

'Why did you want to come back?' Harry enquired. 'You are rich and this place isn't. Did you long for home?'

He could see that James was pleased at the questions.

'It never was much of a home. My father disliked everyone, his servants, his workers. I don't think he even liked his sons and he . . . he drank, just like your father does.'

'I'm sorry.'

James looked at him from less angry eyes. 'It seems you and I have suffered the same fate. Do you hope to get out of here as I did?'

'I couldn't leave my father.'

James looked amazed. 'He's a drunk and he was always hopeless.'

'He's still my father.'

'I salute you, though don't much like your loyalty to him. I have no son.'

Harry looked straight back at him. 'What's stopping you? You're still young.'

James was rather taken aback at Harry voicing his opinions, not just fluently but with a measure of truth in them. He fidgeted for a minute or two and then said, 'I only ever cared for one woman and she decided just before our wedding that she preferred your father.'

'That was a very long time ago,' Harry said. 'If we all went on like that we would never get any further.'

James was still gazing at him.

'You can fish the ponds and the river,' he said, 'and you can shoot over the land as long as you bring no one with you and you don't kill anything you have no intention of eating, and you don't shoot the game out of season. And give pigeons Sunday off, everybody needs one day a week for a little joy.'

'Thank you, Uncle James,' Harry said.

He called himself a toady when he got out of there but he was very pleased to have made his point. It would make a great deal of difference to the meals up at the Hilda House, especially now that the shooting season was underway. His uncle equipped him with a pair of Purdeys. Harry didn't like to say that they were valuable and he should not take them, but he thought his uncle was trying to make a point. He also gave Harry cartridges and a rifle for deer – not that Harry shot deer. He had difficulty shooting anything, he was such a coward he told himself, but it seemed such an unfair way to go about things. However, he couldn't afford to be squeamish. Pheasants were beautiful but they were also good to eat. Grouse he didn't like and he knew that a lot of people didn't like the taste. James also gave him a pair of waders, which fitted him well, and a beautiful fishing rod that once again he felt he should not own.

Also a box, which had probably belonged to the family for a long while, with exquisite flies which his grandfather had apparently handmade.

He scoffed when Harry tried to refuse these things and said that they had been here all the time and that Harry was very welcome to them. It certainly eased their relationship. Harry wanted to see his uncle more often, and he felt that James would have welcomed his company, but he would feel he was betraying his father.

Sarah, however, welcomed all the fish and game and was very pleased to have such variety in their food.

Twenty-nine

Alex was dreading telling the girls that they were going away to school but it was now almost the end of August and could be put off no longer. He was only glad that Hyacinth was there when they were called into the drawing room, and he explained to them that they would be going to boarding school in a matter of days.

They did not look surprised. The big trunks were in evidence in one of the spare bedrooms and the atmosphere in the house had changed.

'I think you will like it,' he said. 'You will make new friends and there will be all kinds of subjects which you can't get at the school here. There'll be gym and hockey and you'll sleep in big rooms so you will have lots of company.'

'It's meant to be the best girls' school in the north,' Hyacinth put in at this point, for which he was grateful.

The two girls said nothing for so long that Alex could hear the ticking of the hall clock as it pondered its way through the day. Doris gazed longingly at the door and in the end Georgina gave him the straight look he had learned to dread and said, 'Will there be a telescope or a laboratory?'

There was of course no positive answer to this. Girls' schools tended to keep off science and stick to the arts, which were supposedly better for their small brains, but he imagined being such a good school all subjects would be included, though probably there would be little to do with stars and planets.

'What is gym?' Doris asked in a small voice.

'It's where you have to run for miles in the pouring rain and learn to jump over high things and climb up walls, or at least thick ropes that rip your hands,' Georgina said.

Doris looked horrified.

'There's a lot more to it than that,' Alex said.

Georgina looked straight at her stepmother. 'You read *Jane Eyre* to us and yet you're sending us away to a place like that.'

Hyacinth had the grace to blush.

'It's not like that,' her father said.

'Have you been?'

'I went to boarding school and loved it,' he said.

'We will have to eat a lot of cabbage,' Georgina said, 'and those dreadful milk puddings that look like frog-spawn. And there will be lots of church services, I just know it. We like Mr Gloucester and Mr Paddy. They teach us all sorts of things. Mr Paddy keeps donkeys.'

What on earth that had to do with anything, Alex wasn't sure, but the pony trial had failed so he couldn't think of anything to say.

'You'll be off in a couple of weeks,' their stepmother said, attempting a smile. 'I've bought you some lovely things to take with you, special brushes and combs and covers to put your night things in, and scented pouches for your handkerchiefs.'

The girls, when the adults had nothing more to say, retired not to the kitchen, where Ada and Fiona would drag it all out of them, but to the garden and consequently to the broken-down summerhouse. Nobody bothered to come here as it was right at the back of the premises and would only have been used by somebody who didn't like other people. Right now that was them.

'Checkmated,' Georgina said, who had learned this game from her grandfather when he had time for her. He turned out not to be very good at it, and after she had beaten him easily three times, they played no more, and it was just as well as she had become very bored.

They sat down in the summerhouse. Luckily it was a fine day because the building was long since past its best and let in rain and snow and wind. They determined to spend a lot of time there now and it was already their secret place. Fiona had given them a tin of toffees recently when she bought some for Ada's family's children, and was generous enough to include her employer's two. *The tin was pretty*, Doris thought, *and had a large black and white dog on the front.*

They chewed their toffee for a while and tried to think.

'There must be something we can do, George,' Doris said finally, and she sounded more determined than ever before, so that Georgina looked at her with respect.

'You think so?'

'We have to. We can't let them send us away. I'm starting to feel like an unwanted parcel.'

Georgina clasped an arm around her sister's shoulders and said, 'Don't worry, it won't come to that.'

Two days later they found Oswald in the yard and Georgina said to him, 'Have you heard that we are going away to school?'

Evidently he had not because he looked hard at them.

'What, one of them schools where you live there all the time?'

'There are holidays,' Georgina said, terrified that he was making it worse.

'We don't want to go,' Doris said. 'Could you take us up to the Hilda House?'

'I can't do that. The doctor would get rid of me if I did things he didn't like. And in any case, Sarah wouldn't be allowed to have you there. The doctor wouldn't let her.'

They went back into the kitchen and the way that Ada and Fiona looked at them they obviously knew as well. They were both so upset that nobody said anything.

Doris sat down by the kitchen stove and wept. 'We'll die like the girl in *Jane Eyre* and never come back,' she said and Fiona picked her up and cuddled her and told her there would be long holidays.

'But when we come back Potty Prudhoe will still be here,' Georgina said.

When the children had gone to bed – and it was very late because they were both too upset to sleep, for which Fiona and Ada didn't blame them – it was something of a relief to both maids.

'Half past nine,' Fiona said, sinking down by the fire. The weather was sultry but they had to keep the fire on for cooking and baking and so the kitchen door and the back door both stood open. After a while they went and sat outside and tried to think of what they could do.

The garden was getting slightly past its best now. It had been dry for so long, and although Oswald did his utmost to keep everything watered, he had to concentrate on the vegetables.

'I thought the worst thing people could do for children was to half-starve them like in my family,' Ada said, 'but it's not true. The poor little souls, nobody wants them.'

'If he was going to send them away why did he marry her?' Fiona said.

'God alone knows,' said Ada. 'I wish I had somewhere else to go. Since she arrived the place has been so bad.'

'Me too.'

Most of all Ada dreaded the mornings when she was called into the drawing room. She wished she had not initiated this herself but then, as she said to Fiona, if she had not it would have happened anyway when Miss Bossypants realized she was in charge.

Something was wrong every day. The beds weren't aired enough. This was rubbish because Fiona pulled back sheets and blankets and opened the windows while it was fine, going back later in the morning to make up the beds and dust and clean. If it was chilly, there were fires lit upstairs every day.

There was too much salt in the light vegetable soup Ada had made so carefully, and although the only pudding allowed was on Saturday nights, it was to be a crème brûlée. Ada thought the mistress wanted this because it had a daft French name. Ada hated making crème brûlée. If you took your eyes off it for a second it separated and left you with an eggy mess and the number of times she had burned the topping of sugar made the kitchen smell of smoke until Sunday.

There also had to be freshly laundered napkins at each meal. This was almost impossible and meant a lot of extra washing and ironing for Mrs Carver, who complained bitterly that the master had got by very well without marrying an upstart for his wife, who was causing great piles of extra washing with her fancy ideas.

It was common knowledge that man and wife slept separately so what had been the point, Ada and Fiona said, but only to themselves. The new mistress had nothing to do but sit about in fancy frocks and complain about the way that they ran the house. It had been a lot easier all round before Mrs Prudhoe became Mrs Blair.

Sarah began to bring Isabella to the market and it became a habit that they called in at the kitchen of the surgery house where Ada and Fiona gave them tea and cake. Also, Sarah thought that since Isabella had nobody to play with up at the Hilda House, it was a good thing to bring her down here to spend time with Georgina and Doris. This would stop, of course, very soon now that the girls were to go away to school.

The two girls took Isabella into the garden to see Oswald and, since she had been friendly with his mother, they also went to see Mrs Leighton as Isabella liked being there.

'I wish I could find a school for her but it's six miles a day to bring her here,' Sarah said. 'Awful that we have opposite problems.'

'It's not going to be much fun around here when they've gone.'

'You can always come and live at the Hilda House,' Sarah said. 'I've got so much work I hardly know where to turn and Hilary does less and less. Harry is doing all the cleaning but there's always a lot for everyone.' Sarah tried not to blush when she mentioned Harry. It had become quite difficult having him there because he seemed to have no idea that she liked him especially, and it was obvious to her that he had never thought about her in such a way. She had a horrible feeling that it took men a lot longer to grow up.

'You've got enough on your plate, what with Luke Leadbetter,' Ada said.

'Luke is a problem and I have to keep an eye on Isabella because she's still scared of him.'

Ada sighed. 'When you think how lovely Mr James is and yet he and Luke were brought up together. Luke was just like his father, never cared for anybody or anything, but he was a real looker. Sad. Neither of them ever got over Isabel Logan. She wasn't well liked. Set her cap at them, she did, and then chose the wrong one. There were a lot of very disappointed lasses in the dale when James went off and Luke got the prize. She was like all the Logans, neither use nor ornament,' Ada said.

'You should think about coming up to us,' Sarah said.

'I don't think so,' Ada said. 'Too many people and too far away from my family.'

'I'm sure Oswald would still help,' Sarah said and then wished she had said nothing since Ada gave her a certain look and said, 'We all know who Oswald wants to help.' But she had stopped accusing Sarah of being after him since they had become better friends.

'I couldn't go and leave the doctor,' Fiona said and she looked away awkwardly. 'I know,' she added, looking at Ada, 'but I couldn't.'

'Fi, give it up,' Ada said. 'He's been married twice and neither time to you. He doesn't even know you exist. I don't think he knows anybody exists other than folk who are sick. He lives in another world. How on earth or why he got himself caught up with her the Lord only knows. She is a first-rate bitch.'

'Ada,' Fiona said reprovingly.

'Well she is. She treats us like muck. She's always complaining. It's Ada this and Ada that and why isn't this done and why isn't that done. Nothing's ever any good for her. It's an insult to cows to call her one.'

That set them off and they had a good laugh, which helped the afternoon along.

Alex couldn't remember being as unhappy as this before. He immersed himself in his work and it would have to do, he told himself. There was always a lot to see to and he was meticulous, going out day and night to the farms and smallholdings, very often heading right up on the tops and into the little villages which lay outside the towns between Wolsingham and the top end of the dale, where it spilled over into Westmorland.

He knew he was doing too much because he was always tired out and bad tempered. He avoided the children, he avoided the servants. He even spoke brusquely to Oswald when he didn't deserve it, but Alex didn't know how to apologize to a servant, and to be fair, Oswald, poor lad, expected nothing more. All he had was his job and living with his mother and the horses. *Sometimes,* Alex thought, *Oswald talks to the horses quite a bit.* Alex didn't blame him; the conversation couldn't have been any worse than Oswald got from Jimmy or his mam, or Alex got from Hyacinth.

She barely spoke. She didn't like him smoking in the house, but then she didn't like him going out without her, except on house calls. She told him it looked bad, and now that the decanters were kept in the kitchen cupboard, he had to make a real performance to get any whisky, and it just wasn't worth the trouble. He was too tired perfecting his work. He was aghast at the very idea of taking her about socially. He didn't want a social life among his patients, and he had the general impression that the people here thought he had chosen his second wife badly.

He knew that they were grateful for his care, and he got a lot out of that, but it was all he got. He slept alone. The food was bad. He wanted to complain, and yet he knew that his servants were put upon, and if he caused more trouble it would only make things worse. He had landed himself with this woman who seemed happy only when she was alone in the drawing room.

She had Sarah make a great many new dresses, even though she never went anywhere. There was only the occasional Sunday when Mr and Mrs Wilson came for dinner, or the Blairs went to them, that she needed to dress up.

Hyacinth tried to make Ada and Fiona go to church twice on a Sunday every week. They didn't mind going now and then, but this really was too much to ask. Ada was angry.

'And how do you think the dinner is going to get made if we aren't here to make it?' she demanded when she had been summoned to the drawing room to be told this.

'You can make it before you go.'

'Is that between getting breakfast for you all and sorting out the rooms, as you insist on having them dusted and swept every day, and with fires made up and kept alight? Meat would burn if left to itself for that length of time. All Mr Wilson has to do is lengthen his sermon by ten minutes, and we'll be sitting down to burned offerings,' Ada said. 'We peel and scrape the vegetables on a Saturday night as it is, while making a meal for you, often another for the doctor if he's out and something different for the bairns. It's like a boarding house!' Ada said and she went out and slammed the door. She then stood just inside the kitchen door, seething.

The bell from the drawing room rang loudly and then again.

'I'm not going back in there or I will kill that woman!' Ada said.

Fiona went through.

Mrs Blair stood white-faced by the windows, which looked across the garden.

'Tell Southern she's to collect her things and leave. I've had enough of her,' she said.

'You can't dismiss her,' Fiona said, shocked.

'Don't tell me what I can and can't do. You coming here with your fancy ideas from God knows where in wretched Scotland.'

'She was just upset.'

'And what does she have to get upset about?' Hyacinth said, glaring at her.

'There's a lot to do.'

'There's two of you, and Mrs Carver comes and does the washing and ironing. Somehow I wonder how you fill your days. I know you make clothes for her family and use the ingredients in my kitchen to make food for them, so don't think I don't. Half your days are spent feeding and clothing other folk in the dale. I don't know how she has the gall to speak to me like that.'

Fiona stood there almost in tears while Hyacinth went to the windows.

'All right,' she said, finally, 'but she is not to behave like that again.'

Fiona fled to the kitchen and Ada swore she would never lose her temper in the future. Her family would starve if she lost her place and by the time Mrs Blair had blackened her name, which she would straight away, Ada would never get another post.

Thirty

In the end, Georgina, unable to think any further, went to her father as he finished evening surgery. She approached softly where he was sitting behind his desk, thinking about his last patient no doubt, or something similar, and he didn't notice her at first. This was perfectly understandable, she had never gone in there before. He was strict about it, family must not go near the surgery.

Eventually she said, 'Papa.'

He looked quickly at her. He said nothing for so long that Georgina almost lost her nerve and ran away but she knew it was her only chance.

'Must we go away to school? We really like it here and Mr Gloucester and Mr Paddy are teaching us things we wouldn't learn anywhere else.'

'That's what bothers your mother and me.'

Georgina hated the woman being referred to like that. 'I like Mr Paddy's telescope,' she said.

'I understand that Mr Gloucester has strange religious views. Mr Wilson would not like that.'

'Mr Wilson wouldn't mind,' Georgina said, having no

idea whether he would or not, since he probably knew very little about the matter. 'He doesn't mind when people don't go to church.'

Church was a sore subject in the family since now the two maids went twice on Sundays with the family, and everybody had to get dressed up. Also the girls went to Sunday school, something they had always hated.

'I'm sure he does,' her father said. 'He just doesn't like to say so. All clergymen love a good attendance.'

'I want to learn all kinds of scientific things and Mr Paddy is teaching Doris about how to deal with animals when they are ill, and how their bones work and stuff like that. I don't suppose you get that at an ordinary school. Mr Paddy left Dublin to come to Newcastle and he was a sailor for many years and knows all sorts about the countries he has been to.'

Her father ignored the reference to Mr Paddy's geographical experience and stuck to the point. 'You will have biology, which is much the same thing, and chemistry and physics and maths and all the things that you need. I won't change my mind about it, so there's no point in protesting. I think you had better go now. I have a lot of work to do.'

She didn't like to point out to him that he was due to dinner shortly, and that he never worked in the evenings unless he had house calls, but that was very often. Sometimes she thought he made them up just to get away from the house. She wished she could do something like that.

The day was getting nearer. Their clothes were being packed into big trunks, which stood like a threat in the centre of Georgina's bedroom. She had to look at them when she went to bed and when she woke up.

'There's nothing else for it,' she told Doris, 'we will go to the summerhouse. We can take things and leave them there and nobody would ever think to look for us. We have to do something, we can't just let them make us go a long way from here. We might never get back.'

Over several days they collected from the kitchen food like apples and bread. They didn't think the maids noticed things missing. Also they filled jugs with water and stored it for when they could not leave the summerhouse. Georgina took several books and paper and coloured crayons, and her favourite tome about astronomy, which was rather heavy. She had to avoid several people while she was taking it there, as it was so obvious.

The last night came and they lay very still in their beds, worrying. Then, when it was very early in the morning and the sun was just rising, they crept away, putting on old clothes and carrying their shoes in their hands in case Fiona or Ada awoke early and began to light the stove.

*

It was Fiona who discovered that the girls had gone. She gave a gasp of surprise and ran downstairs to the kitchen and told Ada. They looked all over the house and in the buildings outside, and called the girls' names in the garden and through the yard. Then they went into the street and all the time Fiona cried, and Ada looked about her as though they would materialize from nothing.

She ran across the yard to where Oswald was in the stables feeding the horses.

'Have you seen the girls?'

'Not since last night.'

'Did they say anything?'

'About what?' And then he looked at her with a guilty expression.

'Tell me!'

'They asked me to help them get away but I said I couldn't or I would be let go and lose the house, and then what would mam and me do? But that was ages ago.'

'When was this?'

'Last week.'

'You could have said.'

'I didn't think they meant it.'

'Go out and look for them.'

Ada was panicked but she couldn't help a certain smugness when she announced at the mistress's breakfast table that the two girls had gone missing.

In the end everybody in the village was alerted and

Oswald even went up to the Hilda House to enquire whether they had fled to Sarah, but they had not.

In the middle of the day rain began to fall. It would have been welcomed, as they had had little rain for weeks now, but it was torrential with a wind behind it, and still the two girls could not be found.

By teatime Fiona had been reduced to tears again and took to blaming the doctor and his wife for their hard-heartedness. She said that she was convinced they had fallen in the river as the Wear was a torrent by then.

In the summerhouse the girls were already bored. The wind and rain soon made their way in through the windows and the door, and where the roof and walls were not quite sound, so that it became cold as night fell. They were rather scared because the darkness gathered early and they could still hear people calling for them.

The search had to be given up after dark but people promised the doctor that as soon as daylight arrived they would continue. The girls couldn't be far away.

The night went on and on. The wind and rain howled around the summerhouse and it got colder and colder. They had not thought of pillows or blankets and sat wondering what to do next.

They waited and waited for daylight to arrive but the rain kept tumbling down and they just sat there, cold and hungry and worn out, both wanting to cry.

Thirty-one

Luke Leadbetter was a problem right from the start. For some reason Harry thought that it would be less trouble now that he had other people to help, but in a way it was as though Luke's presence made everybody suspicious, and with cause. Isabella couldn't bear to be in the same room as him, he didn't sleep or eat, he banged doors and shouted and demanded brandy.

Luke was soon down to the last bottle. Harry tried to ease his father into taking little sips but it didn't work. After only three days Luke found where Harry had hidden a bottle for emergencies and that bottle was soon empty and he was in bed, though it was the middle of the day.

By the time everybody else was ready to go to bed he was just getting up and he made a mess in the kitchen looking for food. When he couldn't find any, he shouted, breaking up everyone's slumber. In vain did Harry try to stop him. He also tried to make his father keep his voice down but Luke either wouldn't or didn't care to, and he shouted so much that Sarah came downstairs and demanded, 'What on earth is going on?'

Luke eyed her. 'I need brandy.'

'We don't have any brandy. We can't afford things like that.'

'Everybody keeps it in for cooking.'

'I don't. Now you can stay up as long as you like, but you can't keep other people from their beds. And stay out of the kitchen. I cleaned it before I went to bed and now look.'

Harry gazed at the heaps of flour and sugar on the floor. Quite aside from the mess, it was the cost that mattered. Aware that his father was about to tell Sarah what he thought of her, he bustled him outside into the warm night.

'You have to stop doing that,' he said. 'They've taken us in and we must be grateful.'

'Grateful? Why should I be grateful for anything? James had no right to come back and take our house.'

'He had every right. It's his house,' Harry pointed out. 'If you weren't drunk you would remember that.'

'He forfeited it when he left.'

'No, he didn't. He was the elder son and it is his. Mr East showed me the papers and he can do what he likes with it.'

'He didn't get everything he wanted,' Luke said with some satisfaction. 'He didn't get Isabel. I took her. She loved me. She never loved him. He thought they were going to get married.' Luke laughed. 'Look at him now, all on his own with nobody to care for.'

Eventually Luke was persuaded into bed and Harry relaxed and finally fell asleep, but when he woke up his father was gone. It was early morning and he found Sarah in the kitchen.

She looked straight at him. 'I'm missing some money,' she said.

'Oh no.'

Harry searched the house and the area outside and then began the descent into Weardale. He walked as far as the grocer's at Frosterley, and when he entered, the man tried to go into the back. Harry had run out of patience by then, so got hold of him and pushed him up against the wall.

'It wasn't my fault, Mr Harry. He threatened me. And he had money.'

'I told you not to sell it to him.'

'He's bigger than me and he come over all nasty. He come in here and yelled and frightened my missus and the bairns. What was I supposed to do?'

'How much did you sell him?'

'Three bottles.'

Harry let go of him with a sigh. He wanted to rant at the grocer but it was not his fault. He ran a shop. He was there to sell things to people who had money and even sometimes to those who didn't have money.

'Do you know where he went?'

'No idea.'

'And don't give him any more. If you give him it on tick I won't pay it.'

Harry scoured Frosterley and when he thought his father couldn't have gone much further, he went back to Wolsingham and there to his horror the gates of his former home were open and the outside doors. He ran up to them and paused in the hall, hearing his father's voice. It was by then mid-afternoon.

Harry ran in, calling his father's name, just in time to see three men bundling him out.

'I'm so sorry, Uncle James,' he managed to say as his uncle, pale faced and ragged with blood on his cheek, said, 'You keep him away from here or I'll have the police on him. The drunken bastard.'

Thrown beyond the gates, Luke passed out in the road. Harry could do little other than go shamefaced to the doctor's and ask if Oswald would take them back up to the Hilda House. Oswald looked sympathetically at him and helped him carry the unconscious Luke into the trap. Harry could not understand why Oswald should care.

'My father was just the same. Luckily he died,' Oswald said shortly.

Not quite the solution Harry had been hoping for, but he was so grateful to Oswald for his forbearance that he thanked him profusely.

After that Luke slept for three days. *One for each*

bottle, Harry thought. He didn't know what to say to Sarah. She worked hard so that they could eat. He did everything he could in return but he was aware that it was not enough.

The following day when there was no brandy, his father was shouting when Harry opened the door of the Hilda House from the back garden, and in the kitchen found his father throwing things out of the cupboards in a desperate attempt to discover brandy yet again.

Sarah looked relieved when she saw Harry but she said, 'This cannot go on. I can't have him here shrieking and shouting. He has Isabella terrified, and the little peace we had has gone.'

Luke resisted when Harry tried to stop him and in the end they had a fight. It had never occurred to Harry that such a thing could happen, but there was no choice on his part and it only ended when Harry put his father so effectively on to the floor that Luke didn't get up.

Harry stared. While they were trying to put the other down he had not remembered this man was his father. He had learned to fight at school so was usually reasonably polite about it, but in this case he had put to use every dirty trick he could think of. He had not realized he was so upset at the way that his father behaved and had always behaved to him. He was aghast when he saw the man down on the floor, unable to get up.

Sarah had made sure nobody else came into the kitchen

but when Luke was finally unconscious and bleeding, and Harry was standing over him almost in tears, she felt so sorry for him that she longed to take him into her arms. She didn't of course but she had never seen anyone quite so upset that she could remember.

Harry was obviously appalled at what he had done, at the hatred that he had felt. Now, in the aftermath of the fight, he was relieved but also felt guilty that he had done such a thing. Sarah could see all these things on his face.

'I'll take him away,' Harry said in forced tones.

'Why don't we try something else?'

'Like what?'

Finally he looked at her from despairing eyes. She could see just a little hope as though he believed in her and why should he not? She had rescued him from the streets.

'That bedroom you share has a key. We could lock him in there and you could have another room. We can easily move one of the beds. You would have to deal with him but if we don't let him out and all he has is food and water we could sober him up so that he stops needing the stuff.'

Harry stared at her. 'I don't think that will ever happen and there's no reason why you should put up with us,' he said.

'I will not be defeated by somebody as hurt and sad as your father. He's given up. We have to help him.'

'It could take weeks to do something like that and even so I don't think he could ever get rid of this addiction. He'll die because of it.'

Harry had to stop himself from sobbing at that point. He couldn't look at her.

'Let's try it,' she said. 'He's too unfit to break down doors and I will lock the windows. God knows why the windows lock, maybe somebody mad was kept in there once, or even small children who could hurt themselves by a fall from so far up.'

Harry hesitated.

'I think we should try,' she urged him.

He looked gratefully at her. 'Thanks so much. You are endlessly kind.'

Sarah's face warmed with blushes but she was rather pleased that she had offered. If it didn't work they would think of something else.

Isabella had been horrified at the idea of Harry's father living in the same house as she did. In vain did Sarah promise her that things would be better and that she was safe. She didn't feel safe and Mr Leadbetter was mad. He took things from the cupboards and threw them on the floor, he shouted and raved and cried until she took to hiding in the bedrooms. In the end, Sarah went everywhere with her but then the problem was solved in quite another way, one that had nothing to do with the mad man at the house. Sarah gave her somewhere to escape to.

Mr Paddy, the man who lived along the fell, had a house there with lots of animals, and people came to help with the animals, including Georgina and Doris.

Mr Gloucester was always there at weekends and he knew a good many stories which he told the girls. Isabella was in heaven. Mr Gloucester spoke Spanish and Mr Paddy spoke a great number of different languages, including Spanish, so she felt more at home there than she had ever felt anywhere since she had left Tenerife.

Also, Mr Paddy had a housekeeper and his servants lived there, which meant she could stay overnight any time she wanted, or any time when Sarah could not see to her personally every minute. Hilary would have helped but she was no defence against the mad man. Sarah apologized and said that things would be sorted out, but Isabella was very happy along at Mr Paddy's house and farm. She and Doris helped him to mend hurt animals that came his way and to feed them.

Mr Paddy's housekeeper, Mrs Mellor, was in charge of Isabella and she was a kind woman. She also had two daughters of about Isabella's age, which made Isabella even happier. Mr Paddy's house was like a big party. Everybody sat down to eat together at every meal and there was a good deal of talk. Isabella had been nowhere like it.

Mr Paddy told her that he had once seen a mermaid but Isabella only laughed and told him that he was silly. No, he said, in the Pacific Ocean he had seen a mermaid on a rock combing her black hair with a golden comb. They laughed but Isabella badly wanted to think it was true because it was such a good story.

Alex was horrified when his children couldn't be found. He wanted to run around like a demented fool, blaming anybody other than himself, in particular his wife, but he was too honest for that. In a way it felt like the day Alice had died.

He felt sick, and that he ought to have been able to better things but as the rain went on sheeting down and night fell quickly the men who had gone out from the village to search for the two girls had to give up until the following morning.

He knew that he should have stuck fast to his resolution not to send them away. That had been the whole point in marrying the blessed woman. Whatever had he been thinking of?

He would never forget how they had looked at him when he'd announced that they would be going away to school. And how could he have forgotten that Georgina had come to the surgery, something no member of his family had ever done before, and he had not listened to her. Why had he not? He didn't know now, just that it seemed like the best thing to do. Theirs was not a happy house, his marriage had ruined what peace there had been.

What if something had happened to them? What if they had fallen down an old quarry or a mine shaft, or that they had been badly hurt in some other way? He could not bring himself to think that they might be dead. The river had swollen overnight and broken its banks in places.

The next day the men of the village and round about went out again searching, shouting the girls' names so that they seemed to echo from every valley and hillside, coming back and back to scorn him.

He went up to the Hilda House to see Sarah and Mrs Nattrass and then to Mr Paddy's house, but although Isabella was there Doris and Georgina had not been seen. Mr Paddy, who came to the door, seemed like a genial man. They had never met before. Alex could see that he was a sensible and learned man and he wished he had not dismissed the two men and their teachings; it would have been a way for his children to stay here.

Mr Paddy and his workers also set off across the fell, miles and miles of it to see if they could find anything. Alex tried to rationalize. If one of them had been hurt surely the other might have been able to go for aid. But then they were children. Doris was nine, Georgina eleven. Doris was so fragile looking and did not remember her mother, Georgina was very clever and plainly spoken and he only saw now how dear they were to him.

Halfway through the third day Alex had to wipe away the tears that did away with his dignity. He avoided Hyacinth. They had said nothing to one another but he felt sure that she blamed him as much as he blamed himself, and what more was there to say? They were his children, not hers, after all.

By the third day Mr Whitty had organized bigger groups of men to search all over the dale. Nobody went to work. They were all stunned by the disappearance of the two children.

Thirty-two

The first thing Luke noticed was his dry mouth. It was nothing new, he had always had to drink a lot of water, regarded it as a brandy chaser and of benefit and also, if he drank water, he could then drink more brandy, so it worked in every way.

It was only when he opened his eyes that he realized he was not where he had thought he was. He was not at home. Home had gone, was lost to him when his evil brother came back. Luke hated him, hated him with a hot, sweeping bitterness that satisfied something inside him.

It had been bad enough trying to cope when James wasn't there. At least he could be glad for all the things he had had that James hadn't. They had never corresponded. James would not forgive him for the fact that he had won the woman James loved, and he would never forgive James for being the firstborn and thinking he was entitled to everything.

He couldn't believe that James was back and that he had been turned out of the house that he had regarded as his for over twenty years. He had thought of it as his birthright. He remembered James turning them into the street but after that it all blurred in his head.

He looked now and remembered he was up on the tops at the old orphanage. He was lying on the bed in a room he had slept in before, quite often. It was very warm. He slid off the bed and attempted to open a window but it wouldn't give. As he pushed harder at it, he could see that it was locked. *How odd*, he thought, *in such warm weather.* He tried the other windows because sunshine streamed into the room but none of them opened.

He went over to the door and tried to turn the handle but it too was locked. He couldn't work it out but as he was trying to decide what to do next, he saw that on the table by the window = next to which stood a dining chair = there were sandwiches, a pitcher of water and a glass.

On the mantelpiece there were several books. He looked at the titles but didn't take much notice. He rat-tled the door more than once and then tried the windows again but had no success. Finally, he hammered on the door and shouted. He kept this up for about five minutes before he sensed a presence at the other side and said, 'Why is the door locked?'

He heard his son's voice. Luke assumed Harry was there to apologize for having treated him so very badly for no good reason. What kind of son knocked his father down and did not feel guilt over it? He listened hard and then harder, unable to believe what Harry was saying.

'Good morning, Father. You have to stay there. You have food and water, a pot under the bed, and books to read.'

'Stay here?'

'That's right. You have to stay there until you stop needing brandy.'

'I don't need brandy, I need my freedom. Open the door.'

'I'm afraid not. No matter what you do or say or how much you shout, you are not coming out of there.'

'I demand that you open this door!'

'No. You have to stay there.'

Luke tried to talk to him but Harry had gone. He tried shouting but nothing happened. There was not much in the room, nothing he could use to break windows, and even if he did it was a sheer drop to the ground from the third floor, and the ground was solid stone, so he could break a leg or even his neck.

There was no knife, fork or spoon. There was a pile of clean clothes and a towel, and cold water in the ewer and soap. And a toothbrush. *There was everything a prisoner needed*, he thought, *but nothing more*.

Harry was true to his word and after a couple of hours of shouting, Luke's voice was so hoarse that he had to take a drink of water and two hours after that he ate the sandwiches. Harry would come back and take away the dirty dishes and hopefully bring some more food, and then Luke would get past him and make good his escape.

He waited. His head thumped as the afternoon advanced and the sunshine lay in long shafts on the carpet. In the end he heard the door unlocking and hid behind it, hoping to catch Harry out when he opened the door, but although he sprung forward Harry was too quick for him and had already closed the door and was able to fend off Luke. It was a shock. He had not realized how weak he was, and then he remembered how Harry had beaten him to the floor with ease.

He watched as Harry turned the key and pocketed it. He had brought food, salad greens and cheese, and some kind of pink pudding.

'You can't keep me locked up like this.'

'Too late.' Harry sounded almost cheerful. It infuriated his father. 'You have had plenty of chances to redeem yourself, and in the end you stole Sarah's money. The money she works so hard for and which feeds us. After that we decided that we couldn't risk your behaviour any longer.'

'You are soft on that girl,' Luke said but his son didn't answer. He put down the food and drink and when Luke attempted to grab him at the door, he just pushed and Luke fell back against the wall. It wasn't a heavy push but it was an effective one. Luke had enough breath to swear at length but by the time he had finished cursing, his son was long gone and only the silence remained.

He was bored. In the end he began to read, though he had no idea what the book was about. He had never been a man who read much. He grew more bored as the evening fell, and when night came he needed brandy.

He called and called and then sobbed in frustration, but nothing happened. He went to sleep when darkness fell and he had horrible dreams where he was burning to death. He awoke with a start and found that he was sweating profusely and needed water. He gulped down two pints of it.

In the early morning Harry came back, and Hilary Nattrass was with him. She didn't even glance at Luke. She took the pot from under the bed and replaced it with another, then took the old one out of the room. Harry put down food and more water.

'I'm fine now,' Luke said. 'Let me out. I swear I won't drink anymore.'

'I've heard it a dozen times, Father,' Harry said, then went out swiftly and closed and locked the door.

Luke felt very strange that morning. He had a headache, he had a need for brandy and he was not hungry. By mid-afternoon – at least he assumed it was mid-afternoon by the light – he found that he wanted the food, and it was good food. Cold bacon and eggs, black pudding, sausages and buttered toast. It tasted almost as good as it would have done hot, but he longed for hot food, even though the weather was warm, especially in the afternoon when sunshine poured into the room. The only good thing about it was that it looked out over the gardens, and he could watch Harry tying up beans and hoeing and raking between the rows, the little dog asleep at his feet after following him round and round. The big sheepdog, which belonged to Mrs Nattrass, was with them too.

Short of anything else to do except read, Luke watched through the window all afternoon. He saw how a little girl came into the garden and ran about, calling to the dogs and singing in a language Luke didn't know, but it was a European language and he recognized the little Spanish girl. What a sweet voice she had. He didn't think he had ever heard anything better.

She looked exactly like Isabel, so he brought his best memories to mind and spent the next two hours recalling their courtship, their marriage, their time together. He pushed from him the harder memories of when she had died and he had lost his little daughter.

Isabella – that was it, she had been named after his beloved wife – Isabella went in, presumably for tea, and then he was left alone again.

That evening Harry brought him a huge salad with warm potatoes in butter and this time Luke ate it straight away.

Thirty-three

On the fourth day Alex began to despair. He couldn't
think of what to do and was convinced by then that his
children were dead. He tried talking to Hyacinth but neither of them could find anything to say. He thought she
had honestly imagined a life at boarding school would
be better for the whole family, and who was to say it
would not have been? He could admit to himself now
that she had never liked them. Perhaps she did not like
any child. Why should she? She had lost her own two at
birth or before it and she had taught because she had no
other option. She had married him because it was better
than starving.

He had long since admitted to himself that it had been
a stupid idea to send the girls away. He had not put them
first. They had been so difficult, but now he wanted to
go somewhere for comfort, for somebody to tell him
that his children would come back, that they were not
dead, that things would get better.

Hyacinth sat looking out at the rain. That was all
she had done for four days. He wished that she had

done something more, but then what more could she do? Everything that could be done was being done by everyone else.

Late in the afternoon he went to her and he realized that rain was falling on to the fire on that dismal day. It made a strange little sizzling noise. They sat in silence for a long time, or what felt like a long time, while the rain continued and the darkness grew deep, and in the end he turned to her in despair and said, 'What if they don't come back?'

'They will.'

What else could she say?

'We got this wrong.'

She gave a short laugh. 'Didn't we?' she said bitterly. 'We should never have got married. I married you because I didn't want to die of hunger in that wretched little village and you married me so that you could have somebody to use in bed and to take your children off your hands.'

He was silent at this, and yes, she was right. He had. He didn't love her and she didn't love him, and they had been so selfish. He left her there and wandered through the hall and into the kitchen.

It was empty. He didn't often go in there. It was the maids' domain but he couldn't think where else to go.

As he stood there Fiona came out of the pantry and started slightly at seeing him.

'Where's Ada?' he asked, for something to say.

'Gone shopping. One of us had to do something before we drove each another mad.'

'I think I'm there before you,' he said and sat down before the stove. 'I should go back out.'

'I don't think any more can be done than what is being done,' she said. 'The rain is so bad nobody can see.'

'Do you think my children are dead in a ditch somewhere?' He looked at her, his face begging her to deny it could possibly happen.

'No, of course not. You must have a little faith.'

Alex gave a short laugh, which was turning into a sob. 'I never had any of that.'

'Try it now.'

He shook his head and as he did so she got down to him and took him into her arms like he was a child.

'I'm sorry,' he said, drawing back a little and then he buried his face in her neck and uttered a deep sigh.

Then they heard the back door open and he was up and gone from the room almost before Fiona could move.

'Any news?' Ada asked, slightly hopeful.

Fiona shook her head.

That night when it was dark, and the maids being able to think of nothing else, and even glad of the night and the chance to lie their weary bones on the feather mattress, Ada went back to something she had thought of about an hour ago and had then dismissed as ridiculous.

'Fi?' she whispered as though anybody could hear, but then she doubted anyone for miles was sleeping. She heard a deep, hopeless sigh. 'Are you asleep?'

'Of course. I sigh in my sleep all the time.'

'I think I know where those bairns might be.'

'Of course you do,' Fiona said in a hard, cold voice. 'We've got the entire dale out looking but you have suddenly decided you're cleverer than anybody else.'

'Yes, but you know those daft police stories where children disappear and are searched for for days and then appear in a closet or under the bed—'

'Are you suggesting that Georgina and Doris are in the house?'

'No. But I do think they might just be somewhere close, somewhere nobody has thought of.'

'We've had people up in the hay lofts, down into the cellars, in every barn and byre and deserted building for miles around. They've been to every mine shaft, every quarry, they've even been through the old quarry ponds and found nothing. So come on, Ada, where are they?'

She turned to Ada, who at once began to doubt herself.

'I know. I just—'

'Where then? We've got nothing to lose if you remember.'

'What about the old summerhouse?'

'What summerhouse?'

'At the very far end of the property where it's over-grown, there's this tiny, awful building completely covered in shrubs and grass.'

'I've never seen it.'

'I think few people have. It's completely invisible. It hasn't been used in all the time that I can remember and there's only one way in, through all the trees and roots and thick, long grass. I came across it one day when I was looking for blackberries, but it's so well hidden that I almost missed the tiny entrance. I haven't actually been in there because I'm too big to get in without hurting myself but for a couple of children—'

She stopped there.

'Do you think the doctor knows of it?' Fiona asked.

'I have no idea. Probably not, since he hasn't been here that long. It's nothing more than a totally disguised cubby hole.'

'You think two children would stay in a place like that for four days?' Fiona said scathingly.

'I don't know, but the worst we can do is get soaked through and feel stupid.'

They lay in silence for about two minutes and then got out of bed, got dressed and went softly down the stairs. Nothing could be heard but the rain banging off the doors and windows and pavements. The streams were gushing fast and furiously under roads and over fords, and in some places the water was so deep that they couldn't see how it went down, which made it dangerous.

The maids put on stout boots and coats, scarves over their heads and opened the back door. Moments later they were soaked to the skin. After the first five minutes Ada could feel even her underwear go heavy with rain, and her boots were letting cold water in at the front, back and sides so that she was sloshing through the grass.

The old summerhouse was a long way off and only Ada knew of it so she took the lead, though her hair kept whipping her face and sticking to her skin. She fruitlessly tried to peel it back as she stepped forward.

The garden went a long way back and to both sides. There was an orchard and, beyond it, a huge second garden, which had long since not been needed, ran down to the fence at the back. Some of the glass in the old greenhouses had smashed and parts of their frames were wrecked. Pieces of wood lay everywhere. Ada had to stand on the glass to make progress and it went brittle and broke into smaller pieces and then smaller still, grainy like sand. She was worried about the glass getting into her boots, but so far that had not happened. She kept stopping because it was so hard to see. The leaves were thick on the trees and continually slapped her in the face as the wind moved them this way and that so very quickly.

At the far end, there was a long stretch of woodland, and away to one side were big planks of wood and various old buckets and a harness. Then the whole thing petered out into bushes of gorse and elderflower and broom, and it was almost wild there, like the fells.

These bushes had been left for years and were almost impenetrable, but somehow there was bare soil packed hard, although slippery now, with the amount of rain which had turned the soil into mud, and from time to time there were big puddles. Finally the tiny path gave way to a wall of bricks with an opening into the summerhouse. Ada felt her way because the blackness was as bad as what the coalminers claimed they saw down the pit. Just nothing.

She called the girls' names and listened into the silence for a few seconds. She struggled on, and then both maids tried to move through the opening. Ada had been right, Fiona thought, it was a huge effort for an adult to get through the tiny door, it was like something people imagined fairies used. They got down on their hands and knees, scraping their bodies as they struggled to go forward, feeling their way, and it was not long before Ada encountered a boot with her fingers, a child's boot. That encouraged them and very soon they had hold of the cold little bodies. Neither child spoke. They were unconscious.

'Go back and get the doctor,' Ada said in a hard voice, 'and hurry up.'

Thirty-four

The days went on until Luke was no longer sure how long he'd been locked up. He begged and pleaded to be let out but Harry didn't listen. All night he lay awake in the silence and longed for brandy. He could not accept that he couldn't have any. Night after night he sweated and his dreams betrayed him with their garish colours and vile sounds and thirsty fires that consumed him, and when he awoke he had sweated though his clothes. He washed every morning and changed them and enjoyed the way that he felt refreshed. His clothing smelled and felt of warm iron to his starved senses.

From time to time he pretended that he was cured, that he didn't want anything but a cup of tea and his freedom, but Harry was deaf to his entreaties and took no notice. Luke got used to the idea that Harry wouldn't listen to him no matter what his mood or how abusive his language, or how disgustingly he lost his temper and threw cups and plates at him.

Harry didn't want to know how bad the withdrawal symptoms were, how horrifying the nightmares and the sweats, but worst of all somehow was the boredom. Luke had not known that he drank because he was lonely. Yes, it was grief but the brandy filled up those ghastly spaces in his head where the pictures of his dead wife and child were. The brandy gave him sweet but clouded joy and bathed his dreams in the life he had lived when she was alive, and he could hold both of them close and safe in his arms. Why had God chosen him to go through this endless grief and pain?

'I can't stand the boredom any longer, Harry, I really cannot.' He didn't know how long he had been there, the days had run one into another. He couldn't bear it. He begged and cried but Harry was stony hearted. Luke cursed him but it didn't make any difference.

Harry was impervious to it all. Luke began to sleep a lot more after the first ten days and he dreamed less, which was a relief in itself. His appetite grew bigger and so did his meals, and Harry began to bring him cups of tea and coffee. Luke thought he had never drunk anything which tasted better.

Soon, Harry added huge pieces of chocolate cake at teatime, and then there was toasted teacake. There was soup, very often a simple soup of vegetables, and fresh buttered bread and big pieces of cheese with chutney.

Harry also added several jigsaws and pens, writing paper, coloured pencils and drawing paper, and sometimes even a newspaper so that Luke could find out what was happening, though he suspected the newspapers were old. Luke also read all the books, and these Harry replaced often. Luke had not known that books could be such a solace. He began to enjoy reading as never before.

Luke had never done a jigsaw in his life but now they filled his attention, and took up a huge space on the dressing table until there was barely room for food and drink, so Harry brought in a tray. There was never a knife, just a fork and a spoon. Luke read for hours and hours a day and grew to enjoy the voice in his head which loved the books, and then he started to sketch the garden. For the first time the nightmares of his loss receded and he began to manage his feelings, to enjoy waking up instead of cursing each day he was alone.

He began to sleep the whole night through in a deep and satisfying way as he had never done before, and it started to make him feel a joy that had long since left him.

He could eat his fill, and when he did dream it was vague and pleasant and he recalled happy times of his childhood before his father drank himself to death. How awful that they had both lost their wives and done exactly the same thing. How very tedious they were. His father was ill-liked in the village even when Luke was a child. People learned to hate and despise the Leadbetters, who thought they were above everybody else when in fact they were more base. They would cheat and take advantage, and they cared for nobody.

Luke hated his father, who had seen to it that people were so ill paid they could barely live, and if they couldn't pay their way he would have them put from their houses. He set spies on them in case they didn't work as long as he thought they should, though in fact he did not pay them sufficiently for the hours they worked.

His father had ill-treated his lovely mother. It was not that he hit her, he ignored her, he would not let her go anywhere without him, he controlled her, that was what it was about. She was less important than his dogs and his horses. Even Luke did not matter. Only James was important because he was the firstborn and the heir, and Luke understood now how the hatred grew. He was always second best. James was given a pony, he had a tutor, he had the best to eat. Luke had no education, no pony, and he had to eat what he was given. Worst of all, his father ignored him and when he was very young Luke wondered whether a servant girl had given birth to him because he was given such rough treatment.

That lack of education was the reason he had sworn to himself that he would send his son to the best school he could afford. He had no life, no freedom, no power. Worst of all, he admitted to himself now, he had done as badly, if not worse, than his father had to him. He had to live with what he had done, with how he had treated people. Was it too late to change? He began to hope that somehow he would be able to make amends.

Luke began to keep a journal based on how he felt, what day it was, what was happening outside and about the books he was reading.

And then Harry proved how cruel he was. He brought him a small glass of brandy. Luke fell on it and then he thought that Harry was trying to outwit him, so he sipped it very slowly. It tasted better than anything had ever tasted in his life. He could smell and taste the sweetness of it and when it was finished he was fine for about an hour. Then he began to cry because he wanted more, and he knew by now that Harry would give him no more.

Every day there was a small glass of brandy and he began by taking a sip and then waiting until he could wait no more. The brandy went, and then he was licking the glass. He saw as if from a distance what he was doing and then the tears slipped down his face and betrayed how stupid he was.

He would triumph over his son. He would get out of here if it was the last thing he ever did. He began to leave the brandy, and Harry would go on letting it sit there until, in despair, Luke emptied it into the pot under the bed. Then he lay down and wept. His son was torturing him to death and would not give up.

To his surprise he began to walk round and round the

room just for something to do. He did a circuit more each day and his legs grew stronger and he began to get a little fatter. There was no mirror in the room, presumably so that he could not smash the glass and push it into Harry's face as he had planned and longed to do so very often. Now he didn't want to. His beard grew and his hair got long but the aches and pains which he had thought would dominate his life forever began to disappear. His dreams sweetened, and his thoughts became less harsh.

He did press-ups as he had done as a youth, just for something to do, to while away the interminable hours, and did more every day. He longed to be outside and spent hours by the window watching the scenery. He became fascinated by the rain and the sunshine, by raindrops and sunbeams. He left open the curtains so that he could watch the moon move across the sky, so that he could work out what time it was. Best of all, when it was dark, he liked the stars. He was lonely but it was different than it had been. He looked forward to Harry's visits even though his son did not speak. At first, Luke would talk at him without any response, until finally he stopped trying to make conversation. But he committed to memory each second that Harry allowed him, every feature, every movement of the boy that he had thought he did not love.

Still he was not allowed out and he thought that Harry

was punishing him for all those awful years at school, for the neglect and the loneliness. Now his father was the one who was lonely and perhaps Harry would make him stay in that room forever and never forgive him. He lost hope of ever getting beyond the four walls which had become his prison.

Thirty-five

The doctor was asleep when Fiona edged into his room. She had seen him like that many times when she had had to rouse him because somebody was ill and, as he sometimes wearily said, more people needed him at three in the morning than at any other time, usually on a Saturday night.

This time was different. She knew that it was the fourth night of this bad dream and he had not even undressed, but just lay across the bed sideways in an exhausted sleep as though his body could bear no more.

He looked younger in sleep, relaxed despite everything. As ever, no matter how many times they had remonstrated with him that he would burn the house down, his candle was alight and had several hours left to it.

She didn't want to awaken Mrs Blair across the landing so she spoke and moved very quietly, but as she said his name he awoke immediately. He always did. It was the way that he lived. He had to be up and on his feet quickly. If he'd undressed, he always left his clothes over a chair, and his black bag was always packed for whatever he might need.

This time he gazed at her and she drew closer and smiled and said, 'Your children are found.'

He carried Georgina home and Fiona carried Doris. Doris was awake by then and crying just a little into Fiona's sopping coat. Georgina went on half sleeping, saying, 'Let me go,' in a dispirited tone but she did not move in his embrace.

They took the children into the kitchen and helped them into warm, dry clothes. Both were fully awake by then. Ada heated milk and put bread into it, and when the children had eaten, the doctor and Fiona took them upstairs and lay with them while they went back to sleep.

The doctor wanted to stay with them all night but just for a few moments he went downstairs with Fiona to the kitchen. Unable to look at them for tears, he said to the maids, 'Thank you both so much.'

'It was Ada,' Fiona said.

'I didn't even know that place was there,' he said hoarsely.

'I came across it by chance,' Ada said.

'I'm so glad you did.'

He went back upstairs and lay down and watched his children sleep.

The next morning, with the two girls safely in the kitchen eating huge breakfasts, Alex went into the dining room where his wife was crumbling toast and trying to drink tea. He sat down beside her instead of at the far end of the table.

'What do you think we should do now?' he asked.

He had awoken her after the children were home, but she had said nothing and so he had crept away in the silence.

She hesitated as though she was about to deny responsibility and then, looking hard at her plate, she said, 'I think we have established that it doesn't matter what I think.'

She seemed so calm but he knew she was relieved and perhaps she felt just as guilty as he did, in another way.

'They aren't going away to school,' he said. 'I shall write today and say so.'

She said nothing to that, but he glanced quickly at her and saw her expression. It was resignation.

'Of course not,' she said flatly. 'Why would you want them to have a good education? After all, they are only girls. The village school will be perfectly adequate.'

'They ran away,' he pointed out unnecessarily.

'They didn't go far. If only you and the other men who were running the search might have realized. They wanted to be found. Now they have won. Much good will it do them when in the future, when they think about what they could have achieved. When it's too late and they end up marrying the wrong men because they have so few choices.'

'Georgina is very clever,' was all he could think to say.

'A village school education will not get her into university and Doris is not very bright at all. She will go nowhere. She'll marry the first unsuitable man she comes across because he tells her she is pretty, and you'll end up keeping them and their feckless children. Georgina may even become an old maid because men want wives who agree with their views and know how to cook and clean and respect them. Because men are so much more intelligent, so much more important than women will ever be. They will end up like I did.'

She stopped there and when he had nothing to say she continued, 'Didn't you think it odd that they hid in plain sight? They have learned early how to manipulate you.'

She left the room then and both wished they never had to meet again.

Thirty-six

When Luke Leadbetter woke up he had no idea where he was for the first few seconds, and then he remembered. He was Harry's prisoner. He felt a great deal better and didn't want a drink. Well, he did, he wanted tea but that was all. He knew where he had been, of course, he had been in hell, and for such a long time that he couldn't remember being anywhere else. He lay still for a few moments and as he did so he could see the light coming through, a tiny sliver, and then he felt the slight breeze and the smell of the tops. It was like nowhere else on earth. Sharp and seared and salt-like as he remembered it, and more than anything else he wanted to get outside into the fresh air.

All the memories flooded back but he tried to ignore them. The room was different than it had been. A merry fire was tall in the grate. He lay there and watched it for a few moments. He thought he had never seen anything quite so wonderful. He felt as though he was being lifted, he was floating, he was free, he was flying, and then he went to sleep again.

He opened his eyes once more and Harry was sitting down on the bed.

'How do you feel?' he said gently.

Luke closed his eyes as the memories flooded back and hurt him so much that he let a tear of remorse slip down his cheek.

'Why couldn't you just let me die?'

'I did keep thinking that the world would be a better place without you but unfortunately I am obliged to try and keep you here.'

That made Luke smile.

'How long have I been like this?'

'A month.'

'It feels like a lot longer.'

Harry said nothing for a few seconds, just nodded, and then he took a deep breath and said, 'I'm sure it does but I had to . . . to try to be right about it, to hope that you would be a lot better.'

There was a pause, and then Harry went on. 'If you want to come with me I can shave you and cut your hair, and you can have a bath and clean clothes. It's Sunday morning and the dinner will be ready by then.'

Strangely, Luke was now afraid. He was afraid of the person he thought he had become, and afraid that the moment he stepped out of the door he would go back to being that person, but he must try. He knew that he must, he owed that to Harry. He owed it to everybody, and most of all to himself, to make an attempt to be a decent person.

So he agreed, and Harry helped him. When he looked into the bathroom mirror after he was bathed and shaved, and his hair was cut and trimmed, and he saw the person that he was, he thought for the first time that he might be able to manage it.

He was pale because he had been inside for too many days, but in a lot of ways he looked better, even younger. The huge red bags were gone from under his eyes, which were clear, and his skin was clear. He was not as thin, at least it was a different kind of slenderness, not haggard, much fitter.

Harry would have taken him downstairs but Luke determined that he would face everybody on his own. He did remember them but only just. His memory was not so good. He didn't know whether it would come back to him, he must take this one step at a time. He felt so confused, like he was setting out for an unknown country.

It felt very odd to walk downstairs, and since he was unused to it he had to hold on to the bannisters at first. The family were gathered in the dining room for dinner and he would be just in time, Harry had said. He was afraid now. He would have given a great deal not to have gone in but he must. He must try to behave like a decent person. He barely knew himself.

He opened the door and then he wished he could run away – or at least walk away. It was full of people and they were about to have a meal. They were sitting at a long wooden table on benches at either side.

Nobody spoke. Luke was suddenly ravenously hungry, and to his delight it was a huge dinner with golden carrots and creamy parsnips and potatoes, which had been roasted in the oven. Better still, in the middle of the table was an enormous piece of beef.

He wanted to say something but he couldn't think of a single thing. He choked. If he could have run at any speed he would have gone. But he felt more tired than he had ever felt before.

'Come in,' Sarah said in welcome, and indicated the chair next to her. 'You can sit right here beside Isabella.'

Luke remembered the child clearly and how afraid she had been, and how awful he had been, and he hesitated. She was so beautiful, so like his Isabel, so like the child he had lost. He hesitated and then smiled very gently.

'Is it all right if I sit beside you?' he said to her.

'Yes, I think so. Sarah says that you are better now.'

'I hope so. I was watching you play outside in the garden. It brought me a great deal of pleasure.' Then he sat down.

Sarah put her fingers on his wrist in a slight caress and he began to eat his dinner. It was the best meal that he could remember. After that he was so tired he went back to bed and slept for the rest of the day and all that night. When he woke up again it was morning, and he felt better than he could ever remember having felt before.

Over the next few days the memories flooded back to him. How he had lost his wife and child, how he had sent Harry away, how awful his life had been and, worst of all, that he had frightened this little girl who was part of his family. He wished that had not happened. And then he remembered the burning of Mrs Nattrass's house, and he was so ashamed of himself that he couldn't speak.

Thirty-seven

It had never occurred to Harry that Sarah liked him. Well, no better than anybody else, anyhow. He liked her very much but she knew all about his family – nobody could have known more, he thought bitterly – so he didn't expect that she would fancy him, as they said around here. He fancied her. It was a first. His life had been so caught up in other things that he had not thought specifically about any girl.

He had been at school forever, where there were no girls, and he'd spent the holidays there too, so saw only the masters' children and they all seemed the same – little, messy and noisy, and then obnoxious as they grew older, ill-mannered and ignoring him. This was quite different and costing him sleep. He had been so worried about his father that until Luke actually began to get better, he'd been unable to think about Sarah more fully, but now he succumbed to feelings he had always pushed away from him.

He wanted to hold her very close, he wanted to know what her mouth felt like, her body. He waited for her to speak, to smile. He was an idiot, he told himself, and worst of all he had taken to finding his face hot and his body awkward around her and he had to keep away.

The trouble was that he had a new project, which he had started thinking about now that his brain was not solely concentrated on his father, and he wanted to know what Sarah thought about it. So, in spite of this clumsiness which he had never had before, he managed to find her when everybody else was busy and he began to outline the plan.

They were in the dining room. She usually laid out her patterns here and mostly the family ate in the kitchen, which was as big as this room, because she was always in the middle of work. The dining room had become her workroom and she often worked here by herself. This morning Hilary was busy in the kitchen and Isabella was at Mr Paddy's house, so Harry got her all to himself. She didn't mind talking while she worked, he knew, when it was not too intricate and she was merely putting in stitches. Then she could think of other things, so all he said was, 'Is it okay if I tell you of an idea I've had?'

Luckily she didn't even glance at him, just nodded, so he didn't get embarrassed. He went ahead, but by the time he was three sentences in, she had stopped working and was gazing at him, half in disbelief and half in amazement that he would even contemplate such a thing.

'That's a magical notion,' she said, 'but how on earth will you put it into practice? Do you know anything about building?'

'Well no, but I think my dad does, and now that he's starting to get better, if we had a major project to do it might make things easier for him. He used to know all the builders and carpenters and such in the area.'

'But what would we pay them with?'

'Well, that's a problem but if I could just consult them, pay them for their knowledge, ask them how to do things and they came and showed me, then maybe Dad and I could do it together and it wouldn't cost much. Do you think it might work?'

'I think it's worth trying,' Sarah said. 'Hilary will be so pleased.'

'It might make her think better of my father, and I think he needs that to happen as much as she does.'

Luke was just as enthusiastic when Harry told him, and in a fit of modesty said, 'I've built a house before. A long time ago but I don't suppose the basics change, and what I don't know we could go and ask. We can pay a little if Sarah thinks it's all right for them to tell us or show us what to do. We've got nothing to lose.'

Hilary didn't realize until later that Harry Leadbetter had brought her to her farm on purpose that cold autumn day. She stood there, barely able to see for tears, and called herself a silly old fool and told him that he was insensitive for bringing her here.

Then he said, and he was crafty, she later acknowledged, 'There is a lot of stone and I think we could work with it.'

'What do you mean? Have it salvaged, taken away, as though your father hasn't caused enough damage here?'

'No, I meant that some of it would go back on to the foundations which are already there.'

He showed her the papers he was carrying, the sketches and the outlines of what it might look like.

'Dad and me, we've been talking to skilled men in Wolsingham and we think we might be able to do most of the work ourselves. We've been shown how to do stone walling and most of the stone is still here. We need wood and various tools, which we can borrow, and I think we might be able to make a start on it now before the bad weather sets in.'

Hilary stared at him as though unable to believe what she was hearing. 'Why, Harry Leadbetter, you great gowk. What in God's name do you think you are doing?' And she punched his arm in play so that she wouldn't show him how excited she was.

Hilary had given up on the idea that she would come back here to live. She had thought her home nothing but a ruin, and she wasn't sure she wanted to live here by herself. She could admit now that she had been very lonely for years and was enjoying life at the Hilda House. There was always something going on, and now that Luke had come back to sobriety, she found that he fitted in there.

She did, however, think it would do Luke and Harry good to have something new to concentrate on. There was no reason why they shouldn't try to bring the farmhouse back to something which could be lived in, even if she didn't go there yet. She hoped that Sarah would say to her that she didn't want to lose her, but then perhaps Sarah imagined that Hilary only endured the life at the Hilda House because she had lost her own home.

'I think it's an excellent idea,' she told Harry, wanting to encourage him to do all kinds of things. Also the house deserved to be rebuilt. It was in such a wonderful place, and the views were the best that she thought she had ever seen. She missed that.

Thirty-eight

By the doctor's orders and with the agreement of the two teachers, every weekend that autumn Georgina and Doris went up to stay either at the Hilda House or at Mr Paddy's farm, depending on the arrangements. The doctor had made changes also at the house and Mrs Carver's sister came in on Saturdays to help Fiona because Ada was gone all day to help with the children. He had got past the idea that he wanted everything done as his wife had chosen. She barely spoke and took little notice of what was going on. It was as though they had separated but were living in the same house. The atmosphere was uneasy but he did not care. He had to put the children first. He didn't see much of them but he was sure he was doing the right thing, and they were happy.

Meals had changed too. Although Mrs Blair presided over the dining room, she said nothing when potatoes appeared on the table, even cheese and butter, bigger portions and quite often a crumble for the doctor of blackberries and apples with thick cream. It was easier in some ways and harder in others. He even said to Ada that she might stay up at the Hilda House for weekends if she chose as she would be looking after his children. He knew that Sarah and Harry would have been kind to them, but Ada was older and it would make things better all round.

Ada was worried about this decision and at first said she would bring the girls back with her on the Saturday evening. After the first weekend, though, she decided it was easier to stay with them and she was much happier spending time with Sarah, helping in the house and with the clothes, which took up most of Sarah's time these days.

When she first went there, she saw a man whom she did not recognize. He was about her own age and he smiled when she saw how taken aback she was.

'I'm Luke Leadbetter,' he said drily and got up from the table to greet her.

Ada, amazed, took the hand he offered to her. She hadn't seen him in years and he looked so good, almost as good as when they had danced together in Stanhope Town Hall now and then. He had had a slight preference for her but even then he was known as a bad lad and, despite his status in the dale financially, Ada knew the family too well and had wanted nothing to do with him.

At first, leaving Fi holding the fort, as it were, back in Wolsingham seemed harder on her friend than on herself. But she well knew that Fiona would never leave the doctor, even if the house fell in on them, and Ada was so glad to get away. Up here on the tops, the life was different. Autumn was in all its glory, the sunny days were crisp with fallen leaves and the girls were happy.

Luke played chess with Georgina, who was very put out when he beat her. Doris wasn't interested and liked jigsaws. Ada could see he was eager to make sure that all three children were at ease with him. Isabella, in particular, his gaze shone on because they were related, and before this he had not thought he would ever see her again without her running from him horrified.

Now she giggled when they played snakes and ladders, she took him to see Mr Paddy and the animals, and they all helped with picking fruit in the orchards at both houses and Sarah and Ada bottled the fruit and made chutneys.

Alex was unsure when he first realized that Fiona McIntyre loved him, but it was the happiest thing that had happened to him in a very long time. He just wished that the timing could have been better. But then he had not seen Fiona as she was, only as his servant, polite and competent with a lovely west lilt to her voice. He had not seen that she was a lady such as Hyacinth would never be. Now he wished he could have married her. She would have run his home and been good to his children;

she would have been there for him when he came home, and he felt certain that she would have been there for him in bed too. He longed for her in so many ways.

He had wished that just once somebody could be on his side and that he could stop being the man whose marriage and whole life was a failure. Now Fiona was.

She had been his servant for years and had looked after the doctor before him. She was forty, quiet and undemanding. It was nothing that she said or did; he just woke up in the middle of the night and felt a slight degree of happiness that there might be some way forward. His marriage was over. He and Hyacinth no longer spoke or sat in the same room if they could help it. Their paths barely crossed.

Also, he had not forgotten how Fiona put her arms around him when he had thought his children were dead. It took someone very special to do that.

What would happen when Fiona decided that she must leave he didn't know, but he had the awful feeling that she would. There was more work at weekends than she could manage, even with Mrs Carver's begrudging help. He didn't like to interfere. Running the household was not his job but he felt reluctantly that he must try to do it and, most of all, he must let Fiona know how much she meant to him.

After all, he now realized that Fiona was there for him and was enduring this for his sake. She did not deserve to have to live in this way. Nobody did. He couldn't say anything, either to his wife or to her. All he could do was work and spend as little time at home as possible.

He could no longer sit over the fire and drink tea and make conversation with a woman he was starting to loathe. He couldn't remember one positive thing about why he had married her. Nothing about it had worked out; there was no redeeming feature. He went to the local pub and played darts and dominoes occasionally; he felt that he had to do something for himself. The house now had nobody in it, much of the time, other than his wife and Fiona, because Ada was up on the tops looking after his children. He could hardly complain after everything she had done for him, but he was hating it all, except for the kind Scots woman who looked after him.

He knew that his work was also suffering because he couldn't leave his home life behind. He wouldn't forgive himself if he didn't get it right and somebody suffered or died. He understood by now that if his wife had had somewhere else to go, she would have gone, and he felt the same. As far as he knew, the woman in the kitchen was the only person in the whole world who cared anything about him.

Thirty-nine

Ada had not thought that she would like being at the Hilda House as much as she did. She wished that she did not have to go back to Wolsingham, but Mrs Carver couldn't be there all the time and it wasn't fair to expect Fiona to look after Sundays on her own, yet she guiltily stayed away as much as she could. She knew that the doctor and his wife still went to church on Sundays and there was a big meal in the middle of the day, but they never had any company now. Although Ada brought the children back in time for school on Mondays, she wished more and more that she could stay up on the tops. She was learning to like it better and better. Also, there was no denying that she was starting to like Luke Leadbetter. She tried to stop herself because she knew what he had been, but he was now so very charming and kind that she could not be unaffected by his presence. What joy there had ever been in Wolsingham was gone. Ada looked forward to her weekends so much that she was too ashamed to tell Fiona what a good time she had up at the Hilda House. She also liked to go and see the progress the men were making on Mrs Nattrass's farm-house. She and Sarah would walk over with sandwiches and cake and tea, and if it was fine they would sit there congratulating one another on how well it was going.

It had never occurred to Ada that she might fall in love. She had always thought such ideas were silly and that having too many children was the result of idiocy. She knew, though, that she had feelings for Luke that were different to anything she had felt before and she was ashamed of herself. She was nobody, and although he might have come down a long way, he was still far above her with his middle-class background and standing in the dale. He was now the man he had been meant to be, even though he had nothing, and she wanted to be with him as often as she could.

Ada knew that such things as building did not come easily to Luke. His hands blistered and bled, his limbs ached and she could tell by the way that he stood, and how pale his face was, that he was not used to doing such things. She admired him the more for his courage. Sarah would put salve on his hands and Ada wished she could do the same, because he looked so gratefully at Sarah and smiled.

Luke seemed to go on in all innocence of her feelings for him, Ada thought. Often he played games with

Isabella, Georgina and Doris – cards or dominoes or snakes and ladders. They had a home-made board for draughts and bottle tops for the pieces. Sarah bought them an old second-hand chess set from the market since Luke had said he played, and they all joined in, except Ada, who didn't understand the game at all and thought she had not the right kind of mind for such things.

'Wouldn't you like to learn?' he asked her one Saturday evening when the girls had gone to bed.

'Me? A thing like that? No, I couldn't.'

'Why not?'

'I hardly went to school. I can only just read and write. How would I manage something so complicated?'

'I don't think that's true. I think you just do your-self down because you assume when people have more schooling they know more, but I don't think that's nec-essarily right. Poor Harry found that out when I sent him to Scotland.'

Ada had painstakingly tried to teach herself to read and write better and was ashamed of her inability. She thought he would make it hard by offering to teach her more reading and writing but Luke was kinder than that. He did not want to embarrass her, she could see.

'Let me at least show you how the pieces work,' he said, and for some reason she only had to be told once. She had seen the others play and had been mystified but was no longer. It became so clear in her mind that she was astonished.

She played her first game with Georgina and beat her, then Isabella, so that she accused them of letting her win. Sarah hated games and refused to have anything to do with it, and Hilary wouldn't either. Georgina was quite good but she lacked patience. After Ada beat Harry, she tried to take on Luke and lost several times, and when she finally won she accused him of letting her.

She was horrified that they had all let her win because she was no good at anything educational. She beat Luke twice before she had the confidence to think that she had done it without any help. She had thoroughly enjoyed doing something which she had had no knowledge of just a few weeks ago.

Luke told her how clever she was and after that Ada began to avoid him. All she wanted was to be in his arms.

When he got the opportunity, when they were outside watching the children gathering and sweeping up leaves for a bonfire one Saturday afternoon, he turned to her and said softly, 'Have I upset you?'

Ada pretended. 'Me? No, of course not.' She took more interest in the leaves. 'How could you? You've been so kind and taught me how to play chess.'

'Since you won so convincingly you've avoided me.'

Ada tried not to admit the sudden warmth in her face. 'No, I haven't.'

'Yes, you have. Did you hate to win, or do you now think I'm beneath you?'

She knew that he was joking, or didn't know what else to say. At that moment Sarah called them in to dinner. Ada looked into Luke's face and saw his eyes and after the girls had run inside, he put his hands at either side of her face and lifted her chin and kissed her. She closed her eyes and savoured the moment.

'Ada Southern, brilliant chess player. I think I love you.'

Ada said nothing, she just slid her arms around his neck and silently thanked God for her luck.

Forty

The gilt was off the gingerbread, James Leadbetter thought. He had come back, full of hope for the future and to settle a few scores as well. He had enjoyed his home, putting it together and throwing out his despised relatives, but when it was all done and he had the place to himself, and had ingratiated himself with the village, he found that he was lonely.

Worst of all, he had seen Luke with Ada in Wolsingham and they were laughing. It hurt that Luke should be happy, that Luke had bettered him once again in the women stakes, that Luke had somehow been given another chance and had taken it in such a way. He was barely recognizable.

Then Luke saw him across the street and came to him. Short of running away and looking foolish, he was obliged to stand and watch his brother walk towards him, holding out his hand. James stared. Luke looked twenty years younger and was clean shaven with his dark hair well cut. He seemed taller and lean and nothing like he had been. He looked to James like the man who had stolen his love away.

'Will you shake hands with me?' Luke said, smiling, but almost humble such as James had never seen. He found he was obliged to shake his brother's hand and even tried to say something to him, but couldn't.

'You do remember Ada Southern?'

She too looked good. Her red hair was taken back into a sleek sweep and her blue eyes were merry. She was wearing the most beautiful black velvet dress that James thought he had ever seen.

'We are going to be married in the spring and would like to have you there with us,' she said.

They had so obviously talked about it that it upset James. He felt bitter. His brother had taken all the aces again, and so it was hard for him to say he was pleased for them, and that certainly he would be at the church on their wedding day. He had been lonely all his life and here was no different than anywhere else. He was always alone and it wasn't something you got used to.

He went for a walk every day, usually by the river. He had to get out, to get beyond the house, which he had thought promised him so much. Now it was silent and it seemed to him that it was peopled with the ghost of the only woman he had ever loved. She had never been his, and now he was reminded of her smile and her walk and her lovely face, her laughter and her joy.

He wanted to take down her picture and place it in the darkness of the attics but he couldn't do it. How cowardly that would have been. She had ruled his whole life so far and he knew that he must try to get beyond that. He had turned her into a saint and there she was, captured forever at her most beautiful when she had been in love with his brother, with the brother who was badly thought of and had achieved nothing, who had treated his son with neglect. Yet now Luke Leadbetter was thriving up there on the tops in the old house.

Harry too came across the street and greeted his uncle with a smile and his hand, and James wanted to run away; he wanted to go back to his old life in Canada. But even the thought of that was filled with bitterness. He knew that you could never go back. You must move forward. What was the saying? Life was a one-way street, there was only forward to go, and if you immersed yourself in the past then you lost everything.

He must stay here and try to go forward and then maybe he could have some chance of happiness. He would live with the portrait; he would not betray it by thrusting it into darkness in the depths of the house or in the attics. If Isabel was to be retained in his memory it must be as she was, not as he had wished she would be for so long.

Forty-one

Fiona heard the doctor come in before she saw him, but it was late and dark on a Saturday night. She had come to hate Saturday nights because Ada was not there and he was mostly out, either seeing a patient or occasionally, she assumed, going to the Black Lion to sit in a corner and talk. He never came back smelling of whisky so she thought it was innocent, and no doubt he felt the need to get away from here when things had gone so very wrong. He was always at home when the girls were here on the other four nights of the week. It was as though he needed to make up to them for not parenting them in a better way, and now he was doing his clumsy best. Fiona couldn't help being glad of that, whereas Mrs Blair barely acknowledged their existence or saw them.

When you fall in love with someone you spend so much time covertly watching them that you know every contour of their faces, every movement of their bodies, the way that they breathe, and it seemed that he recognized her too, even before he turned around.

'Sorry, did I frighten you? I assumed you were long

since asleep,' he said, so quietly that she had never before heard his voice like this: like a caress. It could not be intended for her. Why on earth should he speak to her like this? And then he smiled in the light from her candle.

'Is it whisky you're wanting, sir?' she ventured.

'You read me like a book,' he said and she moved past him and got down the bottle from the cupboard.

There was still a glimpse of firelight from the grate and she was burning only one candle. She found a glass. She could put her hands on every single thing in that kitchen, she knew it so well.

'Will you take a dram with me?' he asked.

She had known that she would never do such a thing, but she was not herself tonight and she thought of what her life might have been, should have been. A husband saying such things to her late at night when the children were in bed and there they were, just the two of them, everything safe and secure. So she took down another glass for herself and then they sat in the old chairs beside the stove. Fiona was suddenly blissfully happy just to see him there, sitting across from her while the candle lit the golden liquid in their glasses. This was the most important moment of her life and nothing could ruin it.

They sat there, she didn't know for how long, and they drank slowly and she could taste the peat and the heather in the whisky, and see the brown streams which gave it its colour. She could imagine the darkness of the lochs and hear the music of the pipes and the sights of the people and the hills, blue or grey, depending on where you were. For the first time in years, she missed her home and wanted to be there.

After they were on to their second drink she could see that he took his courage and, looking into the fire, said softly, 'I should never have married again. I thought I could move forward but I couldn't. Now I don't know what to do and she and I are stuck here like bluebottles when the window closes, doing a lot of useless buzzing with no way out.'

Fiona smiled at him.

'What?' he said.

'It just sounded so strange, you and Mrs Blair as bluebottles.'

He looked at her. 'Do you have a home to go to?' he asked.

'I left there twenty years ago. I'm not sure there is anything to go back to.' And she told him the story of the boy she had not wanted to marry and how her parents had reacted.

'I think it's a fairly typical response,' he said.

'What made it worse – I know people don't say such things – but he was in love with another boy and I was in love with the same boy, so it was a terrible mess. None of us would have been happy.'

'Have you been happy?'

'I've been contented, which is enough, I think. I don't think I wanted to be a married woman in such a place, with everybody beneath me and my husband sneaking out at night to his lover. I could never have competed. Being a servant hasn't been so very bad.'

'Until recently.'

'Until you got married,' she said.

'I upset the apple cart in every way possible. Was ever a man as misguided in his life? When I think back now, I just don't understand how I thought it would work.'

'You needed a home for your children and someone to look after them, and you had not stopped grieving for your first wife, as though you could.'

'I'm aware that Ada is going to leave. I heard about Ada and Luke and I wish her well. Don't stay here for my sake; you could go and live up there.'

'I don't want to leave the children. I am very fond of them and they care for me, and it's an important time for them after everything they've been through.'

'I'm very grateful to you. If you weren't here I don't know what I would do.'

He said nothing after that and looked down at his feet. Fiona put down her glass and went to him, and as he stood up she took him into her arms.

'I've never loved anybody in my life before now and your appalling marriage will not put me off.'

'Are you sure of it?'

354

'Absolutely certain,' she said.

When he put down his glass and drew her up into his arms she was at home like never before. Her life changed when he kissed her. She had read of such things but she thought it was all stories. Nothing had ever felt better than this.

She had never imagined anyone could be so important to her. In the end they tiptoed upstairs with the whisky bottle and the glasses in their hands, and there in the safety of her bed she gave herself to him as she had thought to give herself to someone and never had before. She had waited for so long for the love of her life and now it had happened.

Fiona floated through the next few days, but just when she was starting to think her bubble could never burst the doctor was called out to several homes where there were a lot of children who had scarlet fever.

She had had to tell Ada about Alex or she thought she would burst. Ada was pleased for her but worried too, whereas Fiona was just thankful Ada had found someone to care about and he was not married. He was available and sober.

'He isn't terribly useful,' Ada said in a fit of honesty, 'half a lifetime of sitting about, and he was never taught a thing. He is reasonably decorative these days, which is one thing, but maybe he can start building houses for people.' She had told Fiona how hard it was for Luke to do manual work, but they agreed that it was very good for his humility.

One thing Alex had done immediately when he found out about the scarlet fever was to ask Sarah to take in the two girls, because he was afraid for them after all they had been through, and she had readily agreed. Ada too was to stay at the Hilda House until things improved in Wolsingham.

After the first week Alex was exhausted and came home to Fiona late and they sat by the kitchen fire.

'The problem is that we have houses where the infection has got out of hand already, before I came to know about it, and the children play together,' Alex confided.

All Fiona could do was provide food and whisky and be sympathetic, because he was right. The fever spread. She knew how much he worried about children dying, perhaps even more so than any other doctor, having been through it himself.

From then on he came home very little, and yet he was somehow there for all the other problems and accidents and illnesses. He didn't stop. He would not have eaten had she not forced him to sit down. He didn't sleep until he was exhausted and would fall asleep in a kitchen chair.

Often she would sit with him for hours when he finally came home, enjoying every moment, even when he slept. She was hungry for his look, for his breathing, gazing at his pale, drawn face and wishing that things could have been easier just for a little while, but there was no let up and he went on and on. He had lost his own wife and child, and he knew what that felt like and was resolved that nobody should have to go through what he had gone through.

When he did come home they slept together in her bed, and she had never known how comfortable and comforting it was to have somebody there, so that when you had bad dreams you would wake up and be reassured.

The other problem was that because so many people had big families here, adults got the disease too, and it was just as lethal for them.

He must save them from the pain and the grief and the blights on their lives, so he worked almost every hour of every day. Fiona was convinced that he would kill himself through neglect, and she gave him sandwiches and tea to keep him going. She insisted on him sleeping, while his wife did not seem even to notice whether he was in the house or not. Their relationship was over. Either Mrs Blair was in bed, which she seemed to do out of sheer misery, Fiona thought, or she sat in front of the drawing-room fire, picking at small cakes and drinking weak tea. She barely spoke; she didn't even read anymore. Fiona went in and out on tiptoe so that she should not disturb the mistress's thoughts and all the while felt guilty and wrong and greedy for sleeping with the woman's husband. It was like being two people at the same time.

Fiona felt almost as though she was Alex's wife, and she looked after him as best she could. She was concerned for his welfare, and she both loved and hated how he neglected himself.

It was more than several weeks before he conquered the infection in his area. Several children and four adults had died. She worried he was going to be ill himself. He was very thin and couldn't eat, and hadn't slept properly in so long that his body was no longer operating as it should.

People were so grateful that they sent him gifts, anything they had to spare, anything they could offer. One grateful woman sewed him a beautiful shirt because he had saved her little girl. Others gave him jam or chutney or home-made ginger wine.

The gifts flowed in, and Fiona took them and said how glad he was of them and that he was so relieved to have been of service to the village and the area. She knew that it was a source of satisfaction to him that he could do so much, though he also grieved over those he had not been able to save and blamed himself for each death. She began to understand why doctors did what they did. It was the greatest gift they could bestow. A child's life was everything and he knew to his regret that sometimes he failed. He could not bear to fail.

Fiona was so proud of the work that he had done, but he took personally that people had died on his watch, as though he could save the world.

Forty-two

James spent what seemed like a long time trying to think about what he would do. He had come back here with hopes and dreams and none had come true. Worse still, the opposite had happened. He wanted to laugh himself to scorn but it hurt too much for that. He had to stop living in a world where he won Isabel Logan for himself. He dreamed of her constantly. He tried to think of her at the age she would have been now, middle-aged and having lost her bloom, but he never could think of her as any age other than the one he had last seen her, when she was in her full beauty and just twenty.

Did he have a life to go back to? He had attempted to move forward and felt like a fly caught up in the awful sticky tape that people hung in their living rooms. He could see now that his plans had always been influenced by the idea that life would be better if he came back here. What on earth had made him think that? Everything had moved on. He was older and experienced and he didn't think he wanted to live in a little backwater like Wolsingham. His home in Canada was so much better than this. He hadn't sold it, of course; he didn't need to.

He had laboured long and hard, having gone there with nothing but his health and wits, and they had served him well. He became accepted as he dragged himself up to riches and respect, but he had at the back of his mind a vision of coming back here and somehow marrying the woman he had always loved.

He could have married many times in Canada. He was rich and tall and good-looking and many a woman would have taken him on, but it had never occurred to him that he would do that. He had never taken any of them seriously, and so he was accepted as a confirmed bachelor, that was the phrase for it. He wondered now why he had never understood that the girl he had loved had not just loved and married his brother, but that she had also been dead for many years. Surely he should have understood the basic reality that he could never marry her, no matter how hard he tried. All he had thought was that somehow he could come here and everything would be better. It had been a hollow thought.

Harry's words came back and back to him. Why didn't he marry now and have a son of his own? He wasn't very old, he could do it. Except that it didn't feel that way.

With a heavy heart he rode up to the Hilda House. He was curious about this place, which seemed to have such an effect on everybody who went near it. Maybe it would somehow inspire him, make him feel as though he could change his life yet again.

When he got there he was disappointed. The village was barren, empty, like a ghost town. Only the big house seemed to have any life about it. It was nothing but a big stone edifice surrounded by smaller buildings, all in terraces which were falling down or completely flattened. This place had nothing for him. This area had nothing for him. Perhaps, he thought now, he had needed to come here once again to know that it was time to go on, that he could make something new in his life. Why not?

When he slid down off his horse, he saw that what was exceptional here was the view and the howling gale, which had got worse as he had gone on. He banged hard on the door for fear that he should not be heard. Sarah came to the door smiling and ushered him inside, as though they were the best of friends, and she led him into the kitchen. He had barely been in a kitchen for years, but this was the kind of kitchen that romantics liked to think of.

The whole family, if you could call them that, was gathered there – Sarah, Harry, Luke, Ada, Hilary, the doctor's two children and, best of all, Isabella. He had to stop himself staring at her, she looked so like Isabel. This was what Isabel must have looked like as a child. They were all gazing at him as though surprised but not ill pleased.

Sarah urged him to sit down and Harry engaged him in conversation immediately about the fish on the stretch of river where he and Luke now fished, which belonged to James, and then they talked about the shooting up on the tops. All those times James had been at home and yet left out. He did not belong here. He knew now that the time had come to move on, so he asked Luke very quietly if they might have a word. Luke said yes just as quietly and they slipped outside.

It was very cold up there and quite dark except for a few hours a day. Christmas had been lost in the midst of illness, and the loss of people for so many families, but up here they were away from it all, the air was clean and pure, and it must be standing them in good stead. But suddenly James longed for warmer places, for somewhere he could go now and sit in the sun and think about what he might do next. He could go to Australia; he had always had an inclination for it, and it would be summer there now. Yes, he would strike out and have another adventure. He would start again.

He was beginning to see why people lived in such a place as this village and why it was not for him. The views left nothing out. He could not love it and he was glad that all he had to do was to meet his brother and, if he was tactful enough, it might work out.

'I've decided to leave,' he said, and it brought back memories of the first time he had left, though he threw those out of his mind. He was going to get this right, it would be one of the few things he had got right in his life.

To Luke's credit, he looked disappointed.

James smiled. 'I don't fit here. I never did. I didn't quite know it before now. I thought you had driven me out with your dreadful ways.' He smiled at this. 'Maybe it was for the best. I would never have gone off and made my fortune.'

Luke said nothing about this because he knew that his brother lied. If James had married Isabel he would have been happy and maybe, just maybe, she would not have died in childbirth. Whose fault had that been? He wanted to say that he was sorry but how could he now? It was lost in time and in tears, and in the guilt that he felt.

Sometimes he thought that God had punished him, but that was stupid. God did not have personal vengeance or the time or patience to look at each man in the world and punish him for his shortcomings. God had made people so bleak, so needy, so naive, so stupid, and in a world where you could lie down and die in the cold, in the heat, in childbirth and in poverty. How could God expect so much of each man, so much pain and so much loss and so much grief?

'I'm going to somewhere new. Not Canada. I thought I

might find out a bit more about Europe, and I'd like to see Australia and what it might offer. I don't know. The thing is that I would like you to have the house. I know that by birth it isn't rightfully yours, but in every other way it is. I've been to see East and he has made out the papers so that it is now legally yours, and you will have the income you need to run it and to keep you and Ada and Isabella, wherever she lives. I think the idea of only giving what you have to the elder son is monstrous, so this is your share, which you ought to have had in the first place. I think things would have been so different if it had been this way.

'I never thought much of the dale,' he went on. 'To me it was too small and too insular with little to offer an ambitious young man. But you — you were born to stay here and love it. I want you and Ada, after you are married, to go and live there, and if you want to invite Harry and whoever he marries, and other people too, that is all to the good. The house lacks a mistress. It hasn't had one in so long and I would like Ada to be that mistress now. I have sufficient money to keep it going. I want you to be happy there, as you were for such a short time when you were married.'

Luke still said nothing.

'Will you do that for me? I would like you to. I would like to know that you are there when I set off on my various tours.'

Luke didn't speak.

'Come on, lad, say you are pleased.'

'James—'

'Oh come on, old fellow. We were friends as children. Why should we not be friends all over again? But at a distance.'

That made Luke hide his face and shake his head.

'We can't help who we are. We can't alter essentials. Please don't make me feel guilty,' James said. 'I want you to have a secure life such as I think you always yearned for, so I've put money in the bank—'

Luke tried to stop him but James put up one hand.

'I have other plans. There is more than one woman in the world. There are hundreds of thousands of women. I just was too bull-headed to see it. I'm going to go out and find a wife. Ada is lovely. You do care for her?'

'Very much.'

'All right then. Don't say anything to the others until I'm gone. I'm leaving tomorrow. It's best like this, and you can go down there any time you like, and leave it too, if you want to be up here sometimes. I don't care. I just want you to enjoy it. And I don't want to embarrass Ada, so I will go. You won't mind?'

Luke shook his head.

Luke cried that night but only after the others had gone off to bed. He cried for the childhood that had seemed to be lost, and for the brother that he had thought he had betrayed because they fell in love with the same woman. He thought he had won, but he had lost so very much in that he had lost his brother.

If Isabel had not come between them, might they have married different women and lived a good life there? But no. It would never have worked out. James had always wanted to get away and he never did. When they had talked as boys, James had envisaged the world as his own. Luke had envisaged the dale as his own. So they could not remain friends, and because of Isabel they could not remain brothers.

It was not her fault. Her task had been impossible and he could never work out why she had chosen him. He was the younger son and would therefore inherit nothing. He was idle and feckless and drank too much, even then. He had learned from his father not to value his employees. He had struggled and had tried to do better than his father, but he hated how he had not succeeded.

Men spat upon his name in the streets, he knew it even then, so no matter what he did, he could not be as he had longed to be. He was always his father's son, and then he was James's younger brother. He was not as handsome, not as tall, not as intelligent, not as ambitious, and yet Isabel had loved him. That was all he had, and when she died he was left with nothing. Then he had betrayed her child, sent him away.

You could not turn back the clock or make up for all those times when you made a mess of your life and of other people's lives. His grief had been so great that he had no love to give his son, and yet Harry was a wonderful son, a great person. Luke loved him as he had thought he could never love another human being. You had to be a parent to know that. The one person you would lay down your life for was your child.

He wanted to urge his brother not to go, to say that they would work something out, but he knew that it wasn't so; they were too different and always had been. The distance between them saved them from angry words and blows and disappointments. When you grew up with someone and had so many memories, it was impossible to let go. Yet they must do it, and they both knew they must for the sake of old times and new beginnings, and all the life they had left.

So James got on to his horse and wished his brother all the best and Luke stood by and watched him as he finally went down the hills towards the dale. Luke wished things were different, he wished that he had been a better brother. He blamed himself for so much. How could he blame James when he had taken everything and then frittered it all away in drink and in stupidity and in shame? He did not deserve to be loved.

'Has he gone?' Ada's voice was slight and yet audible behind him. She knew. She came from a big family where disappointments were present every day and she took him into her arms and said with a smile in her voice, 'I will love you, however dreadful you are.'

It made him smile too.

In time, he muttered from the depths of her shoulder, 'What a generous woman.'

Forty-three

In February there was also an outbreak of pneumonia among the older people, and influenza at the same time.

'It takes out those who aren't well to begin with or vulnerable, like children and old people,' Alex told Fiona one night when they were sitting over the kitchen stove very late.

It was almost like being married, Fiona pretended to herself. Yes, she had too much to do but then so did many women. Ada had not come back. Mrs Carver was there at weekends but Fiona liked to play house when it was just Alex and herself. She was happier now than she could remember ever having been before. The children had stayed up at the Hilda House. The weather was too unpredictable for them to go backwards and forwards and with illness in the dale so bad, it was a safer place to be.

'And other people should not come into the house,' he said, and that suited her. 'Germs spread at this time of year when people are inside so much.'

Mrs Blair developed a cough and could not eat the nutritious food Fiona prepared for her. She couldn't stop coughing long enough to eat, so Fiona made a lot of vegetable broth where the vegetables were cooked for so long, they almost disappeared into the liquid itself. Hyacinth managed to take it in and even thanked Fiona several times for her nursing and dedication.

Fiona was a bit surprised at this, and also felt guilty that she was sleeping with this woman's husband.

Mrs Blair was ill for several weeks and lost weight she could not afford to lose, and slept a good deal of the time. Fiona prayed that she would not die. What a stupid situation. She loved this woman's husband and wanted him for herself, but to wish another woman could die so that she could have him was not something she could ever think positively about.

Eventually Mrs Blair succumbed to the flu and then to pneumonia, and it was a bad case. She grew worse, refusing to drink anything but little sips of water. Her voice was hoarse and when her temperature climbed, Fiona then had to keep her cool with damp cloths.

She also tried to ease her breathing, but it got worse and worse, even with steam and vapour rub on her chest, back and neck. The doctor tried to keep people away from the surgery but there were other problems to attend to besides the influenza. In the ice and snow, people who had to leave the house fell and broke bones. There was a fire in one house so he was also treating burns. Oil lamps and candles caused many a fire.

Alex needed help, but the trouble was that the problems were as bad in Alston and Allendale, where the local doctor had just moved on. The area all around them suffered so he and Fiona had to struggle on alone.

At the beginning of March there was a huge snowstorm, which came up to the second-storey windows, and nobody could go anywhere. Despite this, Fiona dug in the garden and gathered what vegetables she could because there was so little left in the house. The doctor was always giving away what he had to the poorer folks in the village and round about. She found that at least when the snow was displaced there was no ice beneath it, and so she managed to pick Brussels sprouts and cabbage, and she had broth mixture in the house, so they lived on that, though the doctor was by then so tired he was of very little use and had no appetite.

The snow could not be got through for two weeks, but then there was a banging on the front door. Fiona went to answer it only to find Ada and Sarah standing there. She burst into tears.

Harry and Luke were with them and they lit fires and had brought supplies. Ada was particularly good with Mrs Blair, who was starting to get better, though Ada told Fiona in a whisper that if the Lord had had anything good about him he would have taken that bitch while she was in his clutches.

'Only the good die young,' Fiona said, and they giggled. It made them feel much better.

The snow thawed and water stood in the fields. The Wear gushed brown out from the dale towards the city of Durham and the sea at Sunderland. There was even a little bit of sunshine, but the scarlet fever and the pneumonia and influenza had taken their toll and most families had lost someone.

There came a night in March when the doctor did not come home. Fiona had grown used to this. He had been out night and morning for months now. But as morning became noon she grew more worried. She thought the problems of his home life and the practice had been too much for him and he was not able to concentrate.

Mrs Blair was now recuperating and she had gone back to complaining about everything. The food wasn't right, the fire wasn't warm enough. She kept ringing and ringing her little bell and when Fiona didn't get in there fast enough she complained even more. *She wouldn't have noticed had the doctor been gone for a week*, Fiona thought in despair.

It was halfway through the afternoon the following day when Mr Whitty arrived, a grave look on his face.

Fiona could see that something was wrong when he asked if he could come in and talk to Mrs Blair. He looked bleak and Fiona was itching to ask him what had happened, but she couldn't do that so she took him through into the sitting room where Mrs Blair toasted herself by a huge fire. She had lost a lot of weight since her illness and complained that she could not keep warm, and sat there wrapped in a huge quilt with cushions at her back. Fiona was terrified now; something had gone wrong. Something had happened, which was why the doctor had not come home and why Mr Whitty was here now. She felt obliged to go out into the hall. She wanted to go into the kitchen, she felt that she ought to, but she hovered, though the oak doors were stout and she could hear nothing.

Less than two minutes later there was a sharp cry from the sitting room, and then Mrs Blair began to scream. Fiona ran in to see what was wrong, to find the woman covering her face with both hands and after the screams subsided, she began to sob and wail and cry. Fiona looked at Mr Whitty's sad and sympathetic face.

'You should stay with your mistress,' he said. 'I think she needs you.' He left as soon as he could without another word, as though he could not wait to get away.

Fiona stared. 'What is it?' she said. 'Has something happened to the doctor?'

'He's dead. He's dead,' his wife wailed.

'What happened?' Fiona stared, and Mrs Blair stopped sobbing for long enough to get out the words. He had come off his horse, hit his head, and the horse had come back to the village alone. Mr Whitty had sent men out to look for him but it was too late.

Fiona was stunned but somehow, she felt bitterly, she had known something awful would take over the sense of happiness she had experienced with this man. Surely it could not be true that he was not going to be there for her anymore?

Mrs Blair was inconsolable and could not speak for tears and the sound of her own voice. Her body began to shudder and shake. Fiona ran into the dispensary and asked Jimmy for his advice. He stared. He did not seem to understand at first, but Fiona just said that the doctor's wife was in a bad way, and news was that he was no more. Once she had got the words out she knew them to be real, and for some reason, which she did not understand, she felt obliged to be kind now to his widow. It was all she could do.

Jimmy stared and then rummaged in the medicine cabinet and took a bottle down and measured an amount carefully into another tiny bottle. He told her to give Mrs Blair this and it would calm her. He would go and find out what had happened. He would go and tell Oswald.

He did not have to. When he was halfway across the yard, Oswald came to him, whey-faced and halting.

'What is it?' Jimmy said. 'What happened?'

'The doctor came off his horse and is dead.'

'The worst of the weather has gone, so why now?'

'I don't know. Only he would have known. Maybe he wasn't paying attention and the horse stumbled. Mr

Whitty says he came over the horse's head and ended up striking his head on a big rock.'

Fiona gave the mixture provided by Jimmy to Mrs Blair, but it was a good hour before the woman ceased to scream and shout. Fiona was convinced it was exhaustion rather than Jimmy's medicine that sent her off to sleep, but she no longer cared. At least now she could think and wonder what had happened, and try to get used to the idea that Alex was not coming back. The doctor's widow lay there on the sofa and Fiona thought the fact that she had just recovered from the flu did not help here.

Fiona left her there and went into the kitchen. She couldn't think what to do. She could only imagine that she was in some ghastly dream, and that when she woke up, all this would be nothing. There would be no scarlet fever, there would be no worn-out doctor. He would come home and everything would be just as it was – and dreadful though that had been, it was not nearly as bad as this nightmare. It could not be.

When Sarah opened the front door to Oswald's banging she knew that something had gone badly wrong just by his face. He could barely speak, but he beckoned her outside and she closed the door, despite the cold weather. After a while she could stand it no more and prompted him softly.

'What is it, Oswald. What's happened?'

He told her very briefly and she called Harry to put the horse into one of the barns. She took Oswald in and gave him tea and she got Ada and Hilary to look after him and Isabella while she went into the dining room with the two girls. There she sat them down and told them as gently as possible that their father had died.

There was a huge silence. They sat there on dining-room chairs, just a little apart, and gazed down at where Sarah's scissors and pieces of cloth and cut-out patterns lay, and nobody said anything. She was not surprised they didn't know how to react; they had seen so little of him, and yet he was their father and had he lived longer, he might have had a much better relationship with them as they grew older. It could hardly have been worse so far, although it was a little better after he decided he would not send them away to school. She felt so very sorry for them. They had been through such a lot and then Georgina said something she had least expected.

She looked up and said, 'Could we have Isabella in here? I don't think she would mind and she knows what it's like to lose both your parents, even though she thinks her father could still be alive.'

Sarah was amazed at Georgina's maturity and then she thought yes, *it was best to have the other child in; perhaps it would help*. So she got up and went to the kitchen and there she collected Isabella, who said nothing. When Isabella was with them, Georgina told her quite clearly that their father had died. It had been exactly the right thing to do, Sarah realized, these children were used to comforting one another, and Isabella let tears come into her eyes and no further. She just sat there. There would be decisions to make, but that could all wait until the children had had a chance to think, Sarah decided. For now, they made a little family together and she was glad of it.

After that, she told Ada because she thought that Fiona would want Ada down there, so Ada got Luke and Oswald to take her back to Wolsingham.

For Fiona the nightmare went on and on, even when Ada was there to comfort her. She could not tell day from night nor what time it was. She couldn't eat or sleep or find any place to be.

Once Mrs Blair had got control of herself she seemed glad to see them as never before, and thanked Ada and Luke for coming and being kind to Fiona. Fiona had no claim to Alex Blair, none whatsoever, she was just waiting for him to come back, waiting and waiting, and each minute became an hour, and each hour a day, and the future stretched unrelentingly and she didn't know what to do.

Mr East and Mr Wilson came two days after the shock of the doctor dying. Presumably they thought his widow would be able to hold herself together by then. Fiona thought there would be a will and there must be a funeral. Strangely, Mrs Blair began to look better. She stopped coughing, and she began to give orders as to what should be done for the funeral. Nobody knew that Fiona was beloved by Alex Blair or that she loved him. It seemed to Fiona that Hyacinth Blair was the person who should not have been here, like she was the intruder and Alex was Fiona's husband. But also she felt sorry for this woman, because she had the feeling that Hyacinth had never had a man who loved her and that was the hardest blow of all.

There was to be a big tea, but because of the number of people who would want to say goodbye to the doctor, the house wouldn't be big enough. So Mrs Wilson said the church hall would be open to the entire village, and there would be food and tea at the house as well.

It was Hyacinth who told Fiona these things.

'Mrs Wilson has offered to help you with the food and drink at the hall and she and the women from the church will come here and help. There will be a number of people needing beds, so all the rooms must be cleaned and dusted and the beds made up. Also, Miss Charles will be calling in later. I sent a note with Oswald and have asked her to come this afternoon.'

*

Hyacinth did not care much about black dresses; she had a more important thing to say to Sarah. Since the moment that Mr East had told her how things had been left, she'd thought a great deal about the children and what would happen to them. She felt that for the first time in her life, she could say what she thought and take control of the situation, and it brought a little light into her life.

When Sarah got there and she had said how sorry she was to hear about the doctor, Hyacinth was polite and asked her to sit down.

'I do want some black clothes made as soon as you can,' she said, 'so that I will not shock the people here by the paucity of my mourning clothes. However, I've got something else that I need to discuss with you. I hope you don't mind. You are the only person I could call on and I know how young you are, but I have nowhere else to go with this.' She took a deep breath and then looked straight at Sarah. 'My husband has left me all that he had, so when things are sorted out legally, I will be fairly well off. There is also a house in Edinburgh, which I think his aunt left him. He . . . he gave me some money to have as my own when we were married and had been paying money into an account for me so that I didn't have to ask him for money for things I wanted for myself. It was . . . it was one of the things he did best.

'I don't want to stay here. I will go to Edinburgh and

then I will either sell that house and buy another or settle there. There is the question of the girls.

'I don't think it's any surprise to you that I have never got on with them. I don't really like children.' She said this softly as though it was a huge fault. 'But I would like to give them the best start that I can after what has happened. I can either take them with me and send them to good schools in Edinburgh and do my best for them, or, if you were willing to keep them for the time being, I would pay the cost. This must have been a great shock to them, so I don't want them to have to make what may feel like impossible decisions now, but if they want to come to Edinburgh to me and to have decent schooling, especially as they get older, I think that might be best. I know that you have an awful lot to deal with, but I wondered whether you might keep them for now. They seem happy up there with you and your . . . and your family.'

Sarah was amazed. She had no idea that Hyacinth Blair could be so sensible. She thought it was surprising what a huge loss did for people, how it cleared the mind. She said that she would tell the girls what was proposed and they would take it from there.

She felt so much better on the way back home. Doris was very small to make any kind of a decision, and she had the thought that, given the chance, Doris would like to stay with Fiona. If Fiona would come up to the Hilda

House to them, that might solve part of the problem. Georgina, she was not so sure about.

She got Georgina on her own. The child looked so tired and it was hardly surprising.

'What else has gone wrong?' Georgina looked almost cynically at her.

'Nothing, Georgie, nothing.' This was what Isabella had begun to call Georgina since her father had died, and Sarah thought it was such an affectionate way of speaking that she wanted to adopt it. She explained the situation to Georgina and, rather than being rude and childlike, as Sarah thought now the poor girl never would be again, she merely sighed.

'We don't have to go with her? Are you sure?'

'Quite sure. You will always have a home with me, just as Isabella will.'

Georgina was not the kind of girl who flung herself at people as Isabella or Doris might have done, she just looked at the floor and nodded her head very slowly.

'I think in the end we might want different things, because I have been thinking that when I'm older, I might like to be a doctor.'

'That's a fine ambition,' Sarah said.

'I will need proper schools for that.'

'You will, yes, and I think it was this that made your stepmother say that you could go to Edinburgh later if you wanted.'

Georgina merely nodded again, and then she got up and walked out.

Fiona had hardly dared hope that Ada would come to see her, but of course she did, and it was all she could do not to fall into Ada's arms. Nobody must know that she was heartbroken, but now was her opportunity to go up to the Hilda House and stay with them. Ada understood, and Fiona could talk about Alex for as long as she wanted to, so all the feelings she had been holding back spilled out in words and sobs.

'I cannot just leave.'

'Fi, you have nothing to stay here for now.' Ada paused there, and Fiona only realized then that this was true, there was nothing to hold her here. 'And there is no reason why you should stay on here with that dreadful woman. You've looked after her, nursed her, put up with her for so long. Why don't you just come back with me? We will pack your things and then you can tell her. And Oswald will take us up to the Hilda House and everything will be much better.'

'She wants me to help with the funeral and everything.'

'Fi, it doesn't matter what she wants now. Please, let me get you out of here. You will be among friends, and the girls will be there. They need you.'

Fiona shook her head. 'I don't think I can.'

'Then what will you do?'

'I don't know. I—' She looked at her friend with such sorrow in her eyes that Ada wanted to weep.

'What is it, my hinny?' she said.

'I think I'm going to have a baby,' Fiona said.

Ada stared, and then she began to smile, and then she gave a cry of joy.

'But, Fi, that's wonderful. You will have something of Alex given to you and you can come and live with us.'

'I don't see how I can do that. People would find out, they would talk. I don't know what to do.'

'It doesn't matter for now,' Ada said. 'Come on, let's put your things together.'

Luke and Ada had planned to be married in the spring of that year but were hesitating. They were reluctant to leave Sarah and Fiona up at the Hilda House to look after everything, until Sarah found that Mr Paddy and his staff were always ready to help, and Mr Gloucester still came up at weekends, so the care would be shared.

There was another complication. Luke had no idea what Harry wanted to do, and he thought he should give him the option of going back to his home and living with Luke and Ada.

Harry was very quiet. Like the girls, he had had too much happen to him, Luke thought, and for so long he had been the parent and Luke the child. Perhaps it was time to turn things around, so he got Harry on his own while Harry tinkered about with the stove in the biggest greenhouse. Luke knew that it was just that Harry needed to do something out of the way of the others, but he felt he had to intrude.

Harry was on the floor, messing with the boiler, and did not look pleased to see him.

'I know, I know, I'm the last person you want to see,' said Luke, 'but it's just that Ada and I have talked to Mr Wilson, and we are going to get married soon. Because of all that's happened, we don't want any fuss, just the ceremony, and after that we are going to move into our house in Wolsingham.'

He stopped there. Harry had not even looked up, as though the greenhouse stove was the most important thing in his whole life and needed all his attention.

'I know that you have very bad memories of that house but James wanted me to have it and to live there with Ada. I just wanted to give you the option of living with your dreadful old man again.' He tried to lighten his voice at this point but it was hard and he needed to take a few deep breaths after it.

He waited until Harry stopped, put down whatever tool he had in his hand and looked up at his father.

'Do I have to decide now?'

'No, no, of course not. I thought that perhaps you and Sarah and Mrs Nattrass would talk it over.'

'The farmhouse is far from finished and I don't think Mrs Nattrass particularly wants to go back there; she's got used to having company. But if we get some decent weather, it could be finished by the spring and that would mean she could either go back or rent it out if somebody wants it.'

'That would leave you and Sarah and Fiona here with three children. You are very young for that amount of responsibility.'

'My biggest responsibility was to stop you from killing yourself,' Harry said flatly, and Luke winced. 'It was good of you to offer and I will think about it.' He picked up the tool and so Luke, dismissed, went back to the house.

Forty-four

It took Harry a couple of days to get used to the idea that he might be able to stay here, which was what he wanted to do. Much as he was fond of Ada, he didn't really want to live with a newly married couple. Fiona was there with them, but she was very quiet. They all knew what she and the doctor had been to one another and also that she was carrying his child. It would soon become obvious, so there was no point in pretending otherwise, Ada had said, but Fiona was hurt and silent and grieving, and it was difficult being around her. Harry kept busy with the jobs he had to do for the most part, since there was nothing he could do about the situation.

Eventually, Sarah and Harry were left alone in the kitchen at the Hilda House, and Harry said, 'My father and Ada are getting married in a few weeks.'

'She told me,' Sarah said, not looking at him, while he didn't look at her. She had needlework to concentrate on; Harry had nothing for his hands to do and kept looking at them.

'He asked me if I wanted to go and live with them.'

'And do you?'

That was when he looked at her. 'I think I've lived with my father for long enough lately, don't you?'

Sarah smiled in sympathy at the attempt at humour. 'You can stay here if you would like to. I do hope you will.' Sarah wasn't looking at him.

Harry was relieved. 'You think so?'

'Of course.'

'You won't go off and marry Oswald?'

Harry wasn't sure whether this was the right thing to say by the way she looked at him, but it was all right, he could see that it was after the first few moments.

'I fixed the stove in the greenhouse. We can grow stuff now from seed.'

'And isn't that the best news I've ever heard,' Sarah said silently to herself.

She had been worried about the situation. She didn't want to be up here without Harry and had hoped and prayed that he would stay. They were both very young, but he was such a big help in so many ways and she could not think about her life without him, however prosaic it all appeared to be.

Ada wasn't quite sure how she would tell her mother that she was getting married to Luke Leadbetter, but she thought that she had better go and see her. She wasn't sure whether to take Luke with her, but when she asked him about it, he said that if her mother still thought of him as the dreadful person the whole dale had known him for, she would be horrified. So Oswald let Luke take the pony and trap and drive them up to Rookhope.

Ada didn't say anything the whole way, she was so worried about what her mother's reaction would be. Luke was also silent, so presumably he was just as worried as she was. All the same, they seemed to make such good time on a dry clear day and were there sooner than she had thought, and still she hadn't worked out what to say. She need not have worried.

Her mother came straight out of the house and she said, 'Our Ada, what on earth are you doing here?'

'Hello, Mam. This is Luke.'

'Very happy to meet you,' Luke said and, having secured the pony's reins, he went up to the house with his hand outstretched.

They had deliberately made it Sunday so that Ada's father was at home. He was a much easier person than her mother, and told her how glad he was to see her. Then he went and shook Luke's hand.

'You seem familiar,' he said.

'Yes, I'm . . . I'm Luke Leadbetter.'

Both Ada's parents stared.

'You'd better come inside,' Ada's mother said, and Ada was horrified for the impression Luke would get, but though poor, the house was clean. She sat them down on shabby kitchen chairs, and Luke's manners would have got him a long way further than this, Ada thought with pride.

'I have asked Ada to marry me, so we thought we had better come and see if you would give us your blessing,' Luke said.

'You're the drunk?' Ada's mother said.

'Mother—'

'Yes, that would be me,' Luke said.

'You don't look drunk.'

'I'm not.'

Ada watched her beloved holding back a smile, and knew that they would laugh about it later.

'I got better. Ada helped me. You probably already know that my brother James came back to our family home, but he is restless and has gone off to see other parts of the world. We are to have the house and a decent income, so I would like Ada to marry me. James says I should have had half what my father left, and I was hardly going to argue with him. I do hope you don't have any objections?'

There were a few anxious moments when Ada thought her mother was unhappy, not because of the way Luke was now, but because of the fear that he might go back to being the drunk he'd once been.

'I promise that I will look after her,' Luke said.

Ada's father looked at her mother and then he said, 'What then, Violet? Shall we give the lad another chance?'

Then Ada's mother visibly swelled she was so proud. For the first time in her life she would be able to boast about her eldest daughter, who was marrying a man who had a huge house with land in Wolsingham.

'Oh, our Ada,' she said, 'I just knew you weren't meant to die an old maid.'

So Ada and Luke's wedding day arrived and it was a fine, though cold, day. Mrs Wilson helped put on a spread in Ada and Luke's house for just the family and a few people for afterwards. Luke and Ada had invited as many people as would like to come. It had been a tough winter for them all; every family had lost somebody, and after the tragedy of the doctor's death, it would be good to be celebrating a wedding. Mr Wilson would officiate, and the reception would be at the Leadbetter house in Wolsingham.

The women sorted out the inside of the house. Oswald and Harry and Luke did everything they could to make the place look good but there was not much need. It had been so well looked after, and the gardens were full of flowers: tulips, daffodils, crocuses in great purple and white carpets. They put out chairs so that those who wished to, if it was a fine day, could sit under the trees in the orchard, and the house was fine, with fires in every downstairs room. Luke did ask Ada if she would like to get rid of the portrait of Isabel, but she said it might hurt other people's feelings, especially Harry's and Isabella's, so the portrait looked down on them all.

Fiona wished that she didn't have to be there. She was so jealous, and yet so glad for her best friend that she had finally found someone to love, and that Luke had regained his life.

All three children were invited to the wedding and were asked to name the colour and style of dress they wanted. Isabella chose green, which went well with her looks. Georgina chose a multicoloured dress that had splodges of pink, purple and yellow, and Doris chose a simple blue dress. Sarah and Ada and Fiona spent many hours making new clothes for them and, for old times' sake, Ada wore the black velvet dress that Sarah had given her, and carried white flowers. Sarah wore red, for the tulips' sake, she said.

Harry was his father's best man. The sun shone and people were cheered, eating and drinking and walking about the grounds, chatting and laughing. After the reception, Luke and Ada were left there at the house in Wolsingham, and Hilary, Sarah, Fiona and Harry took the girls back to the Hilda House.

Mrs Blair was still at the surgery house. The probate for the doctor's will had to be sorted out and she had not yet moved away, though she had enough money. Perhaps she just had to get used to the idea of freedom, something she had never had before.

It was only Fiona who was unhappy. A week went by. She stopped feeling sick but she was getting too big for her waistbands and Sarah let out her dresses. Fiona tried to be happy because her best friend was, but it was a lonely time up there for her, though she tried hard to remain cheerful.

After the first few days, Mr East came up saying that he wanted to talk to her. Since it was a fine day they ventured outside and sat on a stone wall at the back of the Hilda House. The others were all, *possibly tactfully*, Fiona thought, leaving her alone with the solicitor. He must be bringing some news she didn't want to hear judging by the closed look on his face, though as far as she was aware he knew nothing about her past life. There was a small part of her which hoped that Alex had left her something, but if he had done it would have been dealt with long before now. He hadn't known that she was having his child and his wife must not know that he and Fiona had had a relationship, so she put that thought from her mind.

'I've got some bad news,' he said. 'I have had some correspondence with a solicitor in north-west Scotland and he says that your mother has been trying to get in touch with you for a long while, and finally you were traced to here. Your father died some time back and she wanted to see you again because she is far from well. Would you be able to go back to Scotland and see her?'

Fiona stared at him. She had not thought anything like that could possibly happen. She had put her parents into a compartment in the back of her head, and though she thought about them from time to time, it seemed strange now that real things still happened there. She felt awful suddenly. Her father had always been kind in his way, but he had assumed that she would marry a boy he and his wife had chosen, and she could never have done such a thing. She was his daughter, there to do what he wished, she must have no ideas of her own. She had long since understood this and tried not to blame him. It was only what most men thought of their daughters.

Her parents had been essentially good people, but she had run from their goodness because they had tried to make her into something she was not.

'She says that she understands now why you left and although she always wanted you happily married, she sees that you had to go and make your own place in the world.'

'They didn't want me happily married, they wanted me married to a boy I despised, because his family was rich and his people influential,' Fiona said.

Mr East hesitated, but he had obviously thought this through because he said, 'Your mother is getting older, and since you are an only child and will inherit everything your family owns, could you think of going back there and seeing her?'

Fiona didn't know what to say; she felt so guilty and selfish and was silent then for a few moments. She had not imagined she would have to do something so very difficult, but perhaps this had come at the right time. Could she go back? Could she have some kind of life up there, in the place she had called home, the place she had loved?

'Does my mother know where I am?'

'No, of course not. Solicitors don't divulge such things unless the person in question, that's you, wants them to.'

'So she could think that I am living elsewhere?'

'Yes, she could, if that is what you want. Such details are confidential and I am here on your side for whatever you want now.'

'I think I would like to go back there, at least for a short time.'

Fiona went down to see Luke and Ada and to talk it through with her best friend. Ada was so deliriously happy, it occurred to Fiona that it might be difficult for Ada to be anywhere near sensible at the moment. But it was a problem she thought she could deal with right now, whereas going back to Scotland was an altogether thornier prospect.

Ada listened carefully and then said, 'This might just be a solution for you, at least in the short term.'

'But how would I explain the state I'm in?'

'You lie.'

Fiona stared at her.

'You could say that you were married to a doctor in Edinburgh, and that he has died and left you pregnant with his child. It's just an extension to what has happened and it would hurt nobody. I'm sure your mother would be delighted that you are to have a baby and be in the house once again.'

'I don't know what to do,' Fiona said, feeling rather lost.

'Try it. If it doesn't work, there will be another solution, I feel sure.'

'Lie to my mother?'

'You walked out twenty years ago. For her, short of you dying, that was the worst thing you could do to your parents.'

'Oh, thank you,' Fiona said.

'Fi, you need to be realistic here. You can't have the life you want and, to be fair, you never could have had it with the doctor married. At least this is a way out for you. Also, have you any idea what it will be like to inherit a place like that?'

Fiona said nothing. She shook her head.

'You loved it. You would never have left it had things worked out, had you found a man to love. Things do sometimes work out if you give them chance,' Ada said gently.

'I miss him,' was all Fiona said.

'I know you do.'

'Why did the only man I ever loved have to be married to somebody else, and now I can't have even the little of him that I did have?'

'You might learn to love someone else in time. And besides, you are going to have his child. Isn't that some kind of recompense?'

Fiona allowed that it was.

So a few days later, Fiona packed her belongings and went home, with many assurances that she would come back. She didn't mind now leaving Ada in Wolsingham. Well, she didn't mind so very much, now that she had taken action and was going forward in a way, but for some reason leaving the Hilda House was more difficult, and she had no idea why. She had for so long thought this might be a refuge and now she was losing it, though Sarah impressed upon her that there would always be a place for her there, should she want it.

Going home to Scotland was actually easier than she had thought it would be. The moment she got across the border, she began to dream of home. She had bought a plain gold band for her finger when she had to change trains in Newcastle, but that was as far as she could think.

When she reached the island, there was a pony and trap waiting for her with a man she didn't recognize, but he knew who she was. He took her luggage and called her Miss McIntyre, whereupon she corrected him, though she had not known she was going to.

'I'm married now; well, widowed. My name is Fiona Blair.'

The man apologized and corrected himself.

'You couldn't possibly have known,' she said calmly.

To her surprise, her home was nowhere near as big as she remembered it. It was a low farm, painted white, and dearer to her than any other place in the world she knew now. It had been there for four hundred years, surrounded by its gardens, which were mostly given over to fruit and vegetables, herbs and useful plants. But there was also a rose garden, sheltered from the island storms by a big wall. It had always been her mother's favourite spot.

She felt strange now as she was ushered into the sitting room. Her mother, of course, looked so much older and was rather frail, but then she too had lost the love of her life. How awful that they should have such things in common.

Fiona went to her and got down beside her chair,

since her mother had difficulty getting up, and there her mother cried and caressed her and said that she wished everything had been different.

'Alastair still isn't married,' she said, but when Fiona drew back her mother smiled at her.

'I am trying to see why you didn't want him but have long since come to terms with it. I am so glad you found a man you could marry, and best of all that even if he has left you, you will have his child.'

During her first evening back, Fiona wandered into the rose garden. It was too early for roses to bloom, but they were all healthy and in bud. She let fall a few tears for her father and for what she had done to her parents, but as she stood there she sensed somebody behind her, and when she turned Alastair Beaston was smiling at her. He came across and held her hand.

'Fiona,' he said, 'it's been a long time.'

'It has that.' Looking at him now he didn't seem nearly as bad as she had thought he was, but then he was not pretending anymore, she could tell.

He stood, hesitating, as though he couldn't think of what more to say and it seemed to Fiona that he was a much kinder person. Of course, they had both matured and altered as they had tried to adjust to the problems that they had been given.

He had improved beyond measure. His demeanour of good temper had perhaps been learned by bitter experience. There was a look in his dark eyes, which had nothing to do with dreams and all to do with reality.

'I drove you away.'

'No, no.' She couldn't let him feel like that now.

'Aye, I did, with my selfish wants and needs, which had nothing to do with you, as you were very well aware. It was why you left.'

'It was nobody's fault.'

'I have to excuse myself, or I couldn't live with it. When I saw what I'd done = and it took time for me to realize it and blame myself as I should have done right from the start = I was so sorry. You knew who I was and what I wanted, and that I was ready to sacrifice your happiness for my own. I hope you will forgive me.'

She said there was nothing to forgive and that she was so pleased to see him.

'How is Jamie?' she asked.

Alastair found the ground a fascinating place to look at and his voice quivered as he said, 'He died, shortly after you left. It broke my heart. But you . . . you married.'

And so she lied to him as well as to the rest of the world. She told him that she had married a surgeon from Berwick and that he had died a few months back. The lies came so easily to her lips and yet what else could she say? She had to protect herself and her child.

They walked back to the house and she asked him to stay for supper. She knew that her mother would be pleased. Over the meal she embellished the life she had thought up for herself during the long journey, and she became the woman that she said she was.

They talked about her father. Her mother loved hearing tales about him, and about their childhoods. Alastair asked her if she would go riding with him sometime, but she shook her head and said that she was not able to do that at present.

'Oh, I see. Then congratulations are in order, despite the tragedy of your marriage. You'll make a fine mother.'

She was in deep thought when she went to bed, not to the bedroom she had had before, but, at her mother's insistence, in the best bedroom in the house. Her mother said it held too many memories and that she would far rather Fiona took it for hers now. It overlooked the sea. Perhaps now was the time for her and Alastair to be friends, she thought. Perhaps he might be a friend to her child.

It was time for new beginnings. Alex Blair had been the love of her life so far, but she could see now that he was not the right man. She might never find the right man, but if she could enjoy her life here and bring up her child, then at least she had given Alex something and he had enabled her to have a child, which she had thought she never could.

She didn't think he had truly loved her; she thought he had been desperate to hold a warm body in his arms, had needed her there just as much as she had wanted him. He had been intelligent and educated, and if her child had these qualities, plus kindness, then she knew that she could be happy.

Things didn't have to be perfect. They just had to be enough – this place and her child, and a few good friends, and hopefully her mother would be there for a little while yet so that they could get to know one another, even just for a few weeks.

In time she would invite Luke and Ada and Sarah, and Harry and Hilary and the three girls to stay. She so much wanted them to see her here, in this place she had always loved the best. Her luck had brought her many things. She had prosperity and a future. And she knew that they would keep her secrets. Alex Blair would live on in her child.

Forty-five

The three girls were worried. Had they still been living at the surgery house, they might have gone off to the ruined summerhouse out of the way so that they could talk. The day was fine and warm but the fine warm days were bringing on another problem.

Luke and Harry had now finished Hilary's house. It stood there so proudly on the tops and Hilary and Sarah had taken time to furnish it with bits of second-hand goods on sale in Wolsingham. They had made curtains and cushion covers and clippie mats, and there was so little left to do that the three girls knew things would not remain as they were for much longer.

'I think Mrs Nattrass is going to want to go back to the farm,' Isabella said, as they sat as far away from the house as they could so that nobody could overhear them.

'She's looking as if she wants to leave, and after all, there's nobody for her to talk to now, nobody older,' Georgina said.

'Sarah will miss her. There's so much to do with us

three and the house and the animals and everything. It would be much easier if she'd put somebody into the farmhouse as she said she might. That would bring in money too.'

Doris said nothing. She missed Fiona so much and things were changing again, and she just wished things would go along evenly for a while so that she could breathe easily.

'We need to talk to them,' Georgina said.

'About what?' Doris said, suddenly taken aback.

'About Harry and Sarah, silly,' Isabella said. 'They can't live up here just the two of them. They're old enough to get married, even if they are nowhere near as old as the others, and if they can't stay here then neither can we. I wish that just once we could do what we wanted instead of what other people want. It's very trying.'

Georgina sighed. 'Trying isn't the word. All right, so we have to talk to them.'

The other two stared at her.

'We can't do that,' Doris said.

'Then what do you suggest we do? We could be back in Wolsingham and Potty Prudhoe is still there, you know.'

'She won't be,' Isabella said comfortingly, 'not for much longer, Sarah said.'

'I'm not going back there while Potty Prudhoe is still

around,' Georgina said. 'I'll go and talk to Harry but after that, Isabella, you must tackle Sarah.'

Isabella stared. 'How am I supposed to do that? She can be scary when it's something difficult.'

'Just keep Potty Prudhoe in mind,' Georgina said.

Georgina did not want to talk to Harry. She would have given anything to have put it off but she couldn't. She understood more than anything that if you didn't take action, somebody else sorted things out and it was never for your benefit.

You could never find him when you wanted him, she concluded, going all round the garden and the orchard and all over the house. She managed to avoid Sarah, who as usual was seated at the dining-room table lost in work.

Finally, Georgina discovered Harry out the back pegging out the washing. It was a good drying day and the sheets were already billowing in the slight wind. She thought the wind and the smell of the wet washing was wonderful. Harry eyed her as though he knew something awkward was coming and she had to give it to him, his instincts were good.

'Now what?' he said. 'And before you say anything more, the answer is no. We can't afford horses, ducks or anything that Mr Paddy wants to give to somebody else to look after and keep.'

'You have Ernie and the cats.'

'Cats don't belong to anybody,' Harry said.

'Anyway,' Georgina said, 'I wouldn't be a bit surprised if Ernie wanted to go and live with Mrs Nattrass and Bert when they go back to the farm.'

'It hasn't been decided yet.'

That gave Georgina an opening.

'Well, she can't go the way that things are, can she?'

Harry finished his pegging and looked at the effect. *They are like sails on a ship*, Georgina thought, having seen pictures of such things.

'Even if she wants to go to her house she's not going to say so.'

Harry frowned at her. 'What are you going on about?' he said.

Georgina went in for the kill. 'Well, just this. You and Sarah can't live here without her. You must know how that would look. I know you aren't old like your father and Ada, but this is the dale. Word would get round and then what?'

The penny dropped. Finally, she thought.

Harry's face turned beetroot and he walked away back to the house. *Isn't that just like a man*, Georgina thought. *Pretend it isn't happening and then it won't.* She ran after him.

'Have you asked her to marry you?'

'Of course not,' he threw back.

'Why not? You can't pretend that she doesn't like you.

We all know that she's potty about you. We'll start to call her Potty Sarah if you don't.'

'Stop it, Georgie!' He turned around on her.

'Scaredy cat,' Georgina said and went off to the house, ignoring him.

'You've changed your mind about staying here with us,' Sarah said softly to Hilary when they were alone.

'Of course I haven't.'

'You liked being here but you want to go home. I can see it by the look on your face every time we go over there. Be honest, please. The house is beautiful and I would want to go there if it was mine.'

'I can't go and leave you and Harry like that.'

'Like what?'

Hilary concentrated fully on the socks she was darning. 'Together.'

Sarah stared. 'Oh,' she said. 'I didn't think of it like that. Oh, that's all right.'

'It's nothing of the sort,' Hilary said, lips coming together firmly. 'It isn't decent.'

'I never was decent,' Sarah said.

Hilary looked at her. 'You are the most decent young woman I ever met and I won't have your name besmirched after all you've done for other people. I know Harry is stupid, men are, and that you can hardly ask him to marry you, but I do think that a good nudge in your direction would help.'

Sarah said she was to do nothing of the sort.

Hilary looked wisely at her. 'You are far too young to be left alone together,' she said.

'Nonsense,' Sarah said briskly.

Then she went back to the dining room and attempted to sew, but ended up cutting a hole in the material where she shouldn't have, which made her swear.

She was alone in the kitchen later when Isabella came in looking very pale, as though something had gone wrong and she was responsible.

'I thought Harry might have done this veg,' Sarah complained. 'He's had nothing to do all morning. Men always disappear when there's work to get through.'

'I think he's keeping out of the way,' Isabella said.

'The kitchen is always empty when there are jobs to do be done, even Hilary has disappeared. It's just like Auntie Mary.'

'What?' Isabella said, lost.

'It's a local saying. Auntie Mary was always the person who couldn't be found when there was work to be done, so it's known as doing an Auntie Mary.'

'I don't think he has, and I don't think Hilary has either. It's only that things are sort of well, odd . . . '

'What rubbish,' Sarah said, making sure she didn't chop off a finger and didn't look at Isabella.

'Where on earth have you been all this time?' Sarah complained to Harry when everybody else had gone to bed and he was still looking for things, apparently anywhere other than where she was.

'Doing stuff,' Harry said.

'You didn't help with the veg, or the cooking, there's been no cleaning done, and as far as I can see you've made no progress in the garden. You scuttled back for your meals, threw them down and then vanished.'

'I hung out the washing.'

'That was hours ago.'

'Sarah, look—'

She did and then he half-turned away, helplessly, looking like Ernie when he had chewed somebody's scarf.

'I think I ought to go and live with my father and Ada. I think it might be a better idea.'

'Who for?' Sarah blazed. 'What's wrong with here?'

'I just feel in the way.'

'In the way? How am I supposed to manage, especially if Hilary goes back to her house?'

'She probably won't if I go,' Harry managed.

Aware that she really was losing her temper, and she

prided herself that she never did, Sarah said, 'I don't think she wants to be here anymore. I know she did, but then you and your father had no more sense than to make her house look so cosy and homely.'

'You did too.'

'I thought we should furnish it so that it would be easier to let, and now she's changed her mind. If it had still been a ruin we wouldn't have a problem.'

'I knew it would be all my fault,' Harry said, making for the door, but she was nearer and stopped him.

'We might as well have this sorted now,' she said.

'Oh, you think so?'

'Yes, I do.'

'All right then,' Harry said and he reached out and got hold of her. And that was it, and somehow Sarah had known that it would be. She'd been telling herself for weeks that it would never happen, that she would die an old maid, that Harry didn't care about her and that she definitely didn't care about him. But now her arms went around his neck as though it was the only place for them to be, and her throat gave a sweet little sigh as she yielded her mouth.

The three children were sitting on the stairs.

'Well,' Isabella said, 'they've stopped shouting at each other. Do you think that's a good sign?'

'It has to be,' Georgina said.

'I don't like how quiet it is,' Doris said.

'I think there's probably a reason for it,' Isabella said, and they agreed, then tiptoed up the stairs to bed.

Epilogue

A year later

Dear Ada and Luke,

I have a son. We both had a very bad time to begin with but we have recovered and are doing well. He is called Alexander, of course, though the local folk keep shortening it to 'Sandy', which makes me think of beaches.

My mother got much better as soon as she realized I was home for good and has been a big help since Alexander arrived. She is fit enough to tell me that I ought to marry Alastair, though neither of us wants it. I think that although she is pleased with her grandson she would like another, happily fathered by the local Lord of the Isles. I hate to disappoint her but I'm not sure Alastair would be capable of fathering anybody, and I'm certainly now too long in the tooth for another child even if I wanted one. I think my mother thought it would bring her her heart's desire when both our properties were joined together. Mothers never give up, do they? I must remember this when Alexander is grown.

I want my home and land to go to the son of the only man I have ever loved.

Missing you.

God bless you, F.

Dear Luke and Ada,

You are not going to believe this, but I am going to be married. I have the feeling that she very much resembles Isabel, in that she is blonde and green-eyed and no more than twenty-one. I must endeavour to keep my memories in the past where they belong and go forward with joy in my heart. I never thought that I would be foolish enough to fall in love with a woman so much my junior, or that I would have the nerve to ask her to marry me. Her parents are not much older than me but they are in favour of the match. She cannot even be accused of marrying me for my money because she is better off than I am.

Her father and grandfather are very astute businessmen and like that I am older than she is, for there are a lot of young sharks out there hoping the heiress and her money will fall into their greedy arms.

She is American. We met in Florence. The place is full of Americans. I adore her. We will live in New York, where her parents have bought us a beautiful home.

Don't worry that I will be having lots of sons and come back and want the house. It is legally yours, I made sure of it, and I think I may never come back to the dale. You are more than welcome to visit us. It is a long way, but New York is a glorious place. There is a whole world out there beckoning to me and my beautiful Caroline.

Wishing you all the best,

James

Dear Fiona,

It is so good to hear from you and to know that all is well. So pleased to hear about your baby son. What a gift.

Hilary has died. We are all very sad about it. She was spending more and more time with us here at the Hilda House and had become very frail over the past few months. She left instructions that the farm is to be sold and the money invested in the girls' education. We are deeply grateful but miss her so very much. Bert is always trying to get out. He runs back to the farm and I go and try to persuade him to come back here with me, though the tears fall as I cuddle him. He doesn't understand.

We are finding it difficult up here at the Hilda House. It has become the wrong place for us. We are very short of money. Harry's father and Ada have offered to give us some but Harry is loathe to borrow. They have tried to persuade us to go and live with them, but I fear Harry has lived with his father quite long enough and I am not good at sharing kitchens. Ada has become all posh and has a cook and maids. I just wouldn't fit in there and would drive her mad like I used to, wanting to be into everything.

Also, the girls need proper schooling now that they are getting older. We have talked to them sensibly because although they love being here, and Mr Gloucester and Mr Paddy are good with them, we think they need wider experience.

Harry wants us to go to Canada. I think James influenced him more than we had thought. James has written and sent him contacts and money so that we can build a new life there.

I know that Luke would very much like Isabella to live with him and Ada, but she has already talked about Canada. I don't blame her. That is where her father and brother went. I also know that Canada is a very big place, but these things can be surprising and, if she does want to come, I will take her with us.

Georgina and Doris can go and live with Luke and Ada until schooling is sorted out, but after their only experience of the idea of going away to school was so appalling, I'm not sure what will happen. They do not want to leave this area and who can blame them? They have been so very pulled about in their lives. It would be wonderful to see you before we go.

Our best love to you and to Alexander.

Harry and Sarah

To my Stepmother,

I know I should write 'to my dearest stepmother', but I'm trying not to be hypocritical as we were never dear to each other. Harry said I should put 'one another' because it's better grammar but it sounds so formal. I suppose he does know these things since he did Latin and Greek.

I've decided that I want to be a doctor as my father was and since he went to university in Edinburgh, I am writing to ask if I could possibly come and see the city. It might help me to work hard and I would like to see the house where he was born, which is now yours. I don't want to intrude on your privacy. I know that we have no blood relationship and will understand if you want nothing more to do with me. I think that if I asked Luke and Ada, they would bring me and we could stay in a hotel, but it seems to me that for all we did not get on, you have good intentions about our education. Sarah did tell me that you had offered to help. I wouldn't like you to think that you must give us money, but a few days with you and possibly making some kind of friendship would be very pleasing.

All good wishes,
Georgina Blair

Dear Georgina,

I have always thought that every woman would be the better for a good education and know myself what lack of opportunities leaves us with. Choosing to be a wife and mother is all very well, but having had to marry – forgive me – two men I didn't care for, but had little choice, I want your generation to have things better. That was why I said to Sarah that I would like to help. And I will.

I think you are very clever and that you could do whatever you wanted. I would be happy to have you to come and stay with me any time that you like, and will be delighted should you choose to come to university here. It is the most beautiful place I have ever seen.

All good wishes,
Hyacinth Blair

Dear Fi,

Georgina and Doris are especially keen to come and see you and your baby son and I miss you more than I can say. Luke is eager to see your island. When will you be well enough, and have time and rooms enough, to have us to stay? You have left such a hole in my life. Also, Harry and Sarah have decided to emigrate to Canada and take Isabella with them. Luke has said nothing because he knows how big a debt he owes to both of them, but the blow is huge to him. He doesn't want to hold them back but he feels — however unfairly — that he is losing his child for the second time. It would be good for us all to come to Scotland, and then at least I can envisage you in the setting I know you love best.

Thinking of you,
Ada

Dear Fiona,

I miss you. Ada says that you are never coming back, that you have a house and a baby and your mother. You are a very lucky person. Thank you so much for saying we could come and visit. I hope you are telling your baby all the stories you used to tell us and that you will tell them all to me when I see you.

Hugs,
Doris

Author's Note

Bond Isle is a real place in Weardale, but I used the name for a row of houses in Rookhope.

Acknowledgements

I would like to thank my agent Judith Murdoch and my editors Emma Capron, Celine Kelly, Kay Gale and Gaby Puleston-Vaudrey. And, as ever, everyone at Quercus for making such a lovely job of all you do.